Echo Omicron

Ultra Meridian Series: Book 1

Theo Mann

Invisible Publishing Company

Ultra Meridian Series

Contents

Chapter 1

A sonic boom echoed over the desert as the ship plummeted through the atmosphere. It screamed toward the ground in a blinding streak. Its engines reversed to break its fall and kicked up a cloud of dust over the landing site.

Dust stung Sheriff Mace Davenport's throat. He squinted through the glare and grimaced when he read the ship's designation: *Echo Omicron*. Smugglers. He knew that ship and its crew. He didn't relish going out there and facing them.

He pulled his sidearm and checked the ammunition cylinder. He hadn't fired it since he checked it this morning, so of course the cylinder was still full.

He holstered it and pulled his other gun to check it when a gruff voice yelled at him from behind. "Hey, porkchop! Where ya going?"

Davenport didn't look up from his weapon. The ammo cylinder on his second gun had slipped slightly, but when he removed the cylinder, he didn't find anything preventing it from slotting all the way onto the feed pin.

He shoved the cylinder onto the pin and snapped the gun closed. He holstered it and lifted Big Boris from its hook by the door.

He grabbed his face mask to pull it over his nose and mouth when the voice came again. "Hey, porkchop! You goin' somewhere?"

Davenport turned around. A grizzled drunk dangled off the bunk in the cell corner. His head and shoulders drooped halfway to the floor while his legs sprawled on the mattress. He didn't move, but at least he was still breathing.

The other drunk gripped the jail bars with both hands. His lank, grey hair hung around jowls half-concealed by salt-and-pepper whiskers. Greasy, dust-crusted rags covered his hunched body.

"Don't you go running off now, Emmet," Davenport told him. "I'll be back in a minute and then we can play that game of checkers I promised you."

"Checkers!" Emmet bellowed. "What the hell are you....? Hey! You can't just leave us here! We have rights, you know!"

Davenport yanked down his mask and lowered his goggles over his eyes. He chuckled to himself striding across the desert toward the ship. Emmet wasn't going anywhere and his partner Lenny probably didn't even know where he was.

The wind stung every inch of him as Davenport marched across the hard-baked dirt. Sand and grit bit through his thick leather jacket and rawhide pants. It blasted through his face mask and scoured his goggle lenses.

The Ultra Meridian jail stood alone in a vast, sandblasted expanse of desert. The lonely building marked the spot where the Ultra Meridian line intersected the planet Provis' fourth latitude line. No other sign gave any evidence that the spot meant anything—because it didn't.

The *Echo Omicron* loomed over him. The engines reduced to half-power as he approached, but the wind didn't let up. The sand made a hollow sound drumming the hull.

That sound belied the truth. The *Echo Omicron* definitely wasn't empty. It wouldn't land here if it was. Davenport knew enough about the ship's crew to know they were bound to be carrying something contraband.

They wouldn't stop here at all, let alone check in with the local sheriff, if they didn't absolutely have to. They wouldn't get past the Confederate Corps Reserve Wing if they left Ultra Meridian without Davenport's clearance. The Reserve Wing would impound any ship traveling without clearance and pack its crew off to Terminus Anathema.

Davenport was the only authority for a thousand lightyears in any direction and he never shirked his responsibility. He didn't troop all the way out to Ultra Meridian to let the smugglers and gang runners get away with their ill-gotten business.

The *Echo Omicron's* rear gangway unlocked and lowered in front of him as he approached it. He climbed up it into the cargo hold and found two bizarre creatures waiting for him.

The first stood at least four feet taller than Davenport. Curved horns stuck out of his knobbled skull and hooked tusks angled up from his jutting lower jaw. His small, sharp eyes flashed under heavy overhanging brows.

"Good to see you again, Dice." Davenport nodded at the enormous weapon propped on the monster's hip. The giant hand utterly swallowed the trigger grip. "Is that an XQ-75? You had a 62 the last time you came through here."

Dice lowered the weapon so the huge barrel pointed directly into Davenport's face. "It's an 85. Take a good look before I blow your fat head off."

Davenport didn't blink. He kept his gaze locked on Dice's gruesome features. "I'll take a look after I confiscate it. The 85 is contraband outside the Confederacy.....but I guess you already knew that or you wouldn't have bought the gun in the first place. Am I right?"

Dice glared at him and swiveled the gun barrel upward toward the ceiling. "Give us our stamp and get the hell off our ship."

"*Your* ship? Hmm...." Davenport raised his eyebrows, rubbed his chin, and pretended to consider. "I seem to remember this ship landing here a few years ago. It had a completely different crew, a different internal combustion configuration, and even a different identity profile. What do you think about that?"

"I think maybe it was a different ship and the sun is frying your brain on this rock," Dice boomed. "I think all that lard in your diet of laws and regulations probably addled your brain and you don't know one ship from another. That's what I think."

Davenport laughed in his face. "That's a good one, man. You want to hear what I think?"

"No," Dice snapped. "Not really."

"I think you and yours raided this ship, stole the cargo, and jettisoned the crew into space. You know...." Davenport glanced over his shoulder.

He could see the Ultra Meridian jail through the open gangway. It sat alone in the middle of all that nothing.

"I spend a lot of hours on this outpost with nothing to do," he went on. "I might get bored and decide to look into the *Echo Omicron's* movements over the last ten years or so.....but we won't talk about that now. We'll do your inspection and give you your stamp so you can get out of here."

Dice bared his fangs, but he didn't answer. He didn't threaten Davenport again, either.

Davenport waited to make sure Dice didn't pose any further danger to him. Then he turned to the other creature.

It squatted on top of a stack of crates lashed to the cargo hold wall. Its large ears flopped almost to its chin. Long, jointed limbs angled from its shriveled, bony body. Its fingers and bare toes extended too far from its flapping appendages.

Wrinkled skin hung loose all over its naked body, but fortunately for Davenport's long-term sanity, the creature had no visible orifices besides its gaping mouth, bulging eyes, and oversized ears. The rest of its lanky frame was smooth and perfectly innocent.

Davenport fished in his pocket and took out a small square parcel wrapped in oiled paper. He held it out to the creature. "Here you go, Beauty. This one is strawberry."

The creature snatched the food out of his hand, unwrapped the paper with nimble, serpentine fingers, and crammed the square into his gaping mouth.

He smacked his lips and slobbered down his chin while he chewed it up. Then his long, purple tongue slithered over his misshapen lips and his goggle eyes rolled in circles.

Beauty was just about the farthest thing from beautiful that Davenport had ever seen, but Davenport knew better than to alienate the creature. Beauty possessed skills, information, and talents only a fool would underestimate.

Beauty's closest friends and associates didn't know the half of what he was capable of. Davenport learned a long time ago to stay on Beauty's good side no matter what he might think of the rest of the *Echo Omicron* crew.

Davenport noticed Dice glaring at him again. Davenport cast an appraising glance around the cargo hold. Where was it? Where did they hide their illegal cargo this time? He'd busted them too many times for them to chance hiding it anywhere obvious.

They wouldn't put it down here in the cargo hold . It would be somewhere else, somewhere they thought he wouldn't find it. He would just have to prove them wrong—again.

Davenport made one last check on the two crewmembers—the only two crewmembers. He pushed past Dice and didn't even try to avoid bumping into the giant creature.

Davenport strode to the bulkhead hatch on the back wall and entered the ship. Dice's heavy footsteps and Beauty's scuffling ones followed him, but Davenport didn't turn around.

He made his way to the bridge and strolled right in without knocking. A tall, very beautiful woman stood up from where she was bending over the navigation station. Waist-length black hair swished down her back and flint-black eyes glistened in her delicate, ivory-white face.

A mischievous smile twitched the corners of her mouth when Davenport walked in. "You didn't have to bring Big Boris for little old us, Davenport. I might think you were trying to flatter me."

"I'll flatter you for hiding whatever contraband you're carrying where I can't find it. Cut the small talk, Lyons, and let's get your inspection over with so I can get you off my outpost."

She burst into a huge grin. "Aw, Davenport! I thought you liked us visiting Ultra Meridian."

"If you mean I like earning credits for laying successful charges against you, then yes, I do. When are you gonna learn to make your stops at other outposts and quit wasting my time? I thought you were smarter than that. You know you can't pull anything over on me. You'd have better luck with a different sheriff."

She laughed out loud. "Okay, now I know you're flirting with me."

He stuck out his hand. "Where's your cargo manifest?"

She passed him a palm-sized chip. "It's all there. Nothing is missing and you can see it's all straight and above board."

"Straight and above board," Davenport repeated. "That must be pig Latin for 'this cargo will get me forty years in Terminus Anathema'."

"Terminus Anathema," a hissing, raspy voice interrupted.

Davenport turned around to see Beauty climbing on top of the central processor workstation behind the main command podium. He squatted right on top of it and his long fingers danced over the controls while he shot Lyons and Davenport furtive glances with his unnatural eyes.

"Have you been to Terminus Anathema, Beauty?" Davenport asked. "Did you ever meet a prisoner there named Calyx Elkanon?"

Dice let out a thunderous bellow behind Davenport's back. Davenport had to seriously control himself not to spin around and aim Big Boris at the monster.

"Don't tell me," Lyons complained. "You already bribed Beauty with food. You gave him another strawberry ChunkyTender and he told you all our secrets, didn't he?"

Now it was Davenport's turn to laugh. "I should have thought of that. Then I wouldn't have to spend my morning going over this crate with a fine-toothed comb."

"ChunkyTender," Beauty breathed in rapture.

"Beauty didn't tell the sheriff anything," Dice rumbled. "Beauty's our man. He doesn't sing to nobody."

"I bet he sings to you, doesn't he, Dice?" Davenport asked over his shoulder. "I bet Beauty sings you real pretty bedtime lullabies to soothe you to sleep when your XQ-85 just doesn't do it for you anymore. Tell me I'm wrong."

Dice snarled low in his barrel chest and Lyons interrupted. "Can we get our stamp and get out of here? I wouldn't want to keep you from your latest ham sandwich."

Davenport laughed again and switched on the manifest chip. He scanned down the list of goods itemized there. He saw at a glance that the manifest was indeed totally straight and above board. What he was looking for wouldn't be on it.

Chapter 2

D avenport stopped in the middle of the *Echo Omicron's* crew quarters corridor. He glanced up and down it at a dozen doors standing open. "Where are Beauty's quarters?"

"Beauty's quarters!" Beauty barked. "Beauty's quarters—no!"

"Beauty doesn't have quarters," Lyons told Davenport. "You've already taken this damn ship apart piece by piece. When are you going to believe we aren't carrying anything illegal? We're straight, Davenport. I'm telling you the truth."

"You don't know what the statements, 'we're straight' and 'I'm telling you the truth' mean. Now tell me where Beauty sleeps. If he doesn't have quarters, he must sleep somewhere. Now show me where it is. You won't get your stamp until you do."

"Kuniak warthog!" Dice bellowed from behind Lyons. "You're stalling! You can't find nothing so you're pulling this shit out of your tired ass to slow us down."

"I can slow you down even more by standing around arguing about it all day long. I'll tell you what I'll do. I promise you that, if I don't find anything wherever it is that Beauty sleeps, I'll give you your stamp and send you on your way with my blessing. Is it a deal?"

Dice and Lyons exchanged glances. Davenport watched their reactions down to the micron. This must be it. He'd searched everywhere else and hadn't found one thing that wasn't on the manifest. Even Dice's XQ-85 was on the manifest.

"Show him, Beauty," Lyons ordered. "Let's get this over with and get him off our ship."

"No!" Beauty glared up at Davenport with undisguised loathing. He crouched at Dice's heel and crawled after the crew on their interminable inspection through the *Echo Omicron's* many compartments, cabins, and storage cupboards. "I won't show him!"

"Is this the thanks I get for giving you my strawberry ChunkyTender?" Davenport gave the creature a pained expression. "I'm hurt, Beauty. That was my lunch."

Beauty turned his head aside and sulked. Davenport could look right down into the creature's over-large ear canal. "Fine."

Dice and Lyons led the way to the far end of the corridor. Lyons slid aside a panel to reveal a linen compartment set into the bulkhead. "Here. Beauty sleeps here."

Davenport peered into the lightless space barely big enough for a single person. Shelves filled the closet to about three feet off the floor. Clean sheets, blankets, canisters of soap, and a few other innocuous supplies lined the shelves.

A pile of filthy, dirt-smudged blankets lay on the floor underneath. Years of overuse and neglect had compacted them into a thin board of threadbare fabric. A round, body-shaped depression in the middle gave mute testimony that some creature had in fact been sleeping here for a long, long time.

"Mine!" Beauty snarled. "You keep out."

Davenport didn't reply. He squatted down and his scalp prickled when he examined the small, crude bed. This had to be it. Whatever the crew was smuggling must be here. He'd already checked the whole rest of the ship. He didn't believe for a split second that the *Echo Omicron* crew suddenly decided to turn straight and above board.

He shifted Big Boris to his left hand and stretched out his right to move the blankets. Lightning quick, Beauty shot forward and seized Davenport's wrist. He jerked Davenport's arm back with unbelievable strength. "No! You don't touch my place."

Davenport froze. He didn't try to take his arm away. Fighting Beauty would earn him a broken arm and maybe even an amputated one. Beauty might go berserk if Davenport played this wrong.

"Let him search it, Beauty," Lyons told the creature. "As soon as he sees that this imaginary contraband isn't in your bed, he'll give us our stamp and we never have to see his ugly face again."

Not until next time, at least. Davenport remained perfectly still. He didn't even look up. "If you let go, I'll give you another ChunkyTender—a peach one this time."

Beauty let out a low, menacing hiss and unwound his fleshless fingers from Davenport's wrist. Nice and easy, Davenport eased his hand to his back pants pocket.

He took out his last, most treasured possession—his last peach ChunkyTender. He always carried the other flavors for those moments when he needed to ease his hunger or for bribing easily satisfied species like Beauty's.

He kept the peach ones for himself. Most people did. They were too rare and too delicious to waste on everyday fare.

He handed it over. He felt not a tinge of regret when Beauty snatched it from him and wolfed the whole thing. If one peach Chunky Tender earned Davenport whatever the *Echo Omicron* was hiding, the trade would be worth it.

Lyons pulled Beauty away and Davenport heard the creature slurping in the background. Now Davenport could do his work in peace. He picked up the dirty blankets pulled them out of the closet.

Dust and a powerful stench of rot billowed from them. He pushed them away to reveal a perfectly smooth metal floor. Not a single seam, rivet, or connection interrupted the flawless plate.

He bent down and ran his hand over it searching for the tiniest sign. It had to be here. He couldn't believe they might have fooled him.

"You see?" Lyons told him. "There's nothing here, Davenport. When are you going to believe us?"

"You said this would be your last stop," Dice growled. "Give us our stamp like you promised."

He didn't have to turn around to see the three of them standing behind him. He didn't even need to see their expressions to know they were lying. They had to be.

He slid his palm to the left wall and felt along the edge to the corner. He examined every inch of the floor. It was solid, smooth, and secure. It looked exactly the way it should look if it had never been tampered with.

"Give it up, Davenport," Lyons told him. "We're finished here."

He wasn't finished by a long way. He pivoted his weight forward and pressed down on the floor. Sure enough, it clicked downward, locked, and then popped up. It didn't show any extra space around the edges, but that click was enough. It told Davenport everything he needed to know.

He prodded the plate's edges with his fingers and the righthand side swiveled upward toward him. He moved it out of the way to reveal a tiny hollow underneath Beauty's bed.

Another sheet of solid metal plate rested right under the first except this one had a two-inch slot carved in the middle of it. A thin steel cartridge lay tucked it into this slot. Beads of dew clung to its shiny sides. It hardly looked bigger than an ammo cylinder in one of Davenport's sidearms.

He hooked his fingernail around the cartridge and lifted it out. A tiny label on the side read, *Ithium: Highly Toxic. Hazardous Materials.*

"Shit!" Dice whispered.

Davenport stood up and slipped the cartridge into his vest pocket. He pushed past Lyons, Dice, and Beauty and set off down the corridor without a word.

The three smugglers raced after him all talking at once. "What are you gonna do, Davenport?" Lyons asked. "Are you going report us to the Confederate Corps? We weren't at fault. We were only carrying it for a client."

"What do we have to do to get our stamp?" Dice asked. "How much do you want? Name your price."

Beauty hopped up and down around Davenport's legs trying to grab him. "You give that back! That isn't yours."

Davenport didn't answer any of them. He marched straight to the bridge and stopped next to the central processor workstation. "What do you think you're doing?" Lyon's voice spiked a register higher. "Hey! What are you doing? You can't do that! Davenport!"

He popped open the circuitry access partition under the workstation and his gaze skipped over racks and racks of circuits lined up there. He pushed some wires out of the way and snapped a regulator drum off one of the circuit chips.

Beauty charged him, screeching, "No!"

Davenport dropped Big Boris in a heartbeat and shot out his other hand. He hooked the webbing of his thumb and forefinger around Beauty's neck. Davenport held the creature at arm's length while Beauty spat and seethed and raged at the end of his arm.

Just as fast, Dice grabbed Beauty by one arm and hauled him away from Davenport. He wrestled Beauty back while Davenport picked up Big Boris and got to his feet.

He faced the crew with the drum in one hand and Big Boris in the other. "I'm officially grounding the *Echo Omicron* and confiscating your stability gyroscope so you can't launch. You three aren't going anywhere until I report this to the Reserve Wing. As soon as they get here, they'll take you into custody, impound your ship, and I'll hand over the Ithium. Do yourselves a big favor and stay here until they come. Don't do anything stupid like running away or trying to get the Ithium back. You're in enough trouble already."

"You can't do this, Davenport." Lyons's voice trembled. "Don't do this to us."

"I just did."

Chapter 3

Davenport headed back to the Ultra Meridian jail. Those idiots on the *Echo Omicron* were constitutionally incapable of transporting any cargo without doing something illegal. He knew they were carrying something contraband. He just never dreamed it would be something as bad as this.

Ithium—shit! How did they get their hands on it? He shuddered when he thought what they might have done if he didn't find it. If they got their stamp at Ultra Meridian, nothing would have stopped them from delivering it to whatever client hired them to get it.

The cartridge burned a hole in Davenport's pocket. The sooner he got it off his outpost, the better. He passed through the cargo hold with no interference from the three smugglers. They'd be up on the bridge planning what to do next, but that didn't worry Davenport.

Lyons was too smart to try anything on Ultra Meridian. The *Echo Omicron* was the only legal ship on the planet. If they decided to try anything like an escape attempt, they would wait until the Reserve Wing arrived and transported them somewhere else, somewhere with more options.

He pulled on his mask and goggles. He pressed his elbow against his side pocket to protect the Ithium cartridge from the wind and sand. If anything happened to it on his watch, he'd be in as much trouble as the *Echo Omicron* crew—probably a lot more.

He marched back to the jail and stripped off his mask again. He didn't even bother to hang Big Boris on its hook by the door. He headed straight for his desk.

"Hey, porkchop!" Emmet roared through the bars. "You better know I'm filing an official complaint with the Confederate Corps about my treatment in your fine law enforcement establishment. We've been here five hours and you haven't made one attempt to give my partner any medical treatment."

Davenport knelt down on the floor behind his desk, pulled back the floorboards, and exposed the blast-proof safe buried in the rock underneath. "Don't worry, Emmet. I'll be sending a message to my Section chief in a few minutes. You can include your complaint in the same transmission."

"Hey! I didn't mean now!" Emmet blustered. "You can't....."

Davenport ignored him. He spun the dial on the safe, entered his combination, and lifted out the door. He wrapped the Ithium cartridge in his own handkerchief and tucked into the safe along with Emmet's and Lenny's personal effects.

He shut the safe, spun the dial again to lock it, and replaced the floorboards. He finally let himself relax enough to face Emmet. "Now, Emmet. What was this you wanted to say about filing a complaint against me?"

Emmet opened and shut his mouth a few times, but he didn't make a sound. He glanced toward the safe and then back at Davenport. "I only meant....."

"I'll give you ten minutes. If you haven't come up with your complaint by the time I contact my Section Chief, you'll have to wait until the next transmission."

Davenport hung up Big Boris and sat down behind his desk. This promised to be one of the worst days of his life. It started with a simple inspection and ended like this.

Ithium—son of a bitch! He never would have thought the *Echo Omicron* crew had the nerve to get mixed up in something like this. Maybe he underestimated them.

He shook those thoughts out of his mind and opened the draw near his stomach. It slid toward him to reveal a transmission panel dotted with controls.

Ultra Meridian might be the last outpost on the way to nowhere, but the jail had enough power to get help when he needed it.

He might have to wait a few days before he received a reply....or quite a few days. It all depended on how much space dust happened to be floating between here and there at the time.

He dialed up the nearest Reserve Wing relay station at Macron Calypso. He typed out his report and finished with a note to his Section Chief about the case being urgent. He highlighted that a small, domestic-grade combination safe was the only thing protecting the Ithium cartridge from recapture.

"Last chance, Emmet!" Davenport called out as soon as he finished. "Are you ready to write out your complaint now?"

Davenport looked up just in time to see a small, masked head dart around the door-frame right in front of him. Before he could think to react, the petite figure whipped a rifle across the threshold and fired.

The charge whistled into the jail. Davenport dove sideways and the projectile barely missed decapitating him. It smashed into the wall behind his head and the plaster exploded.

He sprang up pulling both sidearms. He popped his head over the desk to see the stranger storming into the jail. In one blink, he saw that it was a woman—a very slightly built woman barely five feet tall.

Whoever she was swiveled sideways and made for the cell. The witch took her attention off Davenport completely and gave him a perfect shot.

He fired both sidearms. One shot clipped the stranger's mask and the invader spun backward from the impact. Davenport's other charge hit the attacker in the shoulder and she whirled in Davenport's direction with a strangled cry.

The rifle swung with the stranger and the attacker opened fire. She pumped the weapon firing again and again with incredible speed. Davenport ducked for cover behind his desk, dove past his chair, and fired again between the desk legs.

The stranger didn't make the same mistake twice. She barged straight for the desk unloading dozens of shots.

Whoever this was didn't come from the *Echo Omicron*. She was way too small and he didn't peg any of the three as stupid enough to attack a Confederate outpost to get anything back, not even a payload as valuable as an Ithium cartridge.

The stranger stormed around Davenport's desk and halted right next to the chair. She whipped her rifle to her shoulder and would have blasted Davenport to pieces if he didn't roll under the desk just in time.

He leapt upright on the other side and got off four shots, two from each sidearm. Now it was the attacker's turn to dive for cover. Davenport bought himself a split second to lunge behind the door and seize Big Boris.

He wheeled the enormous gun around, but his attacker already on her feet. Her rifle went off and he ducked for cover again. He collapsed to the floor and rotated Big Boris around to fire.

He had a straight shot at the attacker and would have blown her into a cloud of blood and powdered bone, but the cell containing Emmet and Lenny stood right behind her. If he fired at her, he would hit the cell, too.

He hesitated for a fraction of a second, and in that instant, a catastrophic explosion struck the jail. The whole building vaporized in a giant thunderclap of dust, fire, and deafening noise.

Davenport came to and rolled onto his stomach gagging on the tang of dust and smoke. He coughed to get his lungs working and tasted blood. He spat it out and struggled onto his knees trying to see something, anything.

He looked around him and had to think twice before he remembered where he was. Blocks of stone, twisted metal, and piles of rubble lay in the center of the plane where the Ultra Meridian jail used to be. Only a few twisted bars remained of the cell that housed the two drunks.

Davenport tried to stand up and crashed down on one knee. His whole body hurt, but when he spotted the woman tottering to her feet a few feet away, he forced himself up. He scrambled to lift Big Boris from the floor next to him. He spotted one of his sidearms not far away and he grabbed that, too.

The woman had the advantage over him. She stumbled through the wreckage to the bars. When she took hold of them, they dislodged from the floor and fell aside.

She hurled them away and staggered into what was left of the cell. She bent over Emmet who lay face down across a pile of broken blocks. "Get up! Get up!"

She hauled him to his feet by his armpits. He swayed and she slung one of his arms across her shoulders. She lugged him away.

Davenport rocketed to his feet and rotated Big Boris to his shoulder. "Stop right there! Freeze!"

The woman pointed a sidearm behind her without turning around. She fired and Davenport had to dodge. He aimed his weapon again, but if he missed at this range, she would almost certainly get away.

He thrust out his sidearm to shoot, but she kept up her own barrage of shots to throw him off balance. She hustled Emmet out of the ruined jail and hit the smooth dirt behind the building.

Davenport saw in a flash that she was heading for the Beast. The skimmer sat parked in its usual place behind the jail. The explosion hadn't touched it. It offered the only escape for these fugitives and Davenport didn't dare to hit that.

He sprang forward to intercept the fleeing pair, but the rubble under his feet slowed him down. He took aim and fired, but he stumbled more than once and missed. His fire only spurred the woman to run faster.

Emmet revived enough to run at her side. She hopped onto the Beast and he swung his leg over behind her. She fired the engine. That sound flaring across the desert stabbed straight to Davenport's guts. He couldn't let them get away—not with his Beast. No way.

He took a gamble and hurdled the last blocks. His boot heels hit the hard-packed soil and he rocketed forward to intercept them. He slung Big Boris's strap over his torso. He wouldn't be firing it at this range and it would only slow him down.

He fired his sidearm again and again. If he hit anything, he didn't hear over the engine screaming. The woman punched the throttle and the skimmer shot forward so fast that Emmet almost toppled off the back.

They streaked past Davenport. In his last act of desperation, he took a running leap to tackle the vehicle. He had to stop them from stealing it, but he still held his sidearm in one hand.

Both wrists slammed down on the bar behind the seat. He scrambled to consolidate his grip, slipped, and finally caught on with his left hand. He floundered to close his right fingers around the bar, too, but his sidearm got in the way.

His brain screamed at him to let go of his sidearm and hold onto that bar. Another part of him argued that he could NOT let go of his sidearm whatever happened. He wrestled between these two urges while the Beast ripped his shoulder from its socket picking up speed.

The woman gunned the engine to the breaking point. The Beast picked up speed shrieking across the flats. Davenport's feet and knees bounced and bumped behind the vehicle each time it hit a little wave of turbulence.

The woman yelled something to Emmet over her shoulder. Emmet turned around and yelled at Davenport. Emmet punched Davenport's knuckles a few times trying to knock him off the Beast.

Davenport tried to swing his sidearm up to shoot Emmet, but the Beast jostled him too much to get a decent shot. Beyond the handlebars, Davenport could see the hills coming up fast. As soon as the woman started driving up into those hills, he would fall off and this whole nightmare would be over.

His shoulder couldn't possibly hurt more than it already did, so he swung his right arm back and crammed his sidearm into its holster. Now he could hold onto the bar with both hands and just in time.

The woman yanked back on the handlebars and rocketed into the hills. She plunged over ridges, into ravines, and up more rocky slopes leaving Ultra Meridian far behind.

Chapter 4

"Stop! Stop!" Davenport bellowed, but he could hardly hear himself over the Beast's engine noise. The motor shrieked to its highest pitch propelling the skimmer up more steep hills into the wilderness outside Ultra Meridian.

The woman yelled something to Emmet again and Emmet went into another frenzy of trying to beat Davenport off the rear seat bar. Once, Emmet succeeded in knocking Davenport's right hand away and he almost tumbled off.

Davenport wound back his free arm and tried to punch Emmet back, but the Beast gave a terrible lurch and he missed. He had to grab onto the bar again to avoid getting dumped into a ditch.

The woman swiveled around a pointed hill and shot almost straight upward trying to get to the summit. She made it halfway when the Beast stalled. She cranked back the throttle, but the engine only howled louder and didn't go anywhere. It struggled for a moment and then started to slide backward down the hill.

She yelled something else. Emmet yelled at Davenport, but the Beast was dead in the water. She cut the engine and the Beast sank to the ground still pointing its nose toward the summit.

The woman hopped off the Beast, ripped off her mask, and stormed around the skimmer. She wound back her foot and delivered a brutal kick to Davenport's side. "Get off, you bastard! You're screwing up the Beast!"

Davenport rounded on her with a roar of pain and rage. "This is *my* Beast, you stupid, murdering thief! You blew up my jail and now you're stealing my Beast right out from under my nose. You're both under arrest. Get down on the ground and put your hands above your heads."

"There's two of us and only one of you, porkchop, and do I need to remind you that you don't have a jail anymore? Where would you put us—assuming you actually *could* get us back to Ultra Meridian—which you can't?"

Something in the way she called him 'porkchop' made Davenport stop and look at her for the first time. Something about her looked familiar, but he couldn't put his finger on it.

She couldn't be over twenty and she wore her shoulder-length brown hair in a no-nonsense arrangement with the top half tied back. The back hung down straight and she wore beaten leather boots, jacket, and vest like most other Ultra Meridian locals.

Her rifle strap slung across her chest bandolier style. A hand-stitched leather ammo pouch draped the other way and two holsters hung from her belt. She presented such a stereotypical picture of an Ultra Meridian desert rat that Davenport immediately thought he knew her.

"You're still under arrest—both of you," he told her. "Emmet, you're guilty of evading arrest and *you*....whoever you are—you're guilty of destruction of public property, attempted murder of a public officer...."

"I didn't blow up the jail, porkchop. Emmet and I could have both been killed in that explosion.....or are you too stupid to realize that?"

"You shot at me and tried to kill me. If you didn't blow it up, who did?"

She sneered at him. "I was trying to free Emmet. If I had been trying to blow up the jail, I wouldn't have done with both of us inside."

Davenport glanced over his shoulder. They'd covered so many miles that he couldn't even see Ultra Meridian from here. Dusty, barren hills surrounded them on all sides.

The events of the day flashed through his mind and he remembered. The Ithium cartridge was still back at the jail.

He didn't think a blast that size could destroy the safe, but either way, the Ithium would be totally unprotected. If it fell into the wrong hands, the results could be disastrous.

"We have to go back." Davenport made a move toward the Beast. "You two are coming with me. Don't make me have to cuff you."

"To hell with you!" she snapped. "I'm not going anywhere except...."

"Yeah." Emmet headed for the Beast, too. "Let's go back to Ultra Meridian."

The woman rounded on him spitting tacks. "Are you out of your mind? You can't go back. He'll lock you up."

"It doesn't matter. My payload is back at the jail. I have to go back."

"What payload?" she asked.

"What payload?" Davenport asked.

Emmet tried to grab the Beast. "Let's go."

Davenport shot out a hand to block his path. "I asked you a question, Emmet. What payload did you leave back at the jail?"

"Don't tell him anything, Emmet," the woman cut in. "He's trying to trap you."

"Can it, Fiddler," Emmet fired back. "I'll handle this my own way."

She scowled at him, but she didn't interrupt. Emmet faced Davenport. "What did you do with my personal effects when you arrested me and Lenny?"

"I put them in the safe the same way I always do. Don't you remember?"

Emmet frowned and thought about it, but he'd been in another world when Davenport took him and Lenny into custody. Emmet was so boozed out that he didn't notice when Davenport relieved him of his personal effects before locking him in the cell.

Emmet made another dive for the Beast. "We have to go back. We have to get it."

Davenport stepped forward, but Fiddler got to the Beast first. She hopped onto the seat and pushed Davenport away. "Get lost, JuicyPie."

Davenport slapped his hand down to his sidearm. He jerked it out and aimed it at her head. "Get your ass off my Beast before I leave your bullet-riddled corpse right here."

Emmet approached the Beast from the other side. "Buzz off, Davenport. This is none of your affair. You can make it back to Ultra Meridian on foot."

Davenport changed his mind in a flash. He swiveled his sidearm downward and pointed it at the fuel tank between Fiddler's legs. He dropped his voice to a dangerous murmur. "If anyone is going anywhere on foot, it will be you two. This is my Beast, and if you don't get off it right now, I'll blow the pair of you sky high. I won't say it again."

Both of them turned to look at him. Davenport didn't pay Emmet any attention at all. The guy hadn't been sober for more than a few minutes in the last twenty years.

Davenport focused all his attention on Fiddler. Anyone with the balls to barge into the Ultra Meridian jail holding a loaded rifle had to be the one in charge here.

Before she could react, the familiar whine of more engines drifted over the landscape. They came from behind the party, from the direction of Ultra Meridian.

All three pricked up their ears. "Who could that be?" Emmet muttered.

"They're following us," Fiddler whispered.

"They're after the payload." Emmet swung onto the Beast. "Drive, Fiddler! We can't get back to the jail now."

She fired the engine. Davenport thought fast. A single glance behind him showed him a dozen skimmers launching over the hills on a dead course for his position. If someone followed them from Ultra Meridian, that meant he couldn't get back to the jail right now, either, especially not without the Beast.

Instinct took over and he jumped onto the Beast behind Emmet. Emmet grabbed Davenport and held him on while Fiddler gunned the engine one more time.

The Beast floundered the same as before. These skimmers weren't designed to carry two people let alone three.

Lightning quick, Fiddler ripped the skimmer sideways and plunged downhill into gullies snaking between the many hills.

The Beast picked up speed now that it didn't have to drive straight uphill. It dove back and forth around corners. Fiddler steered with expert skill, but she only covered a few miles before the pursuers dropped into the gully behind Davenport's back.

Five skimmers flew to intercept the fleeing trio. Gunshots ricocheted off the hills on either side and showered the fugitives in dirt and gravel.

"Faster!" Davenport roared. "They're gaining on us."

"This tub can't go any faster!" Another shot clanged against the fender and knocked the Beast sideways. The skimmer's speed almost sent it spinning into the nearest slope.

Davenport ripped out his sidearm and returned fire, but one sidearm against five attackers wouldn't do anything. The pursuers whipped around a corner and burned up on the Beast.

They got so close that Davenport could see the large Howitzers mounted on their sides. The drivers could fire without letting go of their handlebars.

Another volley punched into the Beast from behind and one of the engines blew out. The Beast wobbled something awful and barely stayed ahead of the pursuit.

"Give me your rifle!" Davenport bellowed over the noise.

Fiddler handed it back. Davenport holstered his sidearm and turned the rifle on his enemies, but he already knew it wouldn't be enough. If he'd been standing still, he could blow them to smithereens with Big Boris, but at this speed, he wouldn't even be able to hit them.

Another shot seared past Davenport's leg and smashed into the Beast's front end. The stabilizers exploded and the Beast jerked hard to the right. Fiddler shrieked out struggling to control the vehicle, "Hold on and get ready to deploy!"

"Deploy?" Davenport yelled. "What are you talking about?"

Only the howl of engines answered him. The Beast slowed even more and it juddered in its dying throes. It couldn't keep going much longer.

The pursuit knew it, too, and they stopped firing. They slowed down and Davenport recognized that they all wore some kind of uniform, but he didn't see any insignia that would identify them.

At that moment, Fiddler jerked the Beast up another hill. The skimmer struggled even more, but just when it threatened to give up the ghost entirely, she dove over a ridge and plummeted down the other side.

The Beast lost stability at the very peak. Instead of righting itself for the downward plunge, the engines died completely. The Beast tumbled head over heel and pitched Fiddler, Emmet, and Davenport off the seat.

All three slammed down hard right behind the ridge. Fiddler jerked over onto her stomach and tore her rifle out of Davenport's hands. "Get ready to repel them!"

"Are you insane?" he roared. "We can't fight them all."

"They're coming!" She scrambled to the ridge and rotated her rifle to her shoulder. "Fire when you see them exposed."

Davenport flopped down next to her and pulled Big Boris into position. The pursuit's skimmers revved at full power. They rocketed up the hill heading straight for the ridge. Davenport measured their trajectory and saw that Fiddler was right. He timed his move down to the millimeter.

The first skimmer zoomed up the slope blasting away with its Howitzers. The three fugitives huddled behind the peak and the shots soared over their heads. The skimmer cleared the ridge and hurtled straight up.

Davenport followed the vehicle with his weapon. At the apogee of its flight, he fired directly into the undercarriage. The blast ripped the chassis in half and the charge blew straight into the fuel tank.

The skimmer ruptured in a ball of fire that flung its rider into the gully beyond, but Davenport didn't have time to celebrate before another three skimmers sprinted in for the attack. He couldn't hit them all.

Fiddler concentrated her rifle fire on one skimmer and Davenport took another. The three pursuers launched over their heads. Fiddler dumped twenty shots into her target. The two skimmers on each end exploded, but the third streaked past them unharmed.

The skimmer whipped around behind the ridge and laid into the defenders with every Howitzer blazing. Just as fast, the fifth skimmer dropped in on top of the fugitives and pinned them between the two vehicles.

Davenport tried to reposition Big Boris, but the Howitzers pounded the ridge with so many blasts that he had to scramble to get away. Emmet and Fiddler tripped over him in their race to escape, but it was too late.

The two surviving skimmers buzzed around the party and showered them with Howitzer fire. Davenport couldn't see the Beast anymore—not that it would do him any good.

He squinted through curtains of spraying dirt and ripped-up sod for any way out when, out of nowhere, one of the skimmers blew. It popped in a sudden starburst of igniting fuel.

The other skimmer wheeled around to face the new threat and that one detonated, too. In half a second, both vehicles disintegrated to nothing.

Chapter 5

Davenport blinked dirt out of his eyes to see four tiny figures standing on the opposite slope. They aimed huge XQs at the clouds of smoke and fumes that used to be the enemy skimmers.

A puff of wind blew the soot and ash away and Davenport found himself looking at four petite women as slight and wiry as Fiddler. Their tiny size made their weapons look even bigger than Dice's, but Davenport couldn't be certain from this range.

The instant the dust settled, the women rushed across the gully and threw their arms around Fiddler. They all started talking at once. "We got here as soon as we could!"

"We heard the noise and figured you were in trouble."

"How did things go at Ultra Meridian?"

"You got Emmet out!"

"Who's that guy?"

Fiddler hugged her friends back. "Thanks for coming to get us."

"We wouldn't leave you out here facing those....." One of the newcomers looked around. "Who were those guys?"

"We don't know," Fiddler told them. "Let's get out of sight and we can talk about what to do."

"What is there to do?" another asked. "You got away from them and you got Emmet. The show's over."

"Who are you guys?" Davenport asked. "Not that I'm not grateful to you for saving our asses and all that, but I like to know who I'm talking to."

"This is Fizzle, Frost, and Flack." Fiddler pointed out each one in turn. "These are my crew. We're the Armageddon Core."

"*Your* crew?" Davenport snorted.

"If you don't know who those guys were, why were they following you?" Fizzle asked.

"Who cares?" Flack replied. "We can't stay out here. More will be coming along any second now. We heard more than five skimmers in the canyons."

"The cavern isn't far away," Frost told everyone. "You can come with us."

"Emmet left his payload behind," Fiddler told them. "He wants to go back to Ultra Meridian."

"So does Davenport," Davenport chimed in.

The four women examined him. "Who's Davenport?"

"He's the Sheriff of Ultra Meridian," Davenport replied. "He was holding Emmet under arrest when Fiddler attacked the jail and blew it to kingdom come."

"Fiddler did NOT blow the jail to kingdom come," Fiddler snapped back. "How many times do I have to tell you?"

"Let me see if I can get this straight." Davenport counted on his fingers. "You attacked the Ultra Meridian jail with a loaded firearm and got into a gun battle with the Sheriff while he was executing his duties as an officer of the law. While this was going on, the jail exploded, killing one man and nearly killing two others, and you seriously expect me to believe you had nothing to do with that? How stupid do you think I am?"

"I....wouldn't ask that question if I was you," Flack muttered, "At least, I wouldn't word it that way if I was in your position."

"I didn't blow up the jail, Davenport," Fiddler retorted. "Yes, I did all those other things, but I could have been killed in that explosion, too."

"The Ultra Meridian jail blew up?" Frost squeaked. "That can't be good."

"It did more than blow up," Emmet growled. "It was completely flattened. It was leveled."

The three women stared at him with huge eyes and then turned to Davenport. "Are *you* really the Sheriff of Ultra Meridian?" Fizzle asked.

"Yes, I am, which means I'm empowered to commandeer any equipment and supplies you might have to bring fugitives to justice. I need you to resupply me with ammo and any way to get back to Ultra Meridian."

"I'm going with you," Emmet told him.

"No," Davenport snapped, "you aren't. Any valuable payload you left at the jail was lawfully confiscated when I arrested you and Lenny. You won't get it back until two things happen. First, you have to be acquitted of any illegal activity or serve a sentence for your original indictable crime. Second, I have to determine that the payload in question isn't contraband that you'd be forbidden to hold in your possession at all."

Flack turned to Fiddler. "Does he always talk like this?"

"He sounds like he ate a computer," Frost added.

"Ignore him," Fiddler told them. "He's in shock after the explosion."

"Do you have ammo, supplies, and equipment or not?" Davenport demanded.

The four young women exchanged glances. Fizzle nodded over her shoulder. "If you're really the Sheriff of Ultra Meridian, you better come with us."

Davenport examined the three young fighters with an unerring eye. He spent far too much time at Ultra Meridian not to recognize that they *were* fighters—experienced fighters.

They wore the same scuffed leather clothing as Fiddler and they handled their weapons with expert ease. They might be young and small, but they must have been doing this kind of thing for a long time.

The Beast lay in pieces at the bottom of the gully. It wouldn't take him anywhere. The four young women started hiking down the hill to the gully bottom, but they didn't go near the Beast.

They followed the bottom through many twists and turns. They kept their weapons trained upward the whole time and covered every possible hiding place the pursuit might use to ambush them.

Fiddler and Davenport did the same thing. The longer this went on, the more relieved Davenport became that he'd fallen in with these....well, he couldn't really think of them as kids. They reminded him of a gang or maybe something more like a military squad—though they didn't look or talk like a military squad.

Anyway, military didn't come out to Ultra Meridian. These women wouldn't call themselves Armageddon Core if they weren't criminal.

If these women were here, dressed like this, and defending themselves and their friends with this kind of precision and discipline, they could only be criminal elements. No other kind of people ever set up shop on Ultra Meridian—except for himself, of course.

Chapter 6

After more than two hours of hard slogging, the Armageddon Core climbed up a hill at an angle to the contour. They ascended to a hidden track running parallel to the slope. It curved around the hill and between some rocks where it entered a concealed tunnel.

The tunnel wasn't four feet high. Davenport and Emmet had to crouch to get into it. The Armageddon Core had to bend over, too, but their miniature stature made the crush less uncomfortable for them.

Davenport straightened up with relief at the tunnel's end. It emerged into a cavern rising to a ceiling carved out of bedrock. The central hall split off into side passages of various sizes, each dotted with more rooms and compartments.

A long counter ran the length of the central cavern's side wall. Another young woman sat there in front of dozens upon dozens of computers. Each one blinked with camera footage, charts, maps—the works.

She turned around and examined the Armageddon Core. "Who the hell is this?"

"Sheriff Davenport from Ultra Meridian," Fiddler replied. "He was just leaving."

The computer technician raised her eyebrows ever so slightly. "It looks more like he just arrived."

Fiddler waved toward the technician. "This is Friend."

"Let me guess," Davenport remarked. "She's your friend."

"The ammo and supplies are over here." Frost entered one of the side passages and showed Davenport a room packed to the rafters with fuel, ration, and equipment canisters. "I guess you can help yourself." She lifted a brick-sized lump out of the nearest canister. "Here. Have a JuicyPie. You look like you need cheering up."

He didn't take the JuicyPie. He was too busy squinting at Friend's computers. "What are you kids getting up to down here? What do you need all this for?"

Flack smacked her lips in annoyance. "What do you think? All the other posses on this planet would wipe us out if they knew we were horning in on their territory. We have to keep them under surveillance. We have to keep tabs on their intelligence and their movements. It's the only way we can have any advanced warning if they're onto us."

Davenport migrated closer to the counter. Friend's hands darted from one machine to the next. She entered data, adjusted the feeds, pivoted certain data sets against others before she fed the results into other spreadsheets.....

"Hey!" Flack yelled at Davenport. "Are you resupplying or not? No one said you could stick your grubby fingers in our business."

Davenport halted right behind Friend's chair. Now that he studied the screens up close, he could see that at least half of them showed locations off this planet. The Armageddon Core wasn't monitoring the other criminal organizations, gangs, bands, and posses at all. That was a smokescreen for a much larger, more complicated operation.

Frost strode over to him and shoved against his arm. "Get over there and resupply like you said. As soon as you take what you want, get out of our cavern and be on your way. We don't want you around any longer than you have to be."

He didn't budge. "If it's happening on this planet, it's my business."

Fiddler rolled her eyes to the ceiling and groaned. "How did I know this was a terrible idea?"

"We can't get rid of him anyway," Emmet chimed in. "He's going back to Ultra Meridian and he's the only way I can get my payload. If I went back without him, he would arrest me again."

"Or worse," Davenport added.

Emmet's eyes popped, but the others didn't notice. "We have to find out who those people were who followed us." Fiddler turned to Friend. "Can you trace where they came from?"

"They came from Ultra Meridian," the technician replied over her shoulder. "I traced them before you destroyed their skimmers."

"Ultra Meridian!" Flack exclaimed. "Did they come from that ship parked near the jail.....What's it called?"

"*Echo Omicron*," Davenport replied, "and those pursuers didn't come from the ship. I'm certain of it."

"What makes you so sure?"

"Because I searched the whole ship about ten minutes before you attacked the jail. They didn't have a single skimmer on board, much less Howitzer-armed skimmers. They also only had three people on board, not twelve, and two of the people who were on board couldn't ride a skimmer even if they had them."

"There he goes again," Frost muttered. "Turn him on and he just doesn't stop talking."

"Those pursuers came from somewhere else." Davenport pointed to one of the maps. "You're tracking Mount Refractory. Could they have sent out those skimmers?"

Friend didn't turn around. She kept tippy-tapping her machines as frantically as ever. She kept swiveling her chair from one screen to the next and rolling her chair up and down the counter. Davenport couldn't figure out how she processed so much information so fast.

"They didn't come from Mount Refractory," she told him. "I monitored them the whole time from when they launched to follow you until you destroyed the skimmers. They came from Ultra Meridian."

"That's impossible," Davenport insisted. "The *Echo Omicron* is the only ship at Ultra Meridian. I already know the skimmers didn't come from there."

"Can you show us footage of where the skimmers did come from?" Fiddler asked. "Did you monitor that?"

Friend didn't answer. She switched one of her surveillance feeds to a camera set up directly over the Ultra Meridian plane. It must be perched on a rock high in the mountains. It gave a bird's eye view of the *Echo Omicron* and the jail...when there still was a jail at Ultra Meridian.

One second, the camera showed the whole scene as blank and still and boring as ever. The next instant, a missile plummeted out of the clear sky. A smoking trail of cloud and fire followed it on a dead plunge.

It smashed into the jail and the whole building went up in smoke. That shot definitely didn't come from the *Echo Omicron* and it didn't come from the jail itself. So much for the Fiddler theory. She was telling the truth. She couldn't have destroyed the jail.

A few seconds later, the Beast streaked away from the site with Fiddler driving, Emmet holding onto her, and Davenport bumping off the back.

The scene over Ultra Meridian went back to still, boring, and uneventful.....until the skimmers rocketed into view. They came from the atmosphere, too, but that shouldn't be possible.

They dove straight downward from directly above the jail. They would have crashed into the ground if they didn't pull up in time. Davenport had never seen or even heard of a skimmer being able to make a dive like that.

"We've seen enough," Frost murmured. "We don't need to see this."

Davenport started to turn away. The image feed went back to displaying the empty plane devoid of everything.....except.....

He stiffened when three figures snuck down the *Echo Omicron's* gangway. They looked both ways to make sure no one was around. Then they sprinted for the jail—at least, Dice and Lyons sprinted. Beauty loped along the ground on all four hands and feet.

"What the holy hell?" Flack muttered. "What are they doing?"

The three smugglers cast furtive glances over their shoulders while they got to work. They lifted the fallen blocks and threw them out of the way. They started taking the ruined jail apart piece by piece. Davenport's blood boiled. "They're after the safe."

"What!" Emmet bellowed. "They can't be."

Davenport whirled around. "I need a skimmer—right now."

"We don't have one," Frost told him.

"You said you did. I'm ordering you, by the power invested in me by the Confederate Corps, to give me a skimmer—now! This is an emergency of the highest priority."

"Yeah!" Emmet chimed in. "Give him a skimmer. We have to get back to Ultra Meridian before they find the safe."

"I told you," Frost countered. "We don't have skimmers. Ammo—supplies—weapons—rations.....yes. We don't have any skimmers."

"Then we need to go back and get the Beast. I need you to help me repair it. It's crucial that I get back to Ultra Meridian immediately." Davenport spun on his heel and stormed back to the supply room. "Go get the Beast—now! Bring it back here and start working on it while I arm up."

"What's the big deal?" Fiddler called after him. "You can't get there quick enough to stop them from stealing your safe. What's the matter? Are you worried they'll steal your stash of ChunkyTenders?"

"My payload is in that safe," Emmet reminded her. "We can't let that go."

"Do you think for a second that the sheriff here cares about your payload?" Fiddler turned back to Davenport. "What's in that safe that's so important?"

Davenport snatched a bandolier of ammo cylinders from the nearest canister and barged back into the cavern cramming them into Big Boris's magazine. "They're after an Ithium cartridge I seized from the *Echo Omicron*."

The whole group froze. They stared at him with large, shocked eyes. Even Friend turned around. "Ithium!" Frost gasped.

"That's right and I don't have to tell you what that means. If deployed the right way, it could contaminate the air or water supply of a large city or even a whole planet. These jackasses wouldn't be so keen to get it if they didn't plan to use it. I put the cartridge in the safe. We have to stop them. I just wish I could figure out how whoever bombed the jail found out about it."

"Maybe someone on the *Echo Omicron* tipped them off," Friend suggested over her shoulder.

"What does any of this have to do with us?" Fiddler countered. "You're the law around here, not us. If you want to go back to Ultra Meridian and get yourself killed, go knock yourself out."

"If you don't help me, not only will you be breaking the law, but you'll be partially responsible for whatever those bastards do with the Ithium. Do you really want that on your conscience?"

The others exchanged glances.

"What about my payload?" Emmet demanded.

Fiddler shrugged. "What about your payload? No payload is worth your life—or mine."

"What *is* your payload?" Davenport asked. "If you tell me what it is, I might be willing to help you get it back—as long as it isn't anything illegal."

Flack burst out laughing. "You're joking, right? Of course it's illegal."

"What is it?" Davenport repeated. "You better tell me. You don't want me finding out from someone else or it could go worse for you, Emmet."

"If I told you, it really *would* go worse for me."

"Now I have to know what it is," Davenport replied. "For a drunk with less than two pennies to rub together, you're awfully concerned about this payload of yours."

Emmet shuffled his feet. "You drive a hard bargain, Sheriff. You know that?"

"I can drive it even harder than this. 'Fess up, Emmet. That's my last warning."

"It's like this, see. I was only.....only posing as a drunk. I wasn't really. Lenny was, but I just rubbed the stuff all over myself and gargled with it so I'd smell like booze."

Davenport's jaw dropped. "You devious little rascal! Here I thought you were a rotten old mud cake. Now I find out you're really a conniving schemer with a fetish for costume parties."

Emmet didn't bite. "You gotta help me get my payload back, Sheriff. You don't know what the client will do to me if I don't deliver."

Davenport froze. "Client? Did I just hear the word 'client' pass your booze-withered lips?" He glanced over at Fiddler and something clicked in his brain. "Oh, I get it."

"I mean it, Sheriff. You don't know....."

"I think I know enough, and if you ever want to see that payload again, you better tell me right now what it is. We're wasting valuable time."

"It's....." Emmet hesitated and looked around at the shining young faces gazing up at him in breathless anticipation. "It's....it's a chip."

"A chip! What kind of chip?"

"How should I know what kind of chip? I'm just a middleman. I get paid to deliver the chip between the supply team and the client. That's all. I was just using Ultra Meridian as a stopover to cover my tracks. I'm not even supposed to be on this stinking planet."

"Well, since I don't have any proof that the chip is illegal, I'll let you come back to Ultra Meridian with me. What happens after that remains to be seen."

"But, Sheriff...." Emmet began.

Davenport ignored him. "What are you all standing around for? Go repair the Beast."

"The Beast is beyond repair," Friend told him, "but there are five more skimmers in the canyon searching for you."

"Perfect." Davenport sliced his finger at all of them. "Arm up. You're coming with me."

The Armageddon Core exchanged more glances. Emmet hustled to the supply room and loaded himself with every weapon he could lay his hands on, but when Fiddler tried to follow him, he stopped her. "Not you. You stay here."

"I'm coming with you. You aren't going out there alone."

"No. You stay here. That's an order."

"Since when do you give me orders?" Fiddler fired back. "Do you think I risked my ass getting you out of jail so I could sit on my hands and watch you throw your miserable life away for some piece of shit payload? I'm coming with you. You don't stand a chance without me."

"Thanks for the vote of confidence, sweetheart," Emmet snarled, "but I think I can take care of myself."

Fiddler snorted. "Please, Dad. Don't make me laugh."

Davenport looked up. "Dad? She's your......?"

"Is that such a surprise?" Emmet rounded on Fiddler. "You aren't going. If I need saving, the sheriff will save me."

"Whoa, whoa, whoa, Trigger!" Davenport blurted out. "Don't go volunteering me to save anything except myself."

"You heard the sheriff," Fiddler told Emmet. "He ordered all of us to go with him. He'll stand the best chance if we all go."

"I seem to recall saying something to that effect," Davenport put in.

"No!" Emmet insisted. "I forbid it."

"And I allow it. So there. Just see if you can stop me." Fiddler shoved past him and dove into the supply room. When Emmet tried to stop her, he met her coming out with two giant XQs, one in each hand.

These tiny women sure favored their XQs. Davenport couldn't wait to see how Dice reacted when he found out they weren't just a monster's favorite weapon. Dice would be furious. He might just swear off XQs for the rest of his life.

Emmet almost walked into Fiddler and her massive guns. She gave him such a ferocious look of challenge that he drew back and said nothing while she trooped out of the room and made her way to the cavern exit.

The others armed up without a word. Davenport led the way outside, but once on the path, he let the Armageddon Core go first.

They didn't go far. They scrambled up into the rocks and arranged themselves at strategic locations on either side of the path leading to their hideout.

Davenport selected a position for himself looking straight down onto the path. Emmet set up opposite him and they hunkered down to wait.

They didn't have to wait long before the all-too-familiar whine of engines howled into the canyon coming closer all the time.

Davenport hefted Big Boris onto his shoulder, but he had to be careful. He slotted an ammo cylinder into the chamber and sighted down the barrel. Just in time, three skimmers roared around the corner and all hell broke loose.

The instant the skimmers appeared, the Armageddon Core attacked with dizzying ferocity. Fiddler and her comrades sprang out from either side. They seized the riders, whipped them off their seats, and hurled them down to the ground.

Fiddler whipped up one of her XQs, aimed, and blasted one of the riders' heads to pulp. She marched from one rider to the next and destroyed them without mercy.

The Armageddon Core got hold of two skimmers and held them long enough to kill the motors. They idled the skimmers while they waited for the next two riders to blunder into their trap.

The third skimmer got away from them before they could grab it. It catapulted into the hill and exploded in a ball of fire. The Armageddon Core looked around them. Frost and Fizzle were occupied holding onto the skimmers. That left Flack and Fiddler to capture the approaching riders.

The enemy hurtled around the corner before Flack and Fiddler could hide themselves. Davenport heard them coming long before they burst into view. He saw the whole thing unfold below him and he never took his eye off his gun sight.

He trained Big Boris toward the corner where he knew the riders would show themselves. His instincts told him where to fire and he released the charge before he saw them.

The blast sailed straight and true. It caught the rider square in the chin and the body ripped off the seat. The rider flew backward and the skimmer streaked straight into Fiddler's grasp. She snatched the handlebars and yanked back on the throttle. The engine died and the vehicle stopped.

The fifth rider hurtled into view. Davenport didn't have time to aim. The rider barreled straight for the Armageddon Core standing in plain sight.

At that moment, Emmet released a second blast. It punched into the skimmer right between the rider's legs and the fuel tank exploded. The vehicle detonated and disintegrated.

Davenport leapt off his rock and slung Big Boris behind him. He took the skimmer from Frost. "Let's go! Grab a skimmer, Emmet."

Fiddler reacted first. She swung her leg over her skimmer. "I'll drive. Emmet can't drive to save his life."

Davenport almost said something and changed his mind. She really was a much more competent fighter than Emmet. If Davenport was going back to Ultra Meridian to face unknown enemies, he'd rather take her than Emmet alone.

Fizzle looked down at the skimmer in her hands. "What do we do with this?"

"Take it home and keep it for the next emergency." Davenport shot her a grin. "Consider it payment for the ammo I took."

He gunned the engine and the skimmer streaked away carrying him back to Ultra Meridian.

Chapter 7

Davenport and Fiddler parked their skimmers behind a rock outcropping tucked in the hills. Davenport looked out over the same view Friend's image feed showed in the cavern. The *Echo Omicron* squatted on its landing gear not far from the pile of rubble where the Ultra Meridian jail used to be.

Dice stood guard with his XQ-85 while Lyons and Beauty rummaged in the rubble. Before Davenport could charge in and confront them, Lyons straightened up holding a square box in her hands.

The three smugglers took off running back to the *Echo Omicron*. "The bastards!" he muttered. "They don't really think they can get away with this, do they?"

"They must or they wouldn't bother," Fiddler remarked. "How are you going to stop them from taking it away?"

"They can't leave the planet. I confiscated their stability gyroscope. They're grounded."

She snorted. "You're cruel."

"I'm a lawman. I wouldn't be doing my job if I left them a way to escape. They might have the safe, but they aren't going anywhere." Davenport checked his weapons. "I'm going down there. You two stay here. I can handle these three on my own."

"What about my payload?"

"I don't know about any payload," Davenport replied. "I only know they took that safe—*my* safe. I'm going to get it, and like I said, if there's anything in it that you're legally entitled to, we'll talk about that after the fact."

"But....."

Davenport held up his hand. "If either of you sets foot on that plane without my permission, you'll never get your payload back—ever. I can promise you that."

He straightened up and stormed down the hill. So those morons on the *Echo Omicron* actually thought they could steal the safe while his back was turned.

He went easy on them when he discovered the Ithium cartridge on their ship. They wouldn't get off so lightly this time. He didn't need a jail to make them regret the days they were born.

He fumed on his way across the plane, but he made sure to enter the cargo hold quietly. If these dunderheads thought for two seconds they could hide the safe from him, he would save time by sneaking up on them and finding out where they hid it. Then he wouldn't have to hunt for it once he clapped the three of them into custody for the rest of their natural lives.

He halted in the cargo hold. No one was around. The three crooks obviously thought Davenport wasn't coming back to Ultra Meridian anytime soon. They must have seen the skimmers follow the Beast into the hills. Maybe Lyons and her crew thought the riders would kill Davenport and leave him to rot. So much for dreaming.

He tiptoed into the corridor and heard voices coming from the crew lounge. Dice's voice boomed through the ship followed by a resounding smash. That dude was biologically incapable of anything resembling subtlety.

"Son of a bitch! This thing is strong."

"Don't break it," Lyons told him. "If you damage the cartridge and release the Ithium here, we won't get paid."

"We won't get paid because we'll all be dead." Was that Beauty's voice? He always talked in broken sentences when Davenport came around. He must have been pretending to be a stupid animal all this time.

"Can't you get us out of here?" Lyons asked. "There has to be a way around it. We can't just sit here and wait until Davenport comes back."

"I can twiddle the engines all you like," Beauty croaked back. "I can even perfect the fuel mixture so the ship runs at the peak of efficiency, but there is no one on this side of the Quezae Seam that can make a ship run without a stability gyroscope. If we tried to launch, we would crash and burn."

"And then we definitely wouldn't get paid. Son of a bitch!" Dice thundered. "This little safe is a lot stronger than it looks."

"Give it to Beauty," Lyons told him. "Maybe he can hack the combination. He can hack anything."

"Not me," Beauty rasped. "Those combination dials are unhackable."

"Unhackable!" Lyons huffed. "There is no such word."

"You hack it, then," Beauty grumbled. "Those dials don't use tumblers and click locks like the hackable ones."

"How are we supposed to get our cargo, then?" Lyons demanded. "There has to be a way."

"There is a way," Dice snarled. "Capture Davenport, twist his pencil-neck until he tells us the combination, and throw his dead corpse into the Fisa Plasma Vein."

Lyons laughed. "That's one way of doing it."

"That doesn't get us off this vile planet," Beauty complained.

"It's real simple," Dice rumbled. "While he's telling us the combination, he can tell us where he put our stability gyroscope. Problem solved."

"We still don't know where he is." A chair scraped across the floor. "Here. Give me the safe."

Davenport had heard enough. He whipped around doorframe and walked right in on them. All three gaped at him in open-mouthed shock, but before anyone could say a word, an unholy ka-boom smashed into the ship. The whole vessel bounced off its landing gear.

"What the hell!" Dice bellowed. "What the hell are you doing to us?"

"I'm not doing anything!" Davenport dove for the safe, but another catastrophic explosion rocked the ship sideways. It tipped upward and flung all four into the wall.

The safe went flying along with all the furniture, food, utensils, and a few crates of equipment stored in the lounge. Everything crashed into the wall and Davenport fell through the open door.

He landed hard in the corridor outside and Beauty landed right on top of him followed by a whole bunch of debris. Continuous pounding booms shook the ship. They rocked the *Echo Omicron* back and forth so no one could stand up.

"We're under attack!" Lyons yelled. "We have to get to the bridge!"

"Screw the bridge!" Dice bellowed. "We have to man the guns and return fire!"

"Who's shooting at us?!" Beauty screeched. His whole idiot creature act evaporated in an instant. "Where are they coming from?"

The bombardment paused for a second and Davenport floundered to his feet. The safe rested in a corner only a few feet away. He took one step and another devastating smash struck the ceiling directly above his head.

Another five shots tumbled the *Echo Omicron* the other way and the crew rolled over each other tumbling back into the lounge. They yelled and shoved trying to right themselves and get each other off each other, but without success.

Big Boris smashed Davenport in the face. He tried to grab it, but another blow tossed the weapon out of his reach. He couldn't even see the safe anymore.

"Get up, all of you!" Lyons ordered. "Get to the guns."

Another momentary reprieve gave Davenport enough time to get his legs under him. He accidentally stepped on Beauty trying to get to the lounge door.

The others got to their feet right behind him and they stumbled over fallen trash to the corridor. The *Echo Omicron* perched at an odd angle. The crew had to walk against the walls to the far bulkhead leading to the bridge.

Lyons pried the door open and the four jumped down to the upward-slanted floor. Beauty scampered to the processor workstation. "We've taken damage, but we can still take off."

"Not without the stability gyroscope." Lyons turned to Davenport. "Hand over the gyroscope. You can't expect us to sit here under this attack without defending ourselves."

Davenport hesitated. In that moment, another blistering barrage pounded the *Echo Omicron* and the ground around its landing gear—if it even had any landing gear left.

Another brutal strike hurled everyone hard against another wall. "To hell with this!" Dice bellowed. "I'm manning the guns."

"How can you?" Lyons demanded. "You don't even know who's shooting at us."

"Who cares?" Dice boomed. "I can still blow them into the next solar system."

He whirled away and staggered to another door in the opposite bulkhead. Beauty pounced onto the processor workstation again. His spidery fingers flitted over the controls. "The shots are coming from the high atmosphere. The ionosphere is masking the attacker's identity profiles."

Lyons thrust out her hand to Davenport. "Give me the gyroscope before we all bite the big one."

Davenport pulled it out and passed it to her. She dove for the processor workstation. Another deafening boom knocked her flat on her stomach where she stayed while she tore into the circuitry access partition.

The shot flung Beauty off the workstation and he hit the ceiling with a squeal before he smashed down hard next to Lyons. "Get to the gun range, for Christ's sake!" she roared over her shoulder. "Give us some cover before we....."

Another crushing smash jolted everyone off their feet. Davenport didn't wait to be told twice. He dove for the bulkhead where Dice disappeared. Beauty scrambled after him and they both plunged through it to the gun range beyond.

The instant Davenport got onto the gun range, more shots tossed the *Echo Omicron* ass over tea kettle again. He slammed against a glass window separating the narrow hall from a bunch of enormous Howitzers mounted into the ship's starboard hull. A huge reinforced window gave a view of Ultra Meridian outside. A second bank of the guns lined the hall's port side.

Dice stood in one of the starboard cubicles wrestling a huge gun upward toward the sky. He squinted into the sun beyond the window, but Dice wouldn't be able to see anything out there. Whoever attacked the *Echo Omicron* did it from too far up in the atmosphere.

Davenport dove to the port range with Beauty right behind him. Davenport grabbed the two-handled firing cradle and swung the gun upward, but he couldn't see anything, either.

He hunkered for cover when another strike tossed the ship into the air again, but he still couldn't find any target.

Beauty screamed something and then dizzying vertigo almost knocked Davenport to the floor. The landscape hurtled past the window as the ship launched into the clear sky leaving Ultra Meridian behind.

The ship vaulted straight up into the ether. Thunderous engine noise vibrated the hull until Davenport could hardly hear himself think. The engines shook the hull almost as bad as the bombardment, but at least they weren't under attack anymore— not yet, at least.

Beauty attacked a control console mounted on the wall and activated it. A huge intricate grid blinked onto the window and displayed a full, 360° view of the sky rushing past the ship.

Other spacecraft appeared on the grid with the *Echo Omicron* rocketing straight at them on a dead course. Davenport swung his Howitzer toward the enemy and the grid showed him exactly where to target.

Lyons plunged the ship into the center of the densest cluster. The enemy all pointed their noses toward the planet unleashing dozens of charges into the atmosphere. If their instruments showed them the *Echo Omicron's* launch, they didn't react fast enough.

Lyons gunned the engines to the breaking point. Seven enemy craft raced past Davenport's window and he and Dice opened up with their Howitzers. Davenport swung to port plastering one ship after another as they appeared on his grid.

They vanished just as fast when Lyons sprinted past them. She looped in a circle for a second pass, and this time, the whole mob rounded on the *Echo Omicron* with a vengeance.

"Crazy bitch!" Dice bellowed. "You'll get us all killed."

Lyons couldn't hear him out on the bridge. Davenport could hardly hear Dice over the noise of so many guns going off. The enemy ships concentrated their fire on the *Echo Omicron*, but that didn't seem to concern Lyons.

She punched the engines and charged straight into them. Her fake worked and the enemy dodged out of her path. They whirled to give chase, but not before Dice and Davenport plastered six with well-placed shots.

Half of them blew and then the *Echo Omicron* vanished in a vapor trail. Beauty sprang to the Howitzer next to Davenport and added his fire to the mix.

Lyons hurtled through the planet's orbit and the remaining enemy dropped into a pursuit pattern. They formed an arrow creeping up on either side. They eased into Davenport's range and he locked his target grid on the nearest ship.

He clenched his fingers around the firing cradle when his battle-frenzied brain noticed something. He'd been so intent on acquiring one target after another that he didn't see it before now.

His enemy slid closer. It lingered there just beyond the window and he stared when he read the identity profile on his grid. *R WCC Dagger Circe.*

Fire, Davenport, he kept thinking. *Fire, you fool!*

His hands refused to obey him. It couldn't be. He refused to believe it, but the profile showed up clear as day in front of his eyes. Could it really be....?

RWCC. Reserve Wing Confederate Corps. Even if he didn't read those words on the enemy ship's profile, he would know it was true. Only the Reserve Wing used Dagger-class ships.

What the hell were they playing at? He saw it all in a split second. The shot that destroyed the Ultra Meridian jail came from the atmosphere. The skimmers that tried to capture him, Fiddler, and Emmet came from the atmosphere. He knew they didn't come from the *Echo Omicron* and there were no other ships around at the time.

These spacecraft right here—they must be the ones who bombarded the jail with him and three other people inside it. They sent the skimmers to hunt him down and now they were trying to destroy the *Echo Omicron*. Why?

"Shoot, you cocksucker!" Dice roared. "What the hell is wrong with you?"

The noise snapped Davenport out of his trance and his fingers jerked against the cradle. He stuttered charges along the *Circe's* flank.

The ship tried to peel off, but he gritted his teeth and followed its course. The *Circe* turned its tail toward his gun and he focused down to the micron.

He increased his assault and dumped charges into the engine exhaust. The *Circe* gunned its engines trying to get away, but a second later, the Dagger burst in a flaming ball of destruction.

Another five ships crept alongside the *Echo Omicron*. They tried to veer in front of the ship, but with all three gunners working to the maximum, they held the enemy at bay.

The Reserve Wing dropped back out of range again. Lyons dodged from port to starboard and back again. She gave the gunners just enough of a view of their pursuers to hold them off while she made her escape into the atmosphere.

Chapter 8

Dice rotated his Howitzer back and forth scanning the sky for any sign of pursuit. Beauty left his gun and returned to the control panel to track the enemy's movements.

Davenport saw his chance and slipped out of the range. Lyons glanced up from the navigation station when he passed through the bridge. Sweat plastered her hair to her face and she flushed with the effort of flying through the Reserve Wing. Did she realize who it was that attacked the *Echo Omicron*?

Davenport headed for the bulkhead. Lyons sprang to her feet, but switching the ship to autopilot slowed her down. Davenport heard her yelling behind him as he stalked into the corridor and down to the crew lounge.

He kicked the junk out of the way and flipped over the upturned furniture looking everywhere for the safe. He worked without stopping until he spotted it under a chair in the corner. He tossed the chair aside and picked up the safe. He turned it over. It was undamaged.

A click made him look up. Dice and Lyons stood in the doorway, both of them aiming XQs at Davenport's head. "We'll take that," Dice snarled.

"You won't get the combination out of me no matter how much you twist my pencil-neck. I heard every word you said and you won't get into this safe without my help."

Dice raised his XQ and powered up the discharge vaporizer. The weapon hummed on the brink of firing. "Either way, you'll be dead. We can hand the safe to our client and take our pay. Getting into it will be someone else's problem."

Davenport indulged in a sad smile. "Can you be certain of that? How do you know your client won't punish you for handing them another problem instead of the item they paid you to retrieve?"

"Quit stalling, Davenport," Lyons interrupted. "The Ithium cartridge is ours."

"Yours?" Davenport pursed his lips. "I'm going to take a wild guess and say it's anything but yours. If it doesn't belong to the secure defense lab you stole it from, it belongs to your client. It definitely isn't yours, and unless you're prepared to shoot an officer of the law in cold blood, you'll never get it back."

"You asked for it." Dice aimed his XQ at Davenport's chest and his thick fingers squeezed the trigger, but Lyons laid a hand on his arm to stop him.

"Shoot him," Beauty wheezed. "Get rid of him."

"Wait," Lyons told him. "He's right. We don't want an aggravated murder charge on our records."

"You mean *another* aggravated murder charge," Davenport corrected. "You've already got several—all of you."

"What are you talking about?" Dice boomed. "Do you have any clue what they'll do to us if we get caught? What do you think he's going to do—let us walk away? He already said he'd turn us over to the Reserve Wing."

Davenport's mind turned over another tooth of its internal gears. The Reserve Wing.....

"The penalty for possession of Ithium is life in Terminus Anathema," Beauty added.

"Fine," Lyons snapped. "We'll kill him."

The pair trained their weapons on Davenport, but he only bent down and picked up Big Boris off the floor at his feet. He set the safe on the floor next to his ankle and rotated the weapon to aim at the *Echo Omicron* crew. "Two can play at that little game, kids. You're gonna have to put on your party hats if you want to kill me."

He powered up Big Boris and watched with satisfaction when Dice growled at him and Lyons shifted her XQ upward to point the barrel at the ceiling.

"Now," Davenport announced, "we're all going to take a wee stroll downstairs. We're going to take a small trip to Macron Calypso and you three are going to spend the rest of the journey in a locked room until I can turn over the goods to....."

He didn't finish. A smash cut him off when Lyons's XQ went off. The shot ricocheted off the ceiling and deflected into the wall behind Davenport's head. The wall exploded and shrapnel pummeled him in the skull. Stars burst in his brain and he buckled.

The next instant, Dice's fist smashed Davenport in the nose and he passed out.

He came to sliding down the corridor feet first. Dice dragged him by one leg while Lyons and Beauty brought up the rear. Beauty cradled the safe in his spindly arms.

Davenport's blurry eyes rotated around the corridor trying to understand what was happening. "He's awake!" Beauty squeaked.

"Kick him in the head!" Dice ordered.

Lyons and Beauty didn't get a chance to attack Davenport again. Dice stormed into the cargo hold and hurled Davenport against the crates stacked there. Davenport flopped onto his stomach and Dice pounced.

He kicked Davenport in the ribs and once in the head. Dice chuckled in sadistic glee when Davenport flipped over and landed hard on his back. "I'm gonna enjoy this. You don't know how long I've been waiting to put an end to your obnoxious jokes."

Lyons came forward and handed Dice his XQ. "Just get it over with and let's get rid of him. We've wasted too much time on this stinkin' planet as it is."

Davenport blinked up at Dice's hideous face trying get his brain to function. Davenport tried to grab his sidearm, but he had difficulty directing his hand where he wanted it to go. He kept telling him to get up, but nothing else seemed to be working right, either.

Dice loomed above him and jammed his XQ right against Davenport's cheek. "Say goodbye to that pretty face of yours, fat head."

No amount of telling himself to do something made any difference. Davenport's stunned senses focused too closely on Dice's fingers tightening around the trigger. He watched each slight movement and pressure change, but he couldn't move to save his own life. The safe. He had to get the safe, but it was across the cargo hold tucked in Beauty's arms.

The XQ hummed down its barrel and into Davenport's skull. He started to relax. If he died right now, someone else would have to take care of the Ithium. He tried, but now it was out of his hands.

A twisted leer spread over Dice's ugly face and he tensed to pull the trigger when another shot rang out. Something hit him in the back and all three smugglers whirled the other way.

Davenport blinked as Fiddler and Emmet sprang out from behind the crates. They ambushed the smugglers exactly the way the Armageddon Core ambushed those skimmer riders.

Fiddler's rifle shot deflected off Dice's enormous bulk. Another shot seared Beauty's thigh. He let out an ear-splitting shriek and the whole cargo hold disintegrated in chaos.

The shock and surprise woke Davenport from his stupor. He hauled himself to his feet and almost got hit by flying charges from Fiddler's and Emmet's guns. They pinned down the three smugglers.

Beauty cowered in a corner still hugging the safe while Dice and Lyons returned fire—until Davenport pulled his sidearms and added his shots to Fiddler's and Emmet's. He aimed for Lyons and the charge pinged off the crate next to her head.

She whirled around and her eyes widened when she saw him. That moment when her concentration broke gave Fiddler and Emmet the opening they needed. They charged forward and Fiddler stabbed her rifle into Lyons's face. "Don't move! Hand over your weapon."

Davenport grabbed Lyons's XQ and Emmet rushed Dice. He disarmed Dice with one well-aimed kick that pivoted Dice's XQ out of the way. Emmet dove in and stuffed his sidearm between Dice's tusks. "Just give me just one excuse, maggot meat!"

Dice stiffened like he wanted to fight, but he must have seen something in Emmet that he didn't like. Davenport held Lyons at gunpoint while Emmet took Dice's XQ away from him.

"You two are a sight for sore eyes," Davenport told Fiddler. "Did you stow away?"

"We didn't stow away. We just followed you." She shot him a grin. "If you want to charge us, I guess we won't try to stop you."

Fiddler sidestepped around him and strode over to Beauty. He hissed and spat and screeched at her in a hysterical frenzy, but when she aimed her rifle at him, he didn't resist her taking the safe.

She turned it over in her hands the same way Davenport did. She smiled first to herself and then at Davenport. A flood of gratitude filled Davenport's chest. He never thought he'd be so happy and relieved to see a couple of criminals riding to his rescue.

Fiddler turned around and called to Emmet. "I have it. Let's go."

"Hey!" Davenport yelled. "What are you doing?"

"We're leaving. We got what we came for."

"How.....what.....?" Davenport's spirits plummeted into his boots. "You can't just...leave!"

She only beamed at him even more broadly. "Thanks for getting our payload back for us. See you around, Sheriff."

Davenport opened his mouth to say something. They couldn't just leave him here with these smugglers who just tried to kill him—never mind the fact that they were all floating around in space with no way to get off this damaged ship.

None of that seemed to bother Fiddler at all if it even entered her head. She strolled over to Emmet and set Lyons' weapon against the crates. Emmet took his sidearm out of Dice's mouth.

Lyons got to her feet. Fiddler and Emmet didn't try to stop her from regaining her weapon. Dice let out another vicious chuckle and Davenport saw the whole situation disintegrating before his eyes.

His gaze darted from Lyons to Dice and back again. What he wouldn't give for Big Boris right now.....or any other XQ for that matter.

Dice pushed himself off the crates. He and Lyons turned on Davenport. They put Fiddler and Emmet completely out of their minds. A sick feeling snuck into Davenport's guts. Now what was he going to do? Fiddler moved farther and farther away and took the safe with her.

Davenport couldn't watch what she did next. Dice and Lyons demanded all his attention and Dice swiveled his XQ back in Davenport's direction.

Dice and Lyons took another step toward and he raised his sidearm. How pathetic it seemed compared to Dice's XQ—not to mention his size.

Davenport backed away and bumped into another stack of crates. He tried to cover both smugglers with one gun, but they spread out to flank him. He prepared himself to make his last stand—his other last stand—when another explosion struck the ship.

Chapter 9

he *Echo Omicron* skidded sideways, tried to right itself, and failed when a vicious barrage peppered its port side. "What the....." The blast jolted Lyons off her feet. She staggered into the crates and lost her grip on her weapon.

Dice steadied himself and looked up at the ceiling. Pounding concussions resounded through the hull. "We're under attack again!" Beauty screeched.

"Get to the gun range—all of you!" Lyons bolted for the bulkhead. She didn't wait for anyone to obey her. She dove through and took off for the bridge with Beauty hot on her heels.

Davenport, Fiddler, Emmet, and Dice exchanged glances. Should Davenport turn his back on these people to defend the ship? If they didn't stand down, he wouldn't, either.

He tightened his hold on his weapon when another blistering crash struck the *Echo Omicron* from behind. It hit right outside the hull wall near Dice's position. The impact hurled the crates against their anchors and the anchors all cracked at once. The crates hurtled across the cargo hold taking Dice and Fiddler with them.

A crate clipped Dice across the shoulder and he pitched face down on the floor. Three more flew at Fiddler and Emmet. They would have pulverized Fiddler, but Emmet tackled her out of the way.

The safe flew out of her hands and rolled a few feet away. The crates tumbled over their heads and smashed into another stack across the bay. The blow shattered those anchors, too, and the crates came loose.

Another crushing blow pounded the ship from above and everything in the cargo hold twirled into the air. Bodies, crates, weapons, and random debris revolved in a jumble as more shots tossed the *Echo Omicron* this way and that.

One more brutal crash slammed everyone down on the floor again. A crate narrowly missed crushing every bone in Davenport's body. When he pulled himself together enough to look around, a carpet of mayhem surrounded him. Crates lay in piles all over the place. He couldn't see the safe anywhere.

Another deafening explosion went off and the rear gangway ramp indented into the cargo hold. Dice and Davenport looked over at it at the same moment and then they looked at each other.

Both men rocketed upright. Davenport ran to Fiddler and Emmet lying crumpled and groaning not far away. "Get up! Hurry! We have to man the gun range! Get up, Emmet!"

Fiddler struggled to her feet first. She and Davenport flanked Emmet and dragged him out of the cargo hold. Dice held the door open for them and he slammed it behind them when they dashed into the corridor.

No one thought of threatening each other now. They barreled to the bridge where Lyons and Beauty already worked to the breaking point dodging countless ships outside.

Dice shoved Davenport, Fiddler, and Emmet onto the range. They sprang to their Howitzers. Fiddler took a fraction of a second to activate the targeting grid and they all started firing as fast as their fingers would work.

Now that he knew what to look for, Davenport saw Reserve Wing identity profiles all over the place. Dozens of Reserve Wing spacecraft surrounded the *Echo Omicron* and pounded the ship to smithereens.

He never would have dared to turn a weapon against the Reserve Wing before today. Now he didn't give it a second thought. He spouted charges at any target that came within range. Adrenaline coursed through his veins and erased every thought besides saving his own miserable life.

One simple concept kept nagging at the back of his mind. The Ithium was still onboard the *Echo Omicron* and he was the only person alive who could stop it from falling into the wrong hands.

Lyons outdid herself flying in maniacal circles around the Reserve Wing. She corkscrewed through their densest clusters and dared them to concentrate their fire on the ship.

They did. They streaked through the skies and bombarded the *Echo Omicron* with countless shots. Davenport braced both legs against the range wall and held onto his firing cradle to stop himself from getting thrown out of position.

Dice and Fiddler took the port range and Emmet occupied the position next to Davenport. They all worked to their utmost, but the instant the grid switched on, Davenport saw that it was hopeless.

Dozens of ships surrounded the *Echo Omicron*. They swarmed the skies so thickly he could hardly acquire a target without the rest distracting him. They whizzed around the ship in clouds and he didn't see any end to them. They covered the entire grid and beyond it.

Lyons raced through them and between them and over them and under them, but enemy craft closed off any avenue of escape. If she set a course to run from them, they hammered the ship's nose and jostled it in a different direction.

Another ten Dagger-class ships and even a few Stalwart-class gunships rumbled alongside the *Echo Omicron*. Davenport and Emmet opened up with their Howitzers, but the enemy unleashed a catastrophic barrage from its own range that obliterated all visibility through the window.

The blow knocked Davenport to the floor. He pulled himself up and got hold of his cradle only to find the grid no longer functioning. A dangerous crack shot through the window. The *Echo Omicron's* hull had been compromised. One more assault like that and the ship would crumble.

The enemy hurtled past the window to target the bridge. Davenport glanced over at Emmet to see the old man blinking at the crack, too. They both turned around to see Dice and Fiddler cowering on the floor while five more Stalwarts decimated the port side.

In front of Davenport's eyes, the Stalwarts' guns smashed through the port window and the pressurized air inside the range whooshed outward through the breach. Fiddler screeched and Dice seized her by the shoulder. He hauled her by force from her cubicle and shoved her into the hall. "Get out!" he boomed. "Get out before.....!"

Another crushing blow struck the range wall and the hull buckled. Davenport and Emmet collided in their haste to get off the range before the whole ship imploded.

The four gunners charged onto the bridge to find Lyons and Beauty already on their feet. They scrambled for the bulkhead while dozens of ships destroyed the bridge. A charge punched through the front observation window. Broken glass, twisted metal, and shrapnel hurtled into the ship.

The expulsion of air ripped Lyons off her feet and almost took Davenport with it. Lyons slammed into the navigation station and whipped over backward. Her hair streamed behind her into the tempest wind rushing through the breach.

She almost cartwheeled over backward to her doom, but Emmet sprang forward and caught her by the arms. He tried to pull her to the bulkhead, but the vortex caught him, too.

Davenport reacted on impulse and rushed them. He tackled Emmet around the middle and ripped the old man over backward. Davenport crashed to the floor and Emmet landed on top of him. Davenport's effort pulled Lyons down, too, and all three fell flat on the floor.

They inched toward the bulkhead, but they made slow progress. Dice shoved Fiddler through the door into the corridor and then he and Beauty fought their way back through the shrieking wind.

Dice grabbed Davenport in one massive arm and Emmet in the other. Beauty picked up Lyons with unnatural strength and practically carried her off the bridge.

Dice hurled Emmet and Davenport into the hall, pushed Beauty after them, and slammed the door with an almighty effort. "Get to the cargo hold! It's our only hope."

Davenport didn't hold out any hope at all. Devastating blasts squashed the ship from all sides. The friends staggered down the corridor crashing into the walls and each other every few steps. Beauty tripped and fell.

Davenport picked the creature up and set him on his feet. Dice shoved them all from behind and bellowed for them to move. His colossal bulk prevented anyone from falling behind him.

Fiddler held the bulkhead door open for them to get into the cargo hold. She waved them through, but no one could hear a word she said over the noise coming from all sides.

The group rushed into a cargo hold as chaotic and deadly as every other part of the ship. Loose crates smashed first one way and then the other each time another barrage pounded the ship.

The party drew back and hesitated to enter. Dice didn't see the danger until he'd already herded everyone inside. Fiddler shut the door and now they had nowhere to run. Flying crates dented the walls and smashed into each other in midair. They disgorged their contents and added more deadly wreckage to the mix.

Davenport pushed Lyons back the way they came. "We have to get out of here! We can't stay here!"

She opened her mouth to yell something back at him when a crushing smash punched through the hull. A charge split the cargo hold wide open and ripped the *Echo Omicron's* tail off. Daylight flooded the cargo hold. Clouds, mountains, and strange canyons twirled past the breach as the ship plummeted through the atmosphere.

The next minute, a catastrophic explosion struck the ship somewhere up front. The *Echo Omicron* upended and everyone in the cargo hold flew in all directions. Davenport soared up, bounced off the ceiling, and cartwheeled toward the breach. His life flashed before his eyes when a crate rotated out of nowhere, clipped him across the back, and knocked him out.

Chapter 10

Something cold touched Davenport's cheek and his eyelids fluttered. He looked up at Fiddler bending over him. The minute he recognized her, she turned her face upward and said to someone out of sight. "He's alive."

"More's the pity," Dice grumbled.

Davenport rolled onto his side. His head pounded, but the rest of him felt unharmed. He sat up and looked around the destroyed cargo hold. Dice and Lyons stood between a few crates not far away. Emmet faced them aiming Big Boris at them. Where did he find it?

As soon as Fiddler saw that Davenport was okay, she joined Emmet confronting the *Echo Omicron* crew.

"This is our ship," Dice snarled. "You and your law buddy can hit the dusty trail if you know what's good for you."

"We aren't going anywhere without our property," Emmet fired back. "We didn't come all this way to leave empty-handed."

"It's *our* property," Lyons returned. "You won't lay a finger on our payload if you want to live to tell the tale."

Davenport dragged himself to his feet. "None of you is taking anything anywhere. You're all under arrest."

Lyons exploded in laughter. "Look around you, Sheriff. You're outnumbered five to one."

"Six to one if you count my XQ-85 here." Dice dropped the weapon into his arms and pointed it at the three people across from him.

"Two can play that little game, remember?" Fiddler hefted another XQ. It didn't look as big as an 85—a 62, maybe—not that it mattered at this range. If she hit Dice with it, it would leave just as big a hole.

Dice let out a mocking chuckle. "Aw! Look at the little squirrel, Lyons. She wants to trim my toenails with her little peashooter! Isn't that cute?"

"Charming," Lyons minced.

"Beauty!" Dice bellowed. "Quit fooling around and back us up! That crate over there has choke shells in it. I can see 'em from here."

A smacking sound answered him. Everyone glanced over to see Beauty armpit deep in a splintered crate spilling JuicyPie packages all over the floor. He tore into them one after the other and crammed the JuicyPies into his mouth too fast to chew or swallow them.

The crusts squashed against his lips and cheeks and the juice ran down his chin in multiple colors. He growled and groaned and rolled his eyes in orgasmic bliss.

"God almighty!" Lyons muttered. "We've lost him."

"I told you we had to keep him away from the food supplies," Dice yelled back. "I told you that a dozen times."

"Don't blame me. It isn't my fault the crate broke open."

"Hey! Cocksuckers!" Emmet bellowed. "You're standing in the way of us reclaiming our payload. Get out of the way before we feed you to the gremlin over there."

"Stow your threats, old man," Lyons returned. "You aren't going anywhere except straight back to jail, and as far as your payload....."

Dice finished the sentence for her by locking up his XQ. It hummed cycling into firing mode.

Emmet responded by raising his own weapon and Fiddler did the same. The opposing crews faced off two against two.

Davenport sidled over next to Fiddler and pulled his sidearm. This puny weapon probably wouldn't even give Dice a massage so Davenport pointed it at Lyons instead.

"Stand aside, both of you. You've committed enough offenses to earn you a death penalty in the Confederacy. I don't think anyone will shed any tears if I drop you both right here."

"You're too much of a Boy Scout to pull the trigger, Davenport," Lyons sneered.

"You think so?" He raised his sidearm and sighted down it to cover her left eye. "Say please like a good girl and I'll make it quick and painless."

"You bastard!" Dice roared and his XQ went off.

Davenport couldn't remember after the fact whether Dice had been aiming at anyone in particular. He couldn't have been aiming very well because the charge smashed into the floor and skidded straight into the crate of scattered JuicyPies.

The shot sizzled under Beauty's feet and exploded in the middle of the pile. JuicyPies soared in all directions showering juices to the four winds. Beauty let out a hair-raising shriek. He sprang into the air trying to catch all the pies at the same time.

Davenport didn't see whether Beauty saved any of them. Dice corrected his aim and fired again, but Emmet and Fiddler anticipated him and fired first.

They both targeted Dice. They rotated their XQs in his direction and fired. He saw and dove sideways. The two charges whistled over his head and smashed into a different crate—an empty one this time.

Davenport charged into the melee firing the only weapon he had. He popped off his sidearm at Lyons. She tried to blast him to death with her own guns, but she wasn't quick enough.

Davenport overran her and elbowed her out of the way. She toppled into more over-turned crates and Davenport bolted to the rear of the cargo hold. He'd last seen the safe here somewhere. He had to get to it before any of the others took it first.

He dodged from one pile of debris to another, searching every nook and cranny, but he didn't see the safe anywhere.

Gunshots went off behind him. Davenport skidded to the right and almost fell to his death through the torn breach in the *Echo Omicron's* tail.

He doubled back. Where was that damn safe? It must have fallen farther forward when the ship crashed nose downward.

He scooted around a different stack and almost collided with Dice coming the other way. Both men dodged and Davenport took off running even faster. He had to find the safe before Dice did.

Dice thought the same thing and rushed after him. He overtook Davenport in a second, but Davenport put on a burst of speed. He barely managed to stay abreast of Dice as they raced through the cargo hold, first around this stack of rubble, then around another.

They passed Lyons, Emmet, and Fiddler, who stood in the same place and stared at Dice and Davenport in a dead race to find the safe. They hesitated and then all three of them all took off after Dice and Davenport, too.

They tripped over each other, bowled each other out of the way, and ran on. They all got so obsessed with outrunning each other that they bumped into things and fell over a few times. None of them thought to shoot at each other and they elbowed and shoved each other so ferociously that they even forgot to look for the safe.

This couldn't go on. Davenport made one last-ditch effort to get in front of Dice. Another large pile of confused junk blocked the way ahead. Davenport timed his attack perfectly and knocked Dice into it.

Dice bounced off the stack and bowled into Lyons, Emmet, and Fiddler following one step behind. They all fell over each other in a tangle of arms, legs, blows, and profanities. Davenport ran on and skated around the corner to find himself.... right back where he started.

Beauty's spine showed above a mountain of empty JuicyPie wrappers. Grunting noises came from underneath the snow of rustling plastic.

Davenport stopped and stared at the grey skin stretched over the bony vertebrae. He had run through the whole cargo bay.

Dice barreled into him from behind and Lyons, Emmet, and Fiddler all crashed into Dice. Dice tried to hook his beefy arm around Davenport's neck, but Davenport slammed his palm into Dice's chest. "Hold it."

The sudden change in tactic startled Dice out of his frenzy and everyone froze. Lyons blinked up at Davenport and a tense silence fell over the cargo hold. "Did any of you see the safe in here?"

Everyone looked around. Beauty's head popped up. Purple, blue, pink, and orange juice stained his jaws, neck, and chest. He stared at the party with his huge eyes and then swallowed.

"Did you see the safe anywhere, Beauty?" Davenport asked.

Beauty cocked his head. "Safe?"

"You don't have to play dumb anymore, Beauty. I know you can talk perfectly well. Did... you... see.... the.... safe?"

Beauty's eyes darted to Lyons and then he wilted. "I didn't see it, but I wasn't looking for it. I.... didn't think to."

"I didn't see it, either," Fiddler said. "We looked everywhere."

"We didn't look very carefully."

"It could have fallen through the hull breach," Emmet pointed out.

Davenport turned around. So did else. They all looked at Emmet. No one wanted to think about the safe falling out of the ship when it crashed.

Davenport saw another race about to break out—or maybe another standoff leading to a gun battle. "Okay, people. Here's what we're going to do."

Lyons rolled her eyes. "You know you're in trouble when he starts calling everyone 'people'."

"We're going to go through this cargo bay one inch at a time—calmly. Do you hear me? Calmly. No shooting, no running, and absolutely NO arguing. Understand? We're gonna find that safe and we'll decide what to do with it afterward. Agreed?"

He examined each person in turn. They stole glances at each other and then nodded.

They split up and spread out. They made a systematic search through all the fallen stuff in search of the safe. Dice even used his massive strength to move the crates so the crew could look underneath them.

They reconvened on the same spot. "That's it," Lyons pointed out. "Now we really have looked everywhere."

"I'm not leaving here without my payload," Emmet barked.

"Hey, Twizzler!" Lyons fired back. "Our payload is just as important as yours."

"We haven't looked everywhere." Davenport strode over to Beauty's JuicyPie kingdom. "Beauty!"

No one answered him. Beauty had burrowed so far into his snowbank that Davenport couldn't see any part of him. Snuffling sounds drifted from under the stained wrappers.

"Beauty!" Davenport hollered. "Come out here. I need to talk to you."

This time, Beauty's head came out at floor level. A wrapper perched on the creature's bald head and his eyes glazed in rapture.

"Did you see the safe anywhere in there?" Davenport asked. "Is it in there with your JuicyPies?"

"He's stupid," Lyons muttered. "He's drunk on JuicyPie juice."

"How many JuicyPies are left, Beauty?" Dice boomed. "You'll finish them soon and then what will you eat?"

Davenport squatted down in front of Beauty and looked right into the creature's intoxicated eyes. "Some people might pay a hefty reward for that safe. Some people might be willing to part with a whole shipload of JimJams."

Beauty's vision cleared instantly. "JimJams?"

"That's right, Beauty. If you like JuicyPies, you must like JimJams, too."

"He loves 'em," Lyon chimed in from behind.

Beauty swallowed again and licked his lips. He opened his mouth to say something and then stopped himself before asking in a very clear, lucid tone, "Do you have any JimJams here?"

Davenport jerked his thumb over his shoulder. "I might have seen some in a crate over there. Now tell me. Is the safe under all your JuicyPies?"

"No, it isn't." Beauty crawled out from under the wrappers. His eyes skipped around the cargo hold. "Where are these JimJams?"

Davenport waved in no particular direction. "I think I saw them over there."

Beauty scampered off leaving a trail of colored footprints behind him. Davenport returned to the others. "The safe isn't in here. I think we can assume it fell out."

Emmet turned away. "We have to go look for it."

The five companions crossed to the hull breach. They stood at the edge and looked down over a vast expanse of labyrinthine canyons twisting and turning into the distance.

The *Echo Omicron* had crashed belly down in a deep crevice. The walls slanted at such a steep angle that they held the ship suspended a hundred feet above the bottom. Davenport couldn't even see the ground from here.

"This is hopeless," Dice groaned. "We'll never find it."

"I have a better idea," Lyons told him. "We can use the ship's scanners to search for the safe. We'll find it much quicker that way than walking around."

"The ship is fried," Fiddler retorted. "You'll never get it powered up enough to run a decent scan."

"We can try it." Lyons turned away. "If you want to go down there and start sifting through the dirt, go right ahead."

She walked away. Davenport waited a moment and then followed her. He found her on the bridge bent over the processor workstation. "Any luck?"

"If by luck, you mean I'm thinking of retiring to a tropical island with all my millions in hard-earned lottery winnings, then yes, I'm having all the luck I can stand."

Davenport had to grin at her. Leave it to Lyons to come up with a smartass remark at a time like this. "I was actually talking about the bank of automatic ballistic warheads you found waiting for us at the bottom of this canyon."

"Sorry. That costs extra, but I did find the safe."

His head shot up. "You did?"

"No. Sorry. Just screwing with you."

Davenport slumped. "Tell me you got the scanners up and running."

"Yep. They're working fine."

"So can you locate the safe or not?"

"Not. The surrounding formations are metallic in chemistry. It's confusing the readings."

"Wonderful," Davenport grumbled. "Just what I want to hear."

She pointed to something on the console in front of her. "There's something over here that's throwing up some strange readings. It's a cube approximately ten inches square and it's a completely different composition from the surrounding rock, so that might be the safe. We'll just have to go take a look."

Davenport straightened up. "It looks like we're going for a walk after all."

"I'll tell Beauty to come up here and adjust the scanners. He might be able to get more joy out of them than I can. That guy could tease a computer to fall in love with him if he really wanted it to."

They returned to the cargo hold to a reception of howls, complaints, and threats from the others.

"This better not be your idea of a trick," Dice snarled at Davenport.

"How could Davenport trick you?" Fiddler jeered. "You're so much smarter than he is. He would never be able to pull one over on you."

"Davenport had nothing to do with it," Lyons cut in. "I ran the scans. We couldn't find the safe."

"So....what are you suggesting?" Emmet demanded. "We aren't leaving without our payload."

"You and your payload!" Dice growled.

"*We* aren't leaving without *our* payload," Lyons countered. "We're going to get it."

She approached the breach again. Davenport, Emmet, and Fiddler watched Dice and Lyons look down. "If you know a way down there," Fiddler remarked, "I'll eat my hat."

Lyons went to a compartment in the wall and took out a twisted steel cable. She anchored it to a bolt hole in the bulkhead and pulled on a pair of heavy leather gloves. She swung onto the cable and slid over the side of the breach followed shortly by Dice.

Davenport waited patiently while Emmet and Fiddler slid down, too. They vanished into the crevice. Then Davenport unbuttoned his leather vest, wrapped it around the cable, and swung out into empty space.

The heat burned his palm through the leather, but he held on all the way down. The cable ended twenty feet above the ground. He spotted the others gathered beneath him. He let himself slide off the cable end and landed among them.

He dusted off his hands. "The signal came from over there."

Fiddler gazed up at the cable end far above their heads. "How do we get back up there?"

No one answered. Dice and Lyons headed off in search of the safe. Emmet stayed right with them all the way. Beauty landed behind Davenport a moment later. He didn't use the cable. He just catapulted out of the ship and bounced on springy legs with no problem at all.

He glanced up at Davenport watching him. "You're a liar, Davenport," Beauty snarled. "There were no JimJams in the cargo bay."

Davenport shrugged. "I did say I *might* have seen JimJams. I guess I made a mistake."

Beauty glared at him with a look of terrible hate. "I'm gonna get you for that, Davenport."

"Would you feel better if I got you some JimJams?"

"You won't give me any JimJams," Beauty muttered. "You're a liar. I'll never believe you again—ever."

He stalked off following the party. They hiked up the crevice for almost a mile. The deep canyon curved to the right and Davenport stopped at the corner.

He looked back at the *Echo Omicron* perched between the sheer walls. At that moment, Dice boomed out some burst of conversation to the others and drew Davenport's attention back to the search. If the others found the safe, he better be on hand to make sure they didn't shoot him in the back to steal it from him.

He started forward to find the other four standing together a few hundred yards beyond. "We should have found the safe by now," Lyons told everybody. "We must have passed it."

"It couldn't be up there." Fiddler pointed at the walls surrounding them. "It would have fallen down here."

"The scans could have confused the safe's location. These formations must have messed up the readings."

"So how are we supposed to find it?" Emmet asked.

"We just have to......"

Lyons broke off as a howling streak plummeted out of the atmosphere. Davenport knew that sound.

The whole party looked up as a ship plunged into view. It streaked up the canyon and slowed to hover over where the party left the *Echo Omicron*.

Davenport recognized the Dagger-class ship instantly, which meant it could only have come from one place: the Reserve Wing. "What the hell?" Dice growled.

Without exchanging a word, the whole crew turned and stormed back the way they came. They made it as far as the curve. They started to walk around it when two Stalwarts boomed up the canyon. They flanked the *Echo Omicron* while the Dagger lowered to the canyon floor.

It landed directly underneath the *Echo Omicron* and disgorged dozens of armed soldiers who swarmed all over the place.

Davenport and the others scurried behind the corner. Davenport glued his eye to the wall and held his breath watching the soldiers surround the ship. The Dagger lifted off and returned to its position hovering near the *Echo Omicron*.

The Dagger extended its gangway and the ramp clanged into the *Echo Omicron's* hull breach. Soldiers filed across to the cargo hold. "Damn it!" Lyons hissed. "There goes our ship."

"It wasn't what you might call functional the way it was," Fiddler remarked. "Half the hull is ruined and the engines are missing."

"Do you have a better idea how we can get out of here?" Dice asked.

"We aren't leaving without that.....!" Emmet burst out.

"Quiet, fool!" Lyons whispered. "If they hear you, we're all finished."

"We aren't leaving without that payload!" Emmet whispered.

"Oh, will you give it a rest with our piece of shit payload!" Beauty squeaked. "If we go snooping around for that stupid safe now, they'll drag us off to Terminus Anathema!"

"Will you all stuff it and listen to me for two seconds?" Fiddler breathed. "I know a way we can get out of here, but we have to get far enough away from the ships that we don't get caught."

"Look," Lyons hissed. "They're spreading out. They're looking for us. We have to go now!"

Davenport didn't argue. Every passing second brought the soldiers closer to their hiding place. Lyons shoved everyone back and they all took off running through the canyon.

More Reserve Wing ships descended all the time. They would search the area hunting for the fugitives. On any other day, Davenport would have marched right out there and met up with them.

Up until today, he never would have hesitated to talk to anyone from the Reserve Wing. He would have been all too eager to tell them all about the Ithium and everything else.

He wouldn't be doing that today. They attacked the Ultra Meridian jail. He saw them do it with his own eyes. These ships released skimmers to hunt him down. Then they shot down the *Echo Omicron* and he could only think of one reason why.

They attacked the *Echo Omicron* only *after* the crew took the safe on board. Now they showed up here. The Reserve Wing was after the safe, too, and they weren't out to do it legally. They wanted to reclaim the Ithium and get rid of everyone who might know about it.

Chapter 11

The party ducked behind another rock formation, flattened their backs against the wall, and caught their breath. "What I wouldn't give for some JimJams right now," Beauty grumbled.

"I know where we can get some," Fiddler told him.

Beauty looked up. "Where?"

Davenport glanced down at him and then at her. "You have JimJams?"

"You got some competition, Beauty," Dice interjected. "You better watch out or Davenport will eat all the JimJams before you get any."

"No wonder he always has the best kind of ChunkyTenders," Lyons observed. "He must be snarfing them in his jail when no one is looking."

"He snarfs them when someone *is* looking," Emmet grumbled. "He snarfs them right in front of the prisoners and feeds us Universal Staples."

"I pay for those ChunkyTenders out of my own salary," Davenport told him. "I only share them with my friends."

"You share them with Beauty," Lyons pointed out.

"Like I said."

Beauty snapped around, scowled at Davenport, and then looked away. "You promised me JimJams. You follow through and then we'll talk."

Davenport didn't answer. He didn't know where he would find any JimJams to get back into Beauty's good books, but he would have to figure out some way. He couldn't have Beauty as an enemy.

Beauty said he would get Davenport for lying to him and Beauty could come up with any manner of torturous methods of revenge.

"You said you could get us out of here," Lyons said to Fiddler. "How do you plan to do it?"

"I can do it anytime. I just want to make sure the Reserve Wing doesn't capture us in the process."

The Reserve Wing. So Davenport wasn't the only one who put two and two together. Why should he be?

The others saw Reserve Wing identity profiles on the gun range's targeting grid the same way he did. They would be stupid not to figure out the whole sequence of events.

Fiddler pulled something out of her pocket and held it up. "All I have to do is push this button, but I want us to move farther away. We're still too close."

"How far do we have to go?" Dice asked. "We could make it all the way back to Ultra Meridian before you call out your mystery rescuers."

"Just trust me. There will be plenty of JimJams for everyone on the other end."

Fiddler set off walking farther up the canyon. Beauty tagged at her heels. He couldn't get to the JimJams fast enough.

The others followed more reluctantly, but she must really have a way to get the party to safety. After what he saw with the Armageddon Core, he wouldn't put anything past her.

No one else had any resources left. They could follow Fiddler's plan or starve out here with no JimJams, no ChunkyTenders, and definitely no JuicyPies after Beauty ate every JuicyPie on the *Echo Omicron* within a few minutes.

Fiddler kept moving without stopping to explain. She walked for two hours until the sun dipped behind the canyon walls.

Davenport looked up at the sky. "If we're going anywhere, we should do it now before we all turn into pumpkins."

"As long as we turn into pumpkins with JimJams in our stomachs, Beauty won't mind," Dice remarked.

"Neither will I," Emmet added. "I'm starving."

"We're far enough away now." Fiddler took her device out of her pocket.

"What is that thing?" Lyons asked. "I've never seen one before."

"It's a homing beacon and you've never seen one before because my friend invented it." Fiddler depressed the button. "That's all there is to it. They should be here in a minute."

"A minute? How can they be? We're thousands of miles from......"

A crash interrupted him and a skimmer hurtled into view. It was the skimmer the Armageddon Core took from their pursuers. Flack and Fizzle rode double on the seat.

The party shrank back to get out of their way. The two riders wheeled the vehicle, came back, and stopped in front of Fiddler. "The whole damn planet is going crazy!" Flack exclaimed.

"We know," Fiddler told her.

"We got caught in the middle of it," Dice complained.

"We're the cause of it," Davenport finished.

Fizzle's eyes widened. "*You* caused it....*Sheriff*?"

"We all did....or rather, *these* nutjobs caused it." Davenport jerked his thumb at the *Echo Omicron* crew. "Now we need you to get us out of it."

"How do you plan to get us to safety?" Lyons asked. "We can't all ride on one skimmer."

"You won't have to. You just have to get into the gateway."

"What gateway?" Davenport looked around. "Last time I checked, we were in the middle of the desert."

"Follow us," Flack instructed. "Whatever you do, don't stop moving. Keep running until you get to the other end. If you slow down even for a second, your atoms will separate and you *won't* come out at the other end."

Before Davenport could ask what she meant, she gunned the skimmer and took off. Fiddler broke into a run behind them. Davenport copied her for lack of anything better to do. If it got them away from the Reserve Wing, he would take his chances.

Flack ripped the skimmer into a side canyon and drove it straight into a vertical wall. Amazingly, the skimmer plunged straight into it and vanished. The solid surface blooped like a giant pool of goo and instantly reformed into solid rock again.

Davenport probably would have aborted then, but Fiddler got to the wall first. Instead of slowing down, she bent her head and charged. She picked up speed and leapt straight for the wall. She dove through it and vanished.

Dice and Lyons followed. They did exactly the same thing and put on speed just like Flack said. They dove in behind Fiddler and Beauty went next. Davenport and Emmet exchanged glances on the run, but there was nowhere else to go. They were the last two left.

Both men increased their pace. Davenport dropped behind Emmet. The next minute, he broke through into some kind of tunnel, but not like any tunnel he'd ever seen before.

This one didn't stand still. It kept moving forward on its own. The whole thing whizzed along at a wicked speed and surrounded Davenport with unending motion.

He slowed down to catch his balance. Instantaneously, a powerful vortex seized him. It wrenched him in all directions at once as though a massive force might tear him apart.

Fear gripped his guts. It almost made him stop again when he heard a scream from farther ahead.

The sound shocked him into remembering Flack's warning. He took off running through the tunnel. This must be the gateway she meant. He ran on and on through swirling iridescent smears of color, light, and shadow. Nothing seemed real, not even himself.

All at once, with no warning, he burst through another....whatever it was. He broke out in the Armageddon Core's hidden cavern.

The rest of his comrades waited for him there and Fiddler passed her hand across her forehead. "I swear I'll never get used to that."

Davenport looked behind him. A wall of solid rock blocked any view of the tunnel. "What was that thing?"

"It's a gateway. Friend created tunnels and gateways and bolt holes all over the planet so we could get anywhere quickly."

"What is it?" Lyons asked. "How did it transport us so far so fast?"

"It's based on naturally occurring space distortions. Friend created a few here so we could travel around more easily."

Fiddler walked over to a shelf near Friend's computer table. She took a handful of disc-shaped, individually-wrapped objects from a box and handed them to Beauty. "These are grape-flavored. Sorry, but that's the only flavor we have."

He attacked them in fury. He snatched them out of her hands, squatted down on the floor, and ripped the wrappers off. He shoved them into his mouth one after the other and swallowed them all in one bite.

He finished them and discarded the wrappers on the floor. He sat back on his haunches, lowered his eyelids to half-mast, ran his long, purple tongue over his lips, and sighed in heavenly delight. "JimJams!"

"You're making me look bad, Fiddler," Davenport remarked.

Beauty's eyes snapped open and he glared at Davenport. "Lying bastard cop!"

Dice laughed out loud. "Beauty knows who his friends are."

Davenport looked away. He didn't like admitting to himself that he was jealous of Fiddler. He would give a lot to lay his hands on a few JimJams about now.

Fiddler took the box off the shelf and passed it around. "Help yourselves."

Davenport didn't take any. He meandered over to Friend's desk. "What's going on out in the wide world?"

"The Reserve Wing is invading the planet."

"Who are they after?"

"Ultra Meridian."

She pointed to the image feed that Davenport saw earlier and he gulped. At least twenty Reserve Wing spacecraft sat in the middle of the plane while soldiers spread out all over the place.

"It looks like they're setting up shop here," Fiddler remarked. "Mount Refractory won't be pleased."

"The Reserve Wing wouldn't set up at Ultra Meridian to take out Mount Refractory or any other criminal organization on this planet," Davenport countered.

"Tell us why they *are* setting up at Ultra Meridian, then, brainless!" Dice fired back.

Davenport bent close to the screen. "What the holy hell is that?"

Friend wheeled her chair over and squinted at the image feed. "Uh...."

The image showed a tall, uniformed man standing in front of a big Stalwart while he talked to some other officers.

In front of Davenport's eyes, the tall man held up a small black cube. Then he strode with it into one of the assembled ships. "They found it!" He spun around fast. "Where's your skimmer?"

"In the supply room," Flack told him. "What do you need it for?"

"I'm coming with you," Emmet announced.

Lyons groaned. "Not that again!"

Davenport marched to the supply room. The skimmer sat there as perfect as ever. He slung his leg over the seat and fired up the engine.

Emmet stepped into the doorway, but Davenport didn't wait. He'd had enough.

He gunned the engine and roared straight for Emmet. Emmet barely sprang out of the way before Davenport blasted past him, ripped the skimmer to his right, and plunged out of the cavern at full speed.

Chapter 12

Davenport slipped off the skimmer and crawled to the ridge. He peered over the side at the plane.

Reserve Wing ships crowded the area around the jail. At least another twenty buzzed overhead going back and forth in different directions or just hovered there awaiting orders.

Davenport picked out the ship where the tall man took the safe. Before he could move, another Stalwart came down to land and cut off his view. It towed the stricken *Echo Omicron* behind it.

The Reserve Wing had sealed the breaches in the ship's bridge and gun range, but the back end still gaped wide open. Davenport could see straight into the cargo bay from here.

Soldiers swarmed all around the ship going in and out through the rear breach. What were they doing? Why would they possibly want to resurrect this wrecked ship when they had plenty of their own?

A Dagger rocketed into the atmosphere followed by two others and the whole squadron started launching in rapid succession. The Stalwart in charge of the *Echo Omicron* fired its engines. It would take off any second now.

A bunch of soldiers went inside through the rear breach and they didn't come back out. They must be planning to man it on the way to wherever they were taking it.

The Stalwart carrying the both the tall officer and the safe launched, too. Davenport made up his mind In a split second. He sprang to his feet and took off running.

Ships all over the plane disappeared into the atmosphere and the Stalwart in front of him started to rise. The *Echo Omicron's* crumpled hull shuddered and a puff of dust escaped from underneath it as the Stalwart towed it skyward.

Davenport sprinted across the plane. The Stalwart lifted the *Echo Omicron* off the ground. It came up to Davenport's waist.

He took a running leap and vaulted into the cargo bay. He tumbled head over heel and the prickle of a galvanic coil rippled down his skin.

The wind died the minute he broke through it. It kept the cargo bay pressurized as the two ships rose through the atmosphere into orbit.

A bunch of crewmen worked all over the cargo bay cleaning up the mess of countless broken crates and their spilled contents. None of them gave Davenport a second glance.

Davenport straightened up and walked halfway across the bay. Still no one paid any attention to him. Two welders sparked their torches near the breach. They must be trying to repair the ship en route.

Davenport ran through a few different possible scenarios on how he should proceed. He didn't plan this in advance and he expected to have more time to consider before he encountered the Confederate crew. He thought he might even have to stow away until he decided how to get the safe back.

Then again, if the Reserve Wing was involved in stealing the safe, he didn't know who to trust. Assuming he got the safe back at all—which looked increasingly impossible with every passing moment—who should he hand the Ithium over to? If the Reserve Wing had been compromised, who did that leave? No one.

He glanced over at the bulkhead. He could go through that door, down the corridor, and find the senior officer on the bridge—hopefully. On second thought, the Reserve Wing might have left a skeleton crew on the *Echo Omicron*. These repair crews might be on their own with nothing but a sergeant in charge.

Just then, a petty officer stormed past him. His name badge read, *Catlin*. He pointed up at the welders and yelled, "Pull it in, Chinny! You're getting too close to the edge."

Catlin glanced over and noticed Davenport for the first time. "Who the hell are you? You aren't on my crew."

Davenport pulled forward the tin star pinned to his vest. He held it out for the man to see. "Sheriff Mace Davenport from Ultra Meridian. Take me to your captain or whoever your ranking officer might be."

Catlin furrowed his brow and scowled. "You're under arrest for trespassing on Reserve Wing property. Hand over your sidearms."

"The hell I am." Davenport fired back. "I'm an officer of the law and I'm here in the line of duty. One of your officers on another ship took possession of an illegal substance stolen from my....."

"You're trespassing on Reserve Wing property," Catlin countered, "and you're under arrest. If you don't hand over your sidearms, I'll have no choice but to detain you pend ing....."

"Did you hear what I just said?" Davenport snapped. "You're in violation of Regulation 4926.459 by interfering with the duties of a sworn officer. *You're* under arrest and so is your whole crew. Now, if you don't take me to your captain this minute, I'll incarcerate you all pending....."

"You don't have the authority to arrest me," Catlin retorted. "I placed *you* under arrest first, and under Regulation 1537. 601, an officer of the law loses all authority at the moment of arrest. You're nothing but a gutter criminal." He turned around and snapped his fingers at some of his crew who stood nearby.

The workers stared first at Catlin and then at Davenport. They listened to this bizarre conversation and didn't move. They stayed where they were trying to make up their minds what to do.

Davenport saw them hesitate and followed up his advantage. "Any of you who interferes with my duties will also be subject to prosecution under Regulation 4938.571."

"And if you don't arrest this man immediately," Catlin countered, "you'll be subject to prosecution under Regulation 2067.934 for failing to carry out a direct order, exposing your ship and crew to unwarranted risk, and....."

"Just take me to your damn captain, already," Davenport barked. "Let him work this out."

Catlin shut his mouth and his nostrils flared when he sighed. "Fine, but I'm placing you under armed guard. I can't allow an armed intruder to enter the ship without a guard."

"Fine," Davenport agreed, "but I'm keeping my sidearms."

Catlin sized him up in a blink. "Fine."

"Fine," Davenport finished.

Both men regarded each other with matched suspicion, but neither of them said anything else. At last, Catlin turned to his crew. "Arm up, you four, and come with us."

The welders sprang to a bunch of steel canisters parked in the corner. These ones bore the Reserve Wing insignia and they were perfectly intact. They hadn't been on the *Echo Omicron* before the Reserve Wing took possession of the ship.

They took out sidearms, rifles, and a few smaller XQs. They armed themselves and returned to the two men still confronting each other in the middle of the bay. The conscripted guards looked surprised to find that Davenport was still waiting for them and that he hadn't started shooting everyone in sight.

They surrounded him, but Davenport didn't care. He just wanted to get to the bridge and see whoever was in charge of this crew. Catlin flashed him another scowl and then led the way out of the bay.

A single officer stood behind the main bridge command podium. The captain paced back and forth supervising technicians and crewmen working all over the bridge.

The front window had been sealed with massive steel plates to cover the breach and the door to the gun range stood open. Welding torches flashed inside the range. The Reserve Wing must be serious about reviving this ship.

Catlin led Davenport over to the captain. "Sir, this intruder hopped on board just before we launched. He claims to be the Sheriff of Ultra Meridian and he's demanding to see you."

The captain turned to Davenport. His name badge read, *Boyne*. His eyes dipped once to Davenport's star and the captain's expression cleared. "What can we do for you, Sheriff? What brings you on board our little derelict?"

"A smuggling crew brought this ship to Ultra Meridian for inspection and I grounded it when I discovered them transporting Ithium on board."

Boyne's eyebrows shot up. "Ithium! That's impossible. The only Ithium in the Confederacy is stored in a secure haz-mat lab on Helios Sanctus."

Davenport restrained himself with an effort. "I know that. They got hold of it somehow or other. They tried to hide it on board to pass it under my inspection for transport to Sacron Enigma. I took the Ithium into custody and then....."

He broke off. Should he tell this captain about the Reserve Wing bombing the jail and trying to steal the safe? Boyne must know all about that. He was part of the squadron that attacked Ultra Meridian.

Boyne watched him intently. "And then?"

Davenport took a deep breath and plunged ahead. "And then, this squadron attacked my outpost and destroyed my jail. Someone on board one of your squadron ships stole the safe containing the Ithium. It's on board one of your sister ships as we speak. I demand that the responsible party be arrested and the Ithium seized."

Boyne's eyes widened even further. "Is that so?"

"Yes. It is. I witnessed the whole incident with my own eyes and I saw one of your personnel take my safe on board your sister ship."

Catlin stepped forward. "Forgive me for wasting your time with this nonsense, Captain." He laid hold of Davenport's elbow. "You're coming with me, dirtbag. You're under arrest under Regulation....."

"Stop!" Boyne ordered. "Don't interfere with an officer during the execution of his duties. Regulations forbid it."

"But, Sir...."

Boyne turned to Davenport. "I'll take up this matter, Sheriff, but you must realize that I can't do anything right now. We're in open space on board a ship devoid of all power. We're under tow by another Stalwart.

"I know," Davenport replied.

"We'll have to wait until the squadron stops at Chiton's Hold to drop the *Echo Omicron* at the repair yard. If you cooperate as far as that, I'll take up this matter personally and ensure that the Ithium gets back to Helios Sanctus where it belongs."

He held Davenport's gaze and didn't blink once when he said this. Davenport measured the man and took a calculated risk. He couldn't fight the whole squadron on his own. He had to trust someone and this captain seemed as good a choice as any. "Fine. We'll wait as far as Chiton's Hold."

"You'll forgive me for saying so, Sheriff," Boyne went on, "but we have to detain you until we get there. I can't have you walking around free. You'd pose too much of a distraction for my crew and.....You'll forgive me for saying this, but you would pose a challenge to my authority. If I leave you walking around free, my crew will wonder which of us they should obey. It will confuse them about who actually is in command of this ship."

"I won't interfere with your crew. I give you my word on that."

"I believe you, but the subtleties of command can affect a crew subconsciously. You've already undermined my authority with Catlin and the cargo bay repair crew. I'm asking you, as a favor to me, to cooperate and allow us to detain you only as far as Chiton's Hold. I'm sure that, as soon as we find and reclaim the Ithium, you'll be exonerated and your position restored. The Admiral might even give you a commendation for your actions."

Davenport sensed Boyne caressing his ego. He ignored the flattery, but he couldn't reasonably ignore the captain's request.

Davenport could well imagine the confusion and disturbance the crew would suffer at having an authority figure on board who challenged their entire chain of command.

"All right," he conceded. "I can go along with that."

Boyne stuck out his hand. "Give me your sidearms, please."

Davenport hesitated again, but in the end, he handed them over. If this plan got the Ithium safely back to Helios Sanctus, what difference did it make in the end?

He might even be willing to go to prison for a long, long time to prevent the Ithium from falling into the wrong hands—if it hadn't already.

Catlin took hold of his elbow again. "Come with me, Sheriff."

Davenport followed him back off the bridge. The crew returned to their work all around him.

Catlin escorted him to the crew quarters. Catlin stopped in front of an empty compartment the *Echo Omicron* crew used as a storage locker.

The doors swept open and Catlin nodded inside. "If you don't mind, Sheriff....."

Davenport stepped across the threshold. At the same moment, Catlin and his men pounced on him from behind. They tackled him to the ground and fists pummeled him all over.

Davenport tried to fight back, but they overpowered him. Catlin delivered a vicious punch to Davenport's jaw and Davenport's head slammed against the floor. He went limp for a moment and the rest of the men attacked even more ferociously.

Davenport felt them dragging him away, but every time he tried to resist, they kicked or punched him again. They flung him against a wall and a crash punctuated the terrible silence that followed.

Chapter 13

Davenport huddled and covered his head against the next blow, but it never came. He peeked out and found himself in a box three feet long and two feet wide—barely big enough for him to curl into. He couldn't stretch out or even raise his head.

He recognized the smell instantly. He was in the closet where he first discovered the Ithium under Beauty's bed. The dirty blankets weren't there anymore, but these idiots didn't see the removable floor.

The ceiling ended an inch or two from the door where a squeak of light entered. He slipped his fingers over the lowest shelf and touched a stack of blankets. That confirmed it. He was in Beauty's closet.

Davenport cursed under his breath. "Cocksuckers!"

He stretched his arm and tried the knob on the inside. Dice and Lyons must have installed it so Beauty could get in and out of his closet when he wanted to.

Davenport tried the knob, but he already knew it was locked. Bastards. Sons of bitches. Davenport would get these fools if it was the last thing he ever did.

Right now, though, he had to get out of this damn closet. He rose off the floor as best he could and started tinkering with the knob. He felt a few screws and tried to wedge his thumbnail into the slot.

He tried to turn it when, without warning, the door yanked open right in front of him. Light stabbed into his eyes and he blinked up at a figure standing over him.

Fiddler looked into the closet and then glanced down when she saw him. "There you are." She squatted down. "Get out of there! We need to move."

"What the hell are you doing here?" Davenport climbed out of the closet, only too glad to straighten his legs. "You're supposed to be back at Ultra Meridian."

"You didn't think we were going to let you go after Emmet's payload, did you? We're here to get it back."

"Emmet's payload isn't here. The safe isn't even on this ship."

She stopped and regarded him for a minute. Then she shrugged. "Well, we'll just have to get it back. Which ship is it on?"

"If I knew that, I'd be there getting it back myself." Davenport paused. "Tell me Emmet isn't here with you."

"We're all here."

"All!" Davenport gulped. "Oh, no. No, no, no, no, no. They didn't."

"Lyons, Dice, and Beauty didn't want to stay behind, either. They came to get the safe. They're looking for it now."

Davenport covered his eyes and groaned. "This is the worst day of my life."

"You should be grateful to us for coming to get you."

"You didn't come to get me, did you? You came to steal the safe from me."

"Well, I did get you out of that closet. You might at least thank me."

"I would rather get myself out of any closets I happen into than for all of you to go blundering around looking for MY safe."

She turned and started walking away. "Fine. Stay here and wait for them to come lock you up again."

Davenport took one last look into the closet he just left and hustled after her. She stopped under a ventilation duct at the end of the corridor. "We have to get out of sight before someone sees us."

"How did you, Emmet, Lyons, Dice, and Beauty get through the cargo hold? I'd really like to know."

"There was no one in there when we came through." She jumped up, grabbed the duct, and pulled herself out of sight.

Davenport followed and hunched in a space not much bigger than the closet except that it ran off in two directions to both ends of the ship. "Now what, Houdini?"

"Now we go back and find the others. They're looking for the safe."

"You mentioned that. I can just imagine how Dice and Beauty are staying hidden on this ship."

She started crawling down the duct. The slightest sound echoed through the whole ship, so she and Davenport mostly slid their hands and knees along the smooth steel. "Here's hoping no one turns on the main furnace."

"I disabled the environmental control." She glanced at him over her shoulder. "How do you think I found you?"

"How *did* you find me? How did you know where they put me?"

"I watched you. I saw you go to the bridge and I knew that was a losing proposition. I followed you to that compartment and then they brought you here. These Reserve Wing guys aren't as observant as they might be."

"They're too busy repairing the damage. They want to restore the *Echo Omicron* for some reason,. They're taking it back to Chiton's Hold for repair."

Fiddler's eyebrows shot up. "Seriously? Isn't that kind of a waste of resources? They're the ones who shot the ship to pieces."

"Don't ask me to explain their logic. Why did the Reserve Wing bomb my jail, try to kill me, and then steal the Ithium in the first place when they're the ones who are supposed to be protecting it?"

"Maybe they were trying to get it back from you."

"If they wanted that, they wouldn't have bombed the *Echo Omicron* when the safe was on board. They were trying to destroy the ship and they couldn't have known the Ithium cartridge was protected by the safe. They could have released the Ithium at Ultra Meridian. In fact......" Davenport stopped himself from saying it. The implications were too terrible even to voice out loud.

"Were you about to say it seems like they were trying to do exactly that?"

Davenport blanched. "You said it, not me."

"Try this one on for size," she countered. "Either the whole Reserve Wing has turned rotten or just this squadron has. I personally choose to believe that only this squadron is involved and the rest of the Reserve Wing is still dedicated to truth, justice, and the Confederate way. I suggest you choose to believe it, too."

Davenport didn't answer. He crawled behind her for a while considering what she said. She was right, of course. Either the whole Reserve Wing had thrown over the very principles upon which the Confederate Corps was founded or else this particular squadron went off on its own.

Like Fiddler, he would vastly prefer to believe the latter. Maybe, hopefully, he might be able to find some forgotten corner of the Reserve Wing where officers still believed in doing their duty. He just might be able to find one person he could trust.

He should have thought of that before he trusted Boyne, but he wouldn't make that mistake again. He would write off this whole squadron and save his trust for someone outside it. He had to choose wisely who to trust and who not to trust.

Fiddler stopped crawling. "Listen!"

Davenport held his breath, but a moment later, he let it out because the noise drowned out any sound he and Fiddler might make. Tremendous bellows echoed up through the ceiling from the corridor below. Davenport would know that deep rumbling voice anywhere.

"You pieces of shit! You stinking bastards! I'll tear you apart! Let go of me, you dipshits!"

Fiddler crawled to the nearest grate that gave a view down into the corridor. A dozen Reserve Wing crewmen wrestled to restrain Dice and even that many men found it nearly impossible to hold him down.

He gouged and slashed his horns and tusks at them until Catlin, that brave and dedicated soldier, dove in and tackled Dice. Catlin hooked his elbow around Dice's neck and twisted Dice's face away.

All the rest piled in and grabbed Dice's limbs. They held him down until they consolidated their grip. Then they dragged him away with Catlin still trailing along behind.

He crushed Dice's neck in such a tight grip that Catlin couldn't stand. The crew had to haul him and Dice together along the floor.

Another dozen men appeared fighting to keep hold of Beauty. The creature contorted in strange shapes and his ear-piercing screeches set Davenport's hair on end.

The crew hauled him away, too, and Fiddler swiveled around in the ventilation duct. "We have to follow them."

"What happened to finding the safe? Are you going to spring them, too? They might tear the ship in half."

"In case we do find the safe, we'll need Dice and Beauty to help us get away from the Reserve Wing. Come on."

Davenport rolled his eyes in exasperation, but he had no other way to move around the ship unimpeded so he went with her.

They followed Dice and Beauty, but when they came to an intersection, Davenport paused. "The crew lounge is over there. Let's go over there for a minute."

"What for?"

"I want to see if they have any JimJams."

Fiddler's eyes popped. "You, too? You're as hopeless as Beauty."

"They aren't for me. I want something to give him when we find him. It's the easiest way to get him to help us."

"How are we going to find Dice and Beauty after you collect the JimJams?"

"I'm sure we'll be able to follow the noise."

She didn't argue and they turned left. He crawled in front now, but when they got to the crew lounge, he looked down into the room full of Reserve Wing personnel.

"The captain says we'll stop off at Chiton's Hold on our way to Atlas Arcane," one of the crew was saying.

"Good," another fired back. "The sooner we dump this wreck, the better. It's stuck together with baling twine and a few strong prayers."

"If that," someone else added and everyone laughed.

"Will we get assigned to stay with it?"

"We better not. I didn't sign on to weld scrap."

"The captain says they want to put it back in service."

"They'll have to melt down this pile of trash and recast it before it's fit for service again."

"The last crew added quite a few aftermarket modifications. Did you see that range processor? You won't see anything like that in the Reserve Wing."

"That's because it's highly illegal. You could get ten years for flying with a processor like that. Only smugglers and cartels use that shit."

Davenport pointed behind Fiddler. She shook her head, but Davenport didn't listen. He scooted around her. She tried to stop him, but he set off anyway. He needed more information and he could think of only one place to get it.

He paused at a few different intersections trying to orient himself. At last, he halted directly above the bridge and listened to Boyne and his 2IC bent over the command podium.

"Yes, Sir," Boyne was saying. "I understand perfectly."

An admiral spoke from the screen in front of them. "As soon as you make landfall at Chiton's Hold, evacuate your crew and return to the *Agamemnon*. I don't want any of our people left behind on that wreck. I'll take the *Devil's Bane* on to Atlas Arcane and you can catch up with us there."

"Did you receive the specs I sent you of the modifications, Sir?" Boyne asked.

"I received them. Update the records. The ship should be listed on our smugglers' database, but you can switch it to the Reserve Wing roster instead."

"Yes, Sir."

"They aren't talking about the safe," Davenport whispered. "Whoever took it must have been working independently."

"Are you saying they bombed the Ultra Meridian jail independently?" Fiddler asked. "No one attacked the *Echo Omicron* independently. The whole squadron attacked at once. They were trying to destroy the ship."

"You heard what he said. They thought the *Echo Omicron* was a smuggler's ship and they were right. They couldn't know I was on it."

Fiddler rolled her eyes to Heaven. "Not even you could be that gullible."

"If Boyne and the admiral knew about the safe, don't you think they'd be discussing it?"

"Not necessarily," Fiddler pointed out. "You already told Boyne about the Ithium. If he wasn't in on it, wouldn't he report it to his superior?"

"Maybe he already did and we just weren't around to hear him do it."

Fiddler looked away. Even Davenport heard how flimsy this sounded. "Maybe whoever attacked us did it to steal the Ithium."

"Maybe the Admiral coordinated the whole thing," she countered. "Maybe he issued orders to his squadron to attack you and then he landed his personnel on the planet to retrieve the safe. Did you ever think of that?"

Davenport didn't answer. He didn't like hearing his own thoughts coming out of someone else's mouth, especially when it meant what this meant.

"Either way," Fiddler went on, "we have to find whoever took the safe."

"If you're right and the Admiral took it, it will be on the *Devil's Bane*. We just have to find a way to get there without going through empty space on the way."

"I'm going to find Emmet." Fiddler squeezed past Davenport and started crawling again. "I have to tell him the safe isn't here."

Davenport crawled after her. "What is it with you and Emmet?"

"What do you think?" she replied over her shoulder. "He's my dad."

"I know, but do you really think it's wise to help him break the law? If you cared about him, you'd stop him from running such dangerous jobs."

She stopped and turned around to stare at him. "You think this is *his* job?"

Davenport froze and then slumped. "I should have seen that coming."

"He's just our runner. I handle the clients."

"By 'our', do you mean your whole gang of......"

She narrowed her eyes at him. "Say it. I dare you."

"Your gang of...." He snorted. He couldn't stop himself. "Miniatures?"

"Uh-huh. Laugh it up while you can, porkchop."

Davenport stifled his laughter. "Okay. I will."

"No," she snapped. "Emmet isn't a member of the Armageddon Core. He isn't....."

"Miniature enough?" Davenport choked on laughter.

"That isn't funny!" Fiddler snapped.

"Yes, it is. It's hysterical."

Her lips twitched. "Okay. It might be a little bit funny, but no, Emmet isn't miniature enough to be in the Armageddon Core. He's also a little too....." Davenport waited for her to finish. "He's too drunk, okay? We couldn't accept him even if he was miniature. I do what I can to help him and he does random jobs for me, but he spends all his pay on booze. The Armageddon Core is a serious organization."

Davenport studied her. "What exactly is the Armageddon Core's business?"

"The others would hunt me down and eviscerate me if I told you." She turned away and started crawling again. "Emmet and I have our own thing going on the side and he runs the stuff for us because he can fly under the radar better than I can. I pull the strings behind the scenes while he goes out in the open. Lawmen like you see a drunk and they don't usually look any further."

Davenport almost said something and stopped crawling. "Do you hear that?"

They both listened and caught the sound of Dice roaring in the background. "Holy shit!" Fiddler whispered. "What is he doing to them?"

"Eating them for lunch, I hope." Davenport turned toward the sound. "Let's go watch the show."

Chapter 14

Dice's bellows got louder as Fiddler and Davenport drew nearer. They could hear curses and insults against the crew's families until, eventually, the walls around Davenport and Fiddler shook with thunderous blows. The pair had to slow down and stop more than once for fear they might burst through the ceiling into the compartments below.

Eventually, Davenport pulled up above a grate overlooking the same empty crew compartment where Catlin and his team attacked and captured Davenport. Now they had their hands full subduing Dice and Beauty—or trying to.

The original ten who captured Beauty piled on top of him in the corner. They smothered him with their bodies and only just managed to pin him down while he screeched and thrashed and scratched and spat. His spidery appendages kept jabbing up between their limbs before they manhandled him back onto the ground.

The rest weren't having near as much joy with Dice. Not only had they called in at least another fifteen crewmen to help, but they even brought in stun guns to shock him into submission.

Five soldiers stood around the confused tangle of bodies. They aimed their stun guns into the jumble, but they didn't fire. Too many other soldiers blocked them from even seeing Dice. They couldn't get off a shot without hitting one of their own.

Dice's thunderous roars tore through the ship. Davenport didn't envy the soldiers trying to restrain him. Every now and then, someone crawled out of the mess cradling some injured body part. More often, they got hauled out by their comrades with punctures, gashes, or flesh torn off.

Catlin stood above them yelling orders at everyone, but no one could hear him over Dice's ferocious bellows. The soldiers punched and kicked Dice, struck him with clubs and weapons, and even shot at him a few times, but nothing penetrated Dice's thick hide. Their best efforts only sent him into an even more dangerous rage.

Finally, Catlin bellowed above the noise. "Flip him over, boys! Roll him this way!"

The soldiers did their best. They grabbed onto Dice and he gouged with his tusks to tear them in half.

He snatched at a few men, and in the mayhem of trying to fight them off, enough of them got hold of his limbs. They flung him sideways onto his chest. The floor protected his back before. Now it lay exposed to the stun guns.

Three soldiers fired at once and their barbs embedded between his shoulder blades. The electrodes struck him. The other two stun gunners pivoted around Dice and fired into his lower back, too. His enormous body convulsed with thousands of volts coursing through it. He bellowed between his tusks, but he couldn't move.

The shock flung the soldiers off. Many fell to the floor bleeding, but the damage was done. Dice twitched and jolted on the floor with electricity streaming down the wires into his body.

He finally lay still and the soldiers stood around in dazed silence staring at him in disbelief. The soldiers came to their senses one by one, limped away, and some started giving their comrades medical aid.

Catlin gave orders to a few people and they rushed away. In a minute, they returned with the enormous secondary docking clamps usually stored in the cargo bay. These huge iron clamps were rated for holding small spacecraft in safe positions during war maneuvers.

The crew loaded Dice with five sets of clamps, and even then, Catlin sent his people to search the ship for more. One set proved sufficient to restrain Beauty, though he kept howling and trying to bite anyone who came near him.

The crew retreated to the door. They left Dice and Beauty lying immobile in the middle of the floor. Catlin ran his wrist across his brow. "Remind me never to deal with one of these things again."

"What is it, Sir?" someone asked. "What is that thing?"

Catlin glanced at Dice and looked away. "I don't know. I've never seen one before and I hope I never find out what it is. Knapp, you run up to the bridge and tell the captain."

Fiddler nudged Davenport and pointed at Dice. The big monster's eyelids fluttered. He was coming around and he didn't look happy at all.

One of the crew nudged Catlin and they all watched with bated breath while Dice's vision cleared. Then he turned his furious eyes on them. Catlin whispered to his men, "Go get the Howitzers."

Five of them scampered off and the others raised their weapons. The stun gunners aimed at Dice again, but he didn't fight the restraints except to turn over onto his seat. He eyed his tormentors and snarled through his fangs.

A minute later, Captain Boyne strolled in. He took one look at Dice and Beauty and turned to Catlin. "Where did they come from?"

"Still not sure, Sir," Catlin replied. "We think he might have come on board with the sheriff. That's all I can figure."

"Scum of the Zuzuk Kanz Stream!" Dice bellowed. "You think you can mess with me? I'll crack your skulls and feast on your filthy, stinking entrails!"

"Keep your mouth to yourself, Adik," the captain snapped. "You're here to answer my questions, not to throw your insults around."

Dice stared at him for a second and then burst out laughing. "A pathetic little Reltoid worm! Do you hear that, Beauty?" Dice pretended to look over his shoulder. "I found me a sad little Staigzein, Dramilon invertebrate. My favorite food!"

Captain Boyne strode over to him and towered over Dice's prostrate body. "Where's the sheriff you helped to escape from confinement? You must have freed him. Where did you hide him?"

"Sheriff?" Dice fired back. "I don't know anything about any sheriff."

Captain Boyne nodded to the stun gunners and they fired again—all of them. Fifteen barbs punched Dice's chest and he went into another seizure of twitching and frothing at the mouth.

Davenport suffered a pang of conscience that Dice was going through this for his sake. Davenport thanked the stars that Dice didn't really know where Davenport was because Davenport wouldn't blame the big guy for spilling everything to spare himself this torture.

Boyne nodded to his men and they reeled in their wires. Boyne waited for Dice to stop quivering and then started all over again.

"You came on board to find the Ithium, didn't you? You knew we confined your friend and you freed him. Where is he? He can't get off the ship and the Ithium isn't here for him to steal. You're all going down to Terminus Anathema, so earn yourself a reduced sentence by telling us where he is."

Dice spat bloody froth out of his mouth. "I don't know anything about any Ithium and I don't know any sheriff. It's just me and my friend here."

Boyne glanced over at Beauty. "All right. Play it your way. If you won't tell us, maybe he will." He sliced his finger at his men and signaled the stun gunners to surround Beauty.

Davenport cringed. Electrocuting Dice was one thing. He could take it, but Beauty was a different story.

The stun gunners took their positions and aimed their weapons at Beauty lying helpless and terrified on the floor. Beauty's bulging eyes darted around the room and a little agonized whimper came from his throat.

Davenport couldn't let this happen. He braced his arms on either side of the vent to jump down into the room. Fiddler tried to hold him back, but Davenport shook her off. He would give himself up before he let them hurt Beauty.

Boyne waited until his men got into position. "Fire!"

"Stop!" Dice bellowed. "I'll tell you everything! Just don't hurt him."

Beauty let out a little sob in the tense silence that followed. Boyne glanced over his shoulder. "All right. Start talking."

The stun gunners didn't move. They continued to hold Beauty at gunpoint. Davenport's heart hammered against his ribs. He held himself stiff and ready to intervene at any second.

"All right, all right," Dice panted. "I'll tell you.....We didn't come on board to find any Ithium. I don't know about any Ithium. We came to find.....the treasure."

Boyne spun around fast. "Treasure! What treasure?"

Dice looked away. Davenport's eyes snapped to the big smuggler's face. Treasure?

Davenport would have found a treasure when he searched the ship—if there was any treasure to find. The *Echo Omicron* crew would have tried to hide that or maybe left it where he *would* find it to distract him from their real cargo—the Ithium.

Boyne marched over to Dice. The captain's eyes sparkled with a strange kind of madness. "What treasure? Start talking fast or the caterpillar gets it."

Dice pretended to hesitate. "All right, all right! Just give me a minute, okay?"

"You don't have a minute, Adik," Boyne snapped. "I asked you a question. What treasure are you talking about?"

"I got hired by the....." Dice hesitated again and seemed to come to a decision. "I got hired by Mount Refractory, okay? You can't tell anyone I told you. They would flay me alive if they knew I told."

"*I'll* flay you if you don't tell me everything!" Boyne's shoulders strained struggling to control himself. "Start talking and don't leave anything out if you want to make it off this ship alive."

"I got hired by Mount Refractory to....to find a hidden treasure stashed somewhere on this ship. Mount Refractory hired the crew to steal the treasure from Ekol Thaine, but they betrayed him and tried to run. They hid the treasure somewhere on this ship. They stopped at Ultra Meridian trying to weasel an inspection out of the local sheriff."

"The sheriff said they were running Ithium," Boyne countered. "He didn't say anything about any treasure."

"I don't know anything about any Ithium. If they were running Ithium at the same time, that's someone else's issue."

Boyne's voice trembled ever so slightly. "What was this treasure?"

Dice shrugged. "You know Mount Refractory. I'd be guessing if I said it was forty or fifty million in gold, jewels, and stolen goods."

Boyne stormed to the door and held a murmured conversation with Catlin. "Did you find anything on the ship?"

"No, Sir, but we didn't exactly look. We were too busy with the repairs. The smuggling crew could have stashed it anywhere."

Boyne strode back to Dice. Was that a mischievous twinkle in the big smuggler's eye? "Where were you supposed to find the treasure?"

"I don't know, okay? I was supposed to find it. Mount Refractory didn't know where it was. That was my job—to find it."

Boyne returned to Catlin. "I'll have to contact the Admiral about this. He'll want to know about this treasure."

"Would you like to contact him here, Sir?" Catlin asked. "This compartment has a communications link."

Boyne looked over his shoulder toward Dice, who peered up at the captain with an anxious expression like he actually worried about what the captain might do.

"The captain can't actually believe this yarn," Fiddler whispered. "Doesn't he even suspect that Dice might be pulling his leg?"

Apparently not. Boyne went out into the hall. Davenport and Fiddler nearly got into a fight trying to go first through the conduit to follow him.

Boyne went to the nearest communications link where he thought Dice couldn't overhear him. He signaled and got the same admiral on the horn.

"We captured two more intruders, Sir. They claim they aren't connected with the sheriff from Ultra Meridian. They say they don't know anything about the Ithium and they came aboard to find some treasure the smuggling crew stashed on board. They claim it's here somewhere."

The admiral perked up immediately. His voice lifted the same way Boyne's did when Dice first told him this crock of steaming horseshit. "What kind of treasure?"

"He doesn't know, exactly, but it came from Mount Refractory so it might be forty or fifty million in gold, jewels, and stolen goods."

"Interesting!" the admiral chirped. "We'll divert right away. I'll question the man and find out the treasure's location."

"He doesn't know, Sir," Boyne told him. "He was supposed to find it and retrieve it. That's what he says, anyway."

"Divert to Scion of Hubris and land at the same spot as before. I'll meet you there."

"Yes, Sir."

Boyne entered the compartment and relayed the news to Catlin. "The admiral will come on board in a few minutes and question you," Boyne told Dice. "You can tell him what you know about the treasure's location. If you play ball with us, you might avoid a long-term sentence."

Dice relaxed in relief and Boyne left the room. Catlin signaled the stun gunners to pull back and leave Beauty alone. Davenport swung his legs forward and poised them directly over the vent.

"What are you doing?" Fiddler hissed.

"What does it look like I'm doing? I'm getting them out. We can't leave them here."

"You don't have a weapon and you heard what Boyne said. The admiral will be here in minutes and you want to...."

Davenport didn't answer. He smashed his feet down through the vent and dropped into the room. He landed in the middle of the thickest knot of soldiers. Fiddler was right. He didn't have a weapon and he didn't need one.

He came to rest right behind one of the stun gunners. He seized the man around the shoulders and whipped him toward his companions. The man's gun came up automatically and Davenport aimed it at the other soldiers. He jerked the man's fingers against the trigger and all the wires uncoiled.

They shot toward the assembled soldiers and the prongs spread out. Three stabbed into three different targets and the power surged down the wires. The victims crumpled to the floor.

The other soldiers wheeled to attack, but Davenport was already springing somewhere else. He leapt for one of the soldiers holding a huge Howitzer. The man brought down his weapon to fire, but it was too big and he missed aiming at Davenport at all.

Davenport grasped the barrel between his elbow and ribs. He rotated sideways pulling the barrel with him. The gun boomed out and flattened six soldiers with one shot.

Davenport spotted Catlin pulling a sidearm. Davenport ducked under the weapon and kicked out. He kicked Catlin's feet out from under him and the man hit the floor with a yell.

Davenport leapt up and spun around to face the rest of the soldiers moving in to grab him. Many held rifles and sidearms with a few more Howitzers. He never doubted he could get away from them, too. Then he would.....”

“Davenport!” Dice roared. “Look out!”

Too late. One of the remaining stun gunners stood apart from the others and unloaded at Davenport from behind. The wires uncoiled toward Davenport in slow motion.

He dodged and missed most of the prongs. The last one whizzed past his shoulder, started to sink, and buried its point in his ankle.

Devastating currents scorched through his body. All his muscles locked and his knees buckled.

“Davenport!” Dice bellowed.

Davenport couldn't move, and the next minute, the soldiers hit him hard. They pummeled him to the floor more brutally than before. He sank beneath them and focused all his effort on protecting his head and body.

Chapter 15

The Confederate crew dragged Davenport out of the cargo hold. He caught a moment's glimpse of crumbling, ruined buildings covered in rust, moss, and creepers. Then the crew flung him against a moldy wall and left him there. They all trooped back to the *Echo Omicron* without looking at him again.

Davenport started to pick himself up, but he hesitated in case they came back and started in on him again. His ribs and back hurt like hell. He couldn't take another beating like that.

The Stalwart rested on its landing gear nearby. The *Echo Omicron* slouched behind it as stricken as ever. Why in the world would the Reserve Wing ever want to repair that ship?

He scanned the area for anyone else preparing to attack him. Three other Reserve Wing ships sat on the ground near the Stalwart. None of them was the ship where the Reserve Wing officer took Davenport's safe.

Davenport stiffened when a single man came out of a nearby ship and strode toward him. The guy walked straight upright with a single-minded directness to his movements. He didn't look around him. He didn't seem aware of or care where he was.

Davenport spotted stars on the officer's collar when the man got near enough. This must be the admiral. He walked right up to Davenport, bent down, and offered Davenport his hand. Davenport recognized him from Boyne's communications link.

"It's a pleasure to meet you, Sheriff. My name is Admiral Killian Joyce. I'm directly attached to Confederate Corps Command on Atlas Arcane. Captain Boyne told me all about your mission to retrieve an Ithium cartridge."

Davenport ignored the admiral's hand and climbed painfully to his feet. "If you know that much, you must know your squadron attacked Ultra Meridian. Your entire squadron conspired to steal the Ithium for criminal purposes. A thinking man might suspect you were involved in that plot."

"I can assure you my squadron knew nothing about any Ithium at Ultra Meridian. We followed ships belonging to Typhon Exelor. We attacked them. If we hit Ultra Meridian itself, I can assure you it was totally unintentional."

"You also attacked the *Echo Omicron*. Your squadron chased it through the atmosphere. That wasn't unintentional."

"Our database lists the *Echo Omicron* as a smuggler's ship—at least, it did. You can't blame us for attacking it. We came to Ultra Meridian to fight smugglers. We had no way of knowing it didn't belong to Typhon Exelor."

"One of your men took my safe with the Ithium cartridge inside it," Davenport insisted. "If you don't know anything about that, you'll make it your mission to find out who took it and return the Ithium to Helios Sanctus."

"Absolutely!" the admiral exclaimed. "I'm as anxious to retrieve the Ithium as you are."

Davenport narrowed his eyes at the man. "I don't believe you. The whole squadron is under your direct command. They wouldn't just randomly miss their target and hit the Ultra Meridian jail instead of Typhon Exelor. Typhon Exelor is on the other side of the planet. You must have given the order to attack. No one else could have done it."

Admiral Joyce only smiled at him. "I understand. You've had a rough day, haven't you? I can see how this misunderstanding might lead you to believe the whole squadron was involved."

"The whole squadron *is* involved."

Admiral Joyce inclined his head. "I can see there's no convincing you. What can I do to show you I'm sincere?"

"How about you show me the safe?"

"All right. I'll do my best. Did you see which ship my man took it into?"

Davenport cringed. "I couldn't see its signature from that distance, but I would recognize it if I saw it."

Admiral Joyce pointed behind him toward the ships nearby. "Was it any of those?"
"No."

An infuriating little smile curled the corners of the admiral's mouth. "Very well, Sheriff. I can see that you do recognize these ships. I will make inquiries and locate the safe for you."

Davenport frowned. "Now?"

"Soon. First, I want you to come with me for a moment. I want to talk to you about this case. There are quite a few details I need to clarify and you're the only person who can enlighten me."

He turned and took a few steps. He waited for Davenport to follow him. The admiral kept smiling in that benign way. Davenport still didn't trust him, but this was better than dealing with armed soldiers.

The admiral strolled between the ruined buildings gazing at everything in delight. "We don't usually stop on this planet. A thriving population used to run a Confederate outpost here, but a terrible epidemic wiped them out. The last hundred and fifty survivors evacuated to Animus Delphi for medical treatment. They left this place to crumble and no one has ever returned to revive it. Isn't that a shame?"

Davenport kept his gaze riveted on the admiral. This was a trap. He sensed it. Any officer worth his salt would have gone to find the Ithium immediately instead of taking a walk around the damn block.

Davenport looked around for a weapon, but not even the Admiral was armed. What could he really do to Davenport here?

He kept leading Davenport farther and farther away from the ships, but Davenport didn't mind. That only meant he was moving farther away from the soldiers. If it came to a fight between himself and the admiral, Davenport didn't doubt he could win.

"I can't tell you how impressed I am that you located the Ithium," the admiral went on. "Not many law enforcement officers in your position would be able to do that."

Davenport stiffened. "How do you know that? You don't know where the crew hid the Ithium."

"They must have hidden it well, though, mustn't they have? They wouldn't leave a cargo like that lying around for anyone to see."

Davenport didn't answer.

"You're obviously a selfless and dedicated officer of the law. Maybe you'd like to reconsider your vocation and join the Reserve Wing. We always need motivated officers with plenty of initiative and critical thinking skills. You've already shown yourself well-endowed with both."

"No," Davenport muttered. "I never considered rethinking my vocation. I'm happy where I am."

"Well, maybe you'll think about it now. Your jail has been destroyed. The Confederacy might not rebuild it and then where will you be?"

Davenport spun around. "Why wouldn't they rebuild it?"

Admiral Joyce shrugged. "Ultra Meridian is a remote outpost—one of the last before the frontier to the vast wastes of Sacron Enigma. Ultra Meridian doesn't get much traffic."

Davenport snorted. "Of course the Confederacy will rebuild it. It's one of the most important outposts in the whole Confederacy *because* it's one of the last before Sacron Enigma. It's the last stop where smugglers like the *Echo Omicron* can get a stamp before they leave the Confederacy. If we didn't stop them at Ultra Meridian, they would get away scot free."

Admiral Joyce waved that away. "You might be right."

Davenport bit his tongue. He knew he was right. He just couldn't figure out why this admiral didn't know it, too. What Confederate admiral in the known universe would even suggest abandoning Ultra Meridian? It was out of the question.

Admiral Joyce motioned Davenport into a doorway. It led to an arched tunnel between two courtyards. "Come this way. I want to show you something interesting."

Davenport ducked under after him. He kept the Admiral in sight at all times in case the Admiral pulled any sudden moves.

The Admiral didn't pull any sudden moves. He walked all the way to the other end and emerged into the second courtyard.

From here, he turned into a large building that, unlike the rest of the ruin, teemed with uniformed Reserve Wing personnel.

The latest technology packed the place along with hundreds of active personnel crowding the building. Lights, computers, communications links—this place had everything.

The personnel scurried from one workstation to the next, discussed their jobs, and reformed in different arrangements.

Admiral Joyce beamed at Davenport's surprise. "Hardly anyone knows about this outpost. We keep it a secret. Everyone thinks Scion of Hubris is a deserted ruin. They don't know we rebuilt it into one of our most sensitive intelligence sections."

Davenport couldn't stop staring at everything in amazement. Did he miss something here? If Scion of Hubris was now one of the Reserve Wing's most sensitive intelligence sections, why was the admiral showing it to a lowly regional sheriff like himself?

The admiral led the way to a spiral walkway that descended between many floors of more high-tech departments.

He talked all the time about the work these people were doing and various threats the Confederacy faced on different fronts far from here.

Davenport didn't hear him. Something was missing—something important.

At last, the Admiral entered a corridor flooded with sunshine. "Anyway, Sheriff, I wouldn't worry too much about the Ithium if I was you."

"Why is that?" Davenport asked.

"Because these things rarely go unnoticed. We usually capture the guilty party and reacquire the dangerous substance before they can do any damage."

"I'll believe that when I see it."

Admiral Joyce smiled. "You're very conscientious."

He opened a door and stepped through it. Davenport crossed the threshold and immediately regretted it.

He stood in a darkened chamber that resembled the ruin outside. The stone walls dripped with fetid water and the room smelled strongly of mold and rot.

"You see, Sheriff," Admiral Joyce breezed, "the man you saw carrying your safe onto the ship has already been caught."

"He has? Who is he? *Where* is he?"

Admiral Joyce turned around to face Davenport. "You're looking at him—but you already knew that, didn't you?"

Davenport gritted his teeth. Here it came. "Yeah. I did."

Admiral Joyce strolled across the chamber to a broken-down section of the wall. "You really don't have to worry about the Ithium anymore, Sheriff. It's locked in a secure vault where no one can get to it."

"So....what are you going to do with it?"

"That is not your concern." The admiral extended his hand and took something out of a notch in the wall. "The Ithium is.....

Davenport saw the gun even before the admiral turned around. He didn't give himself an instant to hesitate. He dove for the admiral in a flying tackle.

The two men hit the ground and Davenport flung out one hand, seized the admiral's wrist, and slammed the gun down hard on the paving stones. The gun fell out of the admiral's grasp and he let out a howl of fury.

The admiral lunged upward to grapple with Davenport, but Davenport prepared himself too well for a trick just like this. He hurled himself past the admiral and grabbed for the gun.

His fingers closed around the trigger grip and he swung the weapon around to aim at the admiral's head. The admiral saw him coming and rocketed off the ground. He strapped his arms around Davenport's chest and slammed him onto his back.

Davenport's many beatings in the last few hours inured him to the pain. Pure hate burned in his veins and he rotate the gun around. He jammed the barrel into the back of the admiral's neck and squeezed.

The metal stabbed into the admiral's skin and he whipped over sideways. The admiral went down, trapped Davenport's gun hand underneath his weight, and kept on going. The admiral used Davenport's weight to fling him farther into the dark.

Davenport didn't see anything over there until the admiral released him. Davenport braced himself for another hard crash on the stone floor, but instead, he sailed into nothing. He fell toward the floor that wasn't there and he plunged down, down into the void.

Chapter 16

Fiddler huddled in the ventilation duct and waited for the noise to die down. She rubbed her arms, but she couldn't stop shivering. She didn't know where the soldiers took Davenport and she didn't want to stick around to find out.

She stole one last peek into the compartment beneath her. Dice and Beauty still lay shackled where the soldiers left them.

Dice looked truly stricken. The anxious, worried act he put on for the captain changed to true concern and he kept glancing toward the door where Davenport disappeared. Beauty went quiet, too. He turned his face to the wall so Fiddler couldn't see his expression.

Fiddler measured the security personnel still stationed by the door. Davenport risked everything to free Dice and Beauty. Fiddler couldn't fail him now, but she needed weapons for that.

She crawled all the way back to the cargo bay and took a left-hand intersection she knew went to the rear corner—or where the rear corner would be if the *Echo Omicron* still had a rear corner.

She lowered herself silently to the floor and got four rifles out of a crate the crew hadn't cleaned up yet. She crouched behind the crates and listened when the crew re-entered the cargo bay, but they left again just as quickly.

She snuck a few more yards and found another crate spilling ammo cylinders all over the floor. She loaded her rifles and her pockets.

She peeked over the crates to make sure the coast was clear and climbed some of the debris to slip back into the ventilation system.

She ran through her strategy on her way back to the crew compartment. She would take a page out of Davenport's book, drop down, and surprise the guards. Only four of the stun gunners remained along with about ten carrying standard weapons.

Granted, some of them sported Howitzers. She kicked herself now for not backing up Davenport when she had the chance, but he struck so fast that he took her by surprise, too.

That wasn't true, really. He did strike fast and he did surprise her, but when she got honest with herself, she had to admit the ugly truth. She froze up.

She thought twice before she jumped down among that many armed soldiers, and by the time she recovered and decided to help Davenport, it was already all over.

She wouldn't make the same mistake again. Dice and Beauty needed her. She had no idea where Emmet and Lyons were, so it was all up to her.

She returned to the same spot, but when she peered down into the compartment, she discovered Lyons there first.

Lyons bent over Dice and whispered to him. Fiddler didn't see any guards or soldiers in the room. How did Lyons get rid of them?

"Take this." Lyons shoved something into Dice's shacked hands. "Don't use it yet. Go along with their interrogation while I look around for the safe. As soon as I find it, I'll help you get out. Then we can dump the others, take the *Echo Omicron*, and leave with the goods."

Fiddler bristled. So Lyons planned to dump Davenport, Emmet, and Fiddler. Lyons didn't know the safe wasn't on the *Echo Omicron*, but she planned to steal it and go on with their original job of delivering the Ithium to their client.

"Where *is* Davenport?" Dice husked. "Did you see where they took him?"

"I don't....." Lyons froze and cocked her head. "They're coming! Remember what I said. Go along with their questions so I can find the safe."

She pressed her finger to her lips and sprang up. She caught hold of the ceiling, pushed her way into the ventilation system, and concealed herself just a few turns away from Fiddler. Lyons didn't see Fiddler hiding there.

Fiddler's hiding place gave her access to the vent over the corridor. She shifted over and looked down at Captain Boyne talking to the admiral she'd seen on the command podium. "We won't see that meddling sheriff again. Davenport won't be able to get off the planet without triggering the station alarm. They'll apprehend him, and by that time, we'll be lightyears away with the Ithium."

Captain Boyne let out a sigh of relief. "I won't be sorry to see the last of him. He knew way too much about our plans."

"He doesn't anymore. The station security chief will alert me when they take Davenport into custody. When they do, I'll come back and eliminate him permanently."

"What about the chip?" Captain Boyne asked. "We still don't have it and we can't use the Ithium without it. The Ithium is locked in a blast-proof safe we can't open, and even if we could, it's useless without the chip."

"We'll find a way to open it. The Ithium will be protected inside the safe until we're ready to take it out. We won't have any trouble finding the chip. The operative carrying it went to ground somewhere at Ultra Meridian. We'll find him and retrieve the chip. I'm not worried about that."

"So do you still want me to take the *Echo Omicron* to Chiton's Hold?"

"Yes," Admiral Joyce replied. "I'll take the *Devil's Bane* back to Atlas Arcane as planned. Once you drop off the *Echo Omicron*, take the *Agamemnon* to Vorax Summa where we'll release the Ithium."

Fiddler's blood ran cold. They were planning to release the Ithium on Vorax Summa of all places. Holy shit!

Davenport was right about that, which meant that he was also right about Fiddler and the others being partially responsible for stopping these assholes. Just knowing what they planned to do made her partially responsible.

These conspirators already had the chip they needed to make their plan a reality. They didn't know it yet, but they would find it when they opened the safe. Then nothing would be able to stop them.

Davenport! Where was he now? Fiddler would give anything to get his advice right now.

Of the whole group, he was the only one who really wanted to stop these bastards from causing a catastrophe that would take millions of lives, maybe billions of lives.

Davenport was the only one who really cared about doing the right thing. Up until this very moment, none of the others cared about anything but getting their damn payloads back.

Fiddler counted herself among their number, too. She got so single-mindedly obsessed with getting the chip that she turned her back on everything else. She never once questioned what their client might do with it.

The admiral said Davenport was on the run somewhere on Scion of Hubris. Well, he was out of Fiddler's reach now. He would have to take care of himself.

That made Fiddler and Emmet doubly responsible for stopping these creeps before they carried out their disastrous plan.

She glanced down the duct to see Lyons crouching over another vent. Lyons peered down at the captain and the admiral, too. Lyons had heard their entire conversation.

The captain turned toward the compartment. "I'll question these prisoners about their treasure. We'll find it before we get to Chiton's Hold and we'll all go back to Atlas Arcane a few million richer."

Both officers laughed and parted ways. The admiral left and the captain entered the compartment. The door slid shut behind him and Fiddler heard voices behind the door.

She almost returned to her place above Dice, but when Lyons crawled forward and lowered herself into the corridor, Fiddler changed her mind.

She pushed the vent open and jumped down right in front of Lyons. "Hold it right there, bitch."

Lyons reared back and then her shoulders slouched. "Oh. It's only you."

"Yeah, it's me, and whatever you think you're going to do, think again."

Lyons strode forward. "Get out of my way, pint-sized. I'm busy."

Fiddler dodged in front of her. Without thinking, she rotated one of her rifles forward and pointed it at Lyons's chest. "You're busy freeing Dice and Beauty and then helping me and Emmet stop these cocksuckers."

"You're right. I'm busy finding the safe, so you don't have to worry about them using the Ithium. We'll be halfway across the galaxy with it by the time they find out. At least we won't have that barnacle Davenport on our asses anymore. He was really getting on my nerves."

"You really need to get your brain re-adjusted," Fiddler fired back. "You're too concerned with your looks and all that brain power is seriously draining your ability to think clearly."

Lyons narrowed her eyes. "You want to pick a fight with me? That would be grossly ill-advised."

"Who the hell do you think hired you to transport the Ithium in the first place? Do you really think your client wasn't a front for these lunatics?"

"You don't know that. You don't know anything about our client. You can't know because *we* don't know anything about them, either. They hired us anonymously."

"Oh, yes, I do know about them. I know they had to have some high-ranking Reserve Wing officer's cooperation. How do you think the thief broke into a secure haz-mat facility like Helios Sanctus to steal the Ithium? That officer would have to be an admiral at least and now this yahoo turns up here planning to kill Davenport to hide the fact that he has the Ithium in his hot little hand. If you're too dim to put those puzzle pieces together, you deserve a one-way trip to Terminus Anathema because you're too stupid to run a smuggling crew."

Lyons scowled and pursed her lips. "Even if you're right, we still have a job to do and that means finding that safe."

"You're in luck, Chippy. The safe isn't on the *Echo Omicron*. The admiral already has possession of it, so there's nothing stopping him from using it."

Lyons frowned even deeper. "Oh."

"Yeah, oh, and they're planning to release it on Vorax Summa. You heard them say that, which means you're partially responsible for what happens. If you walk away right now, all those people's lives will be on your hands the same as ours."

Lyons drew in a long, shaky breath. "If you're right, then how are we supposed to stop them?"

"We can't help Davenport and that's one strike against us. He was one of the few people who might have been able to help us get the safe back."

Lyons groaned and rolled her eyes. "Oh, please. He would have thrown us all into Terminus Anathema at the first opportunity."

"At least he would care more about getting the Ithium to safety to mess with that until after it was all over. With him gone, it means we have to go after the safe ourselves."

"I already said that," Lyons fired back. "You're the only thing stopping me from going after the safe."

"We're going after the safe together." Fiddler raised her rifle and aimed the barrel at Lyons's face. "If you, Dice, and Beauty don't help me and Emmet retrieve the Ithium *and* the chip, I'll treat you as an enemy. I'll treat you as one of them and you won't end up near so pretty. Take my word on that."

Lyons hesitated and then relaxed. "All right, but first we have to...."

A deep rumble cut her off and both women listened to the vibrations coming through the hull. "We're launching!" they both whispered at the same time.

They looked at each other and Fiddler read her own expression on Lyons's face. They regarded each other with appraising intensity.

"Our first job is to free Dice and Beauty," Fiddler finished. "After that, we'll figure out how to get from one ship hurtling through space to another ship hurtling through space."

A sly smile spread over Lyons's face. "Once we get Dice and Beauty back, we'll take it from there. Maybe something will turn up."

Fiddler nodded. "Sounds like a terrible plan. Let's do it."

Chapter 17

L yons and Fiddler crab-walked into the ventilation duct and repositioned themselves over the same ceiling vents. Fiddler had to part with two of her rifles to arm Lyons, but at this point, she didn't mind too much. She still had her sidearms and the bulk of the ammo.

Lyons crept to the other vent several feet away. The two women flanked the captain, who stood over Dice in his previous position. "Now, you're going to tell us where this treasure is."

"I told you I don't know where it is. I came on board to search for it. I couldn't tell you without hunting around the ship for a while."

"You don't have a while. If you and your friend want to save your own lives, you better come up with something pretty spectacular pretty quick. My patience is wearing thin."

"Okay, okay," Dice blurted out. "I'll tell you what I know and then you'll be able to find it."

"I'm waiting," Boyne snapped. "Start talking."

"Okay. It's like this. Mount Refractory hired a bounty hunter to rob the Sultan of Kigruili. The bounty hunter's contract promised him 40% of the take and they fitted him out with a new ship and all the guns and ammo he could carry."

"Is this turning into some kind of fevered bedtime story?" Boyne snarled. "I'm losing interest."

"Just stay with me for a little longer. The bounty hunter traveled to Kigruili and snuck into the Sultan's palace at night. He loaded a chest with gold and jewels and riches from all over the palace, but when the time came for him to get away with the goods, he had to go through the princess's bedroom. He took one look at the princess and fell madly in love with her."

Fiddler glanced over to see if Lyons was catching Dice's fairy tale version of the facts. Lyons rolled her eyes again and opened and closed her hand in a talking motion. She opened and closed her own mouth in a silent pantomime of talking about nothing.

"The bounty hunter fell on his knees by her bed and opened the chest. He professed his undying love and promised to change his ways if the princess would only open her eyes and look at him—just once."

Boyne snorted. "Now I've heard everything!"

"She roused from her sleep and sat up to see the most handsome man she'd ever laid eyes on kneeling by her bed and holding out a chest loaded with riches." Dice's voice became soft and silky. Was he getting as carried away by his tale as he sounded? "She fell instantly and madly in love with the bounty hunter. So great and overpowering was their love that they both forgot all about the treasure. They had eyes only for each other."

"Is this going somewhere?" Boyne demanded.

"They clasped each other's hands and their lips floated toward each other for their first magical kiss when, without warning, the doors exploded open and the Sultan's honor guard stormed into the room. The crown prince, the Sultan's only son and the princess's twin brother, led the charge. He drew his sword to strike down the criminal who dared to steal the princess. He took a great swipe at the bounty hunter, but the bounty hunter's training kicked in and he dodged. The sword hit the princess and she was killed instantly."

Boyne stared at Dice, captivated. "What happened then?"

"The prince was so devastated that he fell on his knees and burst into tears. With her dying breath, she made her brother promise that he would give the chest of treasure to the bounty hunter as restitution for robbing him of his only love. The prince tried to do just that, but the bounty hunter swore revenge."

"I bet he did," one of the soldier guards chimed in.

"He took the treasure, but such was his grief, that he decided not to return it to Mount Refractory at all. He decided to keep it all for himself and he ran off to the Vindictus Vein and joined the pirates."

"Did he take the treasure with him?" Boyne's voice strained. Dice had caught him with this wild tale.

"Of course he took it with him. He was so out of his mind with rage and grief that he was beyond reason. He believed the treasure belonged to him and he even started to think of the treasure itself as a substitute for his lost love. He became obsessed with it and even slept with it."

"Wow!" someone breathed from the back of the room.

"He offered to pay the pirates to help him go after the prince to seek his revenge, but when they got near the palace for the second time, the pirates betrayed him. They attacked him in the dead of night, cut his throat, stole his treasure, and threw his body into the nearest black hole."

"So how did it get on *this* ship?"

Dice shifted on the floor. "I'm getting to that."

Of course he was. He had to think of the next phase of his story before Boyne realized what a bunch of hogwash Dice was spinning for him. Farther down the duct, Lyons made rude gestures to match Dice's fabrications. Fiddler had to fight back laughter.

"Eventually, word got back to Mount Refractory that their man had gone on the run and taken refuge in the Vindictus Vein. Mount Refractory sent out a raiding party and attacked the pirate ship on its way home from the Sultan's palace. They killed everyone on board....."

"So they got the treasure back," Boyne prompted. "They took it home with them."

"No, they didn't because the treasure wasn't on board. It turns out that, while the pirates were drinking and feasting and celebrating the bounty hunter's demise, the cabin boy snuck into the cabin, took the chest, and squirreled it onto a Vagrant-class the pirates carried around for emergencies. He slipped away about an hour before Mount Refractory struck. They kept five pirates alive and tortured them to tell them where the treasure was, but they couldn't tell. They were as confused about the treasure's disappearance as anyone, but of course Mount Refractory didn't believe them. They......"

"That's enough," Boyne interrupted. "If this treasure is real, you're going to help us find it." He turned to his men. "Get him up—the other one, too."

The guards went into a flurry. They picked up Dice and tried to set him on his feet, but they'd loaded him with so many shackles that he tipped over. He crashed on top of three guards and crushed them under his bulk.

A muddle of bodies floundered on the floor for a few minutes. Even Boyne got involved in trying to unwrap Dice from the men. The soldiers struggled to get hold of him and get away from him at the same time.

Fiddler had to stifle giggles at the sight. The crew took far too long to realize that they could simplify the process by unshackling Dice, but they delayed doing it until they tried absolutely every other option first.

"To hell with it," Boyne snapped. "Unshackle him."

"Sir...." one of his men squeaked.

"I've had enough. Unshackle his ankles, at least."

Boyne stood back and watched while they freed Dice's legs. They propped him upright and he actually smiled at Boyne now that he could stay that way.

Boyne positioned himself right in front of Dice and glared up at him. "Now you're gonna lead us to the treasure, and if you try anything, your exploded corpse can orbit Gladius Orion for the next hundred years."

Dice smiled innocently down at him. "Sure. I won't try anything. I want to get out of here as much as you want...."

"Don't shine my ass with your bullshit. Just take us to the treasure."

"Okay. Mount Refractory said something about it being hidden in the aft exhaust flue."

"The aft exhaust flue got blown up in the battle."

Dice shrugged. "Oh, well. So much for that, then."

Boyne gritted his teeth and narrowed his eyes. "You better not be messing with me or you'll be sorry."

Dice only beamed at him. The guards marched Beauty to Dice's side. The two crewmates exchanged a glance, but the guards propelled them forward before they could say anything.

Boyne led the way. They paused just long enough for the door to open, and at that second, Lyons and Fiddler plummeted through their vents right on top of the crew.

Fiddler aimed her boots at the back of Boyne's neck. She nailed him hard and he folded beneath her. She spread her legs and landed straddling his unconscious body.

Lyons flanked the crew from their other side. Both women rotated their rifles forward and opened fire. They dropped four guards before the crew realized they were under attack. The guards spun their Howitzers around and Dice went ballistic.

He tore his shackles apart with one flex of his massive shoulders. The metal rent and the scraps thumped to the floor. He let out a devastating roar and flew straight into the Howitzers' path.

The guards fired, but Dice wasn't as clumsy and brutish as he looked. He came to rest between two Howitzers aimed at him and he clamped his arms around both barrels. He crushed them against his sides and twisted the barrels into useless curves.

One guard yanked his hand away, but he couldn't dislodge his fingers from the trigger guard. He gaped up at Dice's enraged face and screamed.

The other guard reared back and accidentally fired his weapon. The charge ricocheted back from the bent muzzle and the Howitzer exploded in the guard's face.

The other soldiers raced in to attack, but Dice didn't go for them. He turned to Beauty and, with one brutal jerk, he tore Beauty's shackles off, too.

Beauty screeched and vaulted at the guards. He pounced on two of them and landed a foot on each of their shoulders. He gouged their eyes and ripped at their mouths.

Fiddler whipped her rifle one way and then the other. She took a split second to make sure none of her friends were in her line of fire and then pulled the trigger. She dropped as many guards as she could see until no one remained but the four friends.

Dice hurled the bleeding bodies into a corner. "Let's get out of here. Where's Davenport?"

"He's gone," Fiddler replied. "The admiral left him behind on Scion of Hubris."

Dice hesitated and bowed his head taking in the news. Then he shrugged. "Well, that's it, then."

He lunged for Boyne and flipped the captain over. Dice snatched Lyons's rifle from her and pointed it at the captain's head.

He slapped Boyne and Boyne's eyelids fluttered. "I'm talking to you, mister."

"Take it easy on him, big guy," Lyons told him. "If you hit him too hard, he won't be able to tell us anything."

Dice ignored her. "You're taking this ship to Chiton's Hold, aren't you? How many crew do you have on board?"

"Huh?" Boyne blinked the stars out of his head. "How many.....?"

"I asked you a question, dipshit! How many crew do you have on board?"

"Uh....forty—no fifty!" Boyne raised his arms in front of his face when Dice pulled back his hand and threatened to slap him again. "Don't! We're just a maintenance crew—that's all."

"You're a lying sack of shit, is what you are," Fiddler snapped. "You're in league with the admiral to release the Ithium on Vorax Summa. We heard you with our own ears."

Boyne's eyes widened. "I don't know what you're talking about."

Lyons bent over him and held out her hand. "Hand over your security key."

"Www...what security key?"

She nodded at Dice. "Rip his arms off."

"No!" Boyne screeched.

"I'll give you to the count of five to stop messing with us and then I'm going to hand you over to Dice to pay you back for shocking him like that." Lyons held out her hand again. "Hand it over now."

Boyne cast terrified glances at Dice while he rummaged in his pocket. He handed over a thin plastic card and Lyons grinned down at him. "Good boy. You'll go far in the Confederate Corps."

She nodded to Dice again and he delivered a devastating punch to the man's face. Boyne flopped to the floor, unconscious.

Lyons led the way to the door while Dice and Beauty relieved the crew of their many weapons. Dice took two stun guns and handed one to Beauty. "Take this, son. We'll find you some food soon."

"We're likely to encounter resistance between here and the bridge," Lyons announced. "Try to keep as many of the crew alive as possible. We'll need them to repair the ship before we get away."

She stepped out of the room and the party followed her out into the corridor. She used the captain's security key to lock the compartment with everyone inside.

"What's the plan?" Dice asked.

"We take the ship," Lyons replied. "I suggest we start with the bridge. We can use the captain's security key to lock the rest of the crew in their compartments so they can't bother us."

"And then what?" Fiddler demanded. "This ship doesn't even run anymore. The engines are shot to hell."

"Not for long. I spotted a bunch of the crew trying to repair them."

"They can't repair them," Beauty interjected. "The engines were blown clean off when the Reserve Wing shot us down."

"I don't claim to understand the workings of their inner genius," Lyons replied. "I only know they're trying to get the ship up and running. Why else would they take it back to Chiton's Hold?"

"Maybe to scrap it," Fiddler suggested. "That's about all it's good for anymore."

"That's my ship you're talking about," Lyons snapped. "Show some respect."

"You stole this ship from Yolo Barnes," Fiddler returned, "so don't give me that shit about showing you respect. You're a thief and a smuggler."

"And what are you?" Lyons sneered. "You're nothing but a desert rat."

"I'm a thief and a smuggler and I'm proud of it," Fiddler countered. "I don't get all high and mighty about anybody defending my ship."

Lyons opened her mouth to argue, but Dice cut her off. "I can't believe I'm wading into a pissing match between two thief-smugglers about which of them is the biggest thief-smuggler with the biggest attitude, but we might want to get off the street if you see what I mean. We're in a public place, remember?"

Lyons and Fiddler glared at each other, but with cooler heads prevailing, the group set off for the bridge. Lyons and Fiddler went first with Dice and Beauty behind.

They made it as far as the bulkhead leading to the bridge. Lyons peeked through the porthole. "Everything looks quiet. None of the bridge staff is armed."

"That's wishful thinking, isn't it?" Fiddler pointed out. "These are Reserve Wing crewmen from the *Agamemnon*. They'll all be armed."

Lyons snorted, raised one eyebrow, and looked down her nose at Fiddler. She started to make another cutting remark that would sorely tempt Fiddler to slap her, but before Lyons could get the words out, ten charges smashed into the wall right next to her head.

The whole group ducked and bolted as charges ricocheted up the corridor. Fiddler crouched low and raced from one corner to another searching for any way out.

Blasts pinned her down. Not even shooting behind her into the corridor could get her out of this.

She dove back across the corridor and slammed into the wall. She was just making up her mind to do a kamikaze charge on her unseen attackers when three charges punched through the sheathing right next to her head.

They ripped a hole in the panel. She looked through the smoke at a space falling to the cargo bay beneath her.

She took a chance and shimmied through. More charges exploded behind her and propelled her faster than she planned. She tumbled between the ship's frame structure and crashed into Dice passing underneath her.

She toppled off his shoulder and hit the floor. He helped her on her way by shoving her off and snarling. "Clumsy little maggot! Watch where you're going!"

Fiddler scrambled to her feet and looked around for the enemy. "Where's.....?"

Dice clapped an enormous hand on her shoulder and tugged her half off her feet. "Keep quiet!" He bellowed louder than any noise she made. "You'll get us all caught."

He towed her to a corner of the cargo bay where piles of goods hid them from view. He flung her out of sight where Lyons and Beauty were already waiting for them.

Chapter 18

G unfire spat down on Davenport's head. He fired the admiral's gun, bolted away from the hole through which he'd fallen, and took off running.

The pit widened into some kind of catacombs. He dodged one way and then the other. If the admiral cared at all about getting rid of Davenport, he would send a security team down here to track him.

Davenport ran until his side cramped. He paused to check his surroundings and noticed a wink of daylight ahead. He ran toward it. A crumbling wall let light shine through the fallen bricks and he peeked past a curtain of overhanging foliage to a wide paved street outside.

Uniformed Confederate personnel strolled to and fro on their business. Weeds and small trees split the pavement. An overgrown wall blocked Davenport from view.

He tiptoed onto the street and observed the Confederate workers from a safe vantage point. A clear demarcation line separated the newly constructed intelligence station from the ruins left behind by previous inhabitants.

The Confederate personnel paid no attention to the ruined parts of the city. The station didn't appear to have any security detail at all—none Davenport could see. Maybe they thought that setting up on an uninhabited planet would protect them...or maybe the security detail was just on the other side of the station right now.

In any case, they hadn't sent out any patrols to find him—not yet. He scooted behind the wall and got himself good and lost in the ruins. He turned several corners when a cluster of ships rocketed into the atmosphere behind him.

A bunch of Reserve Wing Daggers raced away from the planet followed by five Stalwarts. One of them towed the wrecked *Echo Omicron*. In half a second, they passed out of sight and didn't return. He was alone.

He kept moving until he traveled miles from the intelligence station. If he had to stay on this planet for years, that would still beat getting killed any day.

He turned another corner and stopped. He stared all around him at a run-down dump of a town like so many others he'd seen in his time.

None of the buildings sported the sparkling glass or state-of-the-art technology of the intelligence station. Weather-beaten walls, sagging rooves, and shambling, homemade houses dotted the crooked streets.

Davenport studied the place until he spotted a ramshackle establishment at a different corner. Staticky music drifted from a broken window and Davenport understood. This must be the auxiliary settlement—the place where hopeful and less-than-funded fortune-hunters came to make money off the Confederate paychecks coming out of the intelligence station.

The Confederacy only offered its personnel approved forms of recreation. The other half came along and built this town where Confederate workers could get everything else they wanted—unapproved forms of recreation. They just had to slip through a few miles of ruin to a place where the Confederacy would never find out what they were up to.

Davenport knew towns like this only too well and they knew him. He knew exactly what to expect in a place like this.

He sauntered onto the street. People slouched in their various establishments and not one of them wore a uniform. They wouldn't dare.

He wouldn't find anyone around here who knew about his run-in with the admiral or anything else that happened at the intelligence station.

He followed the music and pushed open a creaky door hanging off one hinge. Dusty tables, chairs with one or two legs missing, drunks lying in pools of nameless fluid in corners—oh, yes, he understood places like this.

He walked up to the bar. A hunched Ozriel barely looked at him and went on polishing the glasses with two of its arms. It cleaned the taps with two others, counted the money in the till with another two, and mopped the floor with the last two. "What'll you have?"

Davenport looked around him at the refreshments on offer. How many years had he refrained from indulging in these illicit delights? Should he do it now? Would sampling them just once lead to the beginning of the end?

"If you aren't going to order anything, then get out," the Ozriel growled. "I don't have time for vagrants."

"What kind of flight craft do you have?" Davenport asked. "Anything in the Acrien range?"

The Ozriel's many arms stopped moving and the creature looked up. He locked his flecked eyes on Davenport, blinked once, and then bared his teeth. "No Acriens."

"What *do* you have?" That look told Davenport in an instant that this creature really did have some flight craft. Davenport would work out later how to pay for it.

The Ozriel put down his glasses, propped his mop in a corner, shut the till, and threw down his rag. The creature slouched out of the bar without a word and slammed the door behind him.

Davenport scanned the establishment one more time. Oh, well. If this grouchy alien couldn't give him a flight craft, someone else in town would do it. Davenport could trade his skills for a ship to get off this rock.

The same door crashed open and a tall man strode in. He took the Oziel's place behind the bar and scrutinized Davenport for a moment. Then he wilted and supported himself on both arms against the bar. "Davenport! Shit, you gave us a scare!"

"What are you doing here, Donavan? I thought you were in Terminus Anathema."

"I was, but you know....." Donavan shrugged. "I got out. Now I'm here."

Davenport glanced toward the door. "What's wrong with your bartender? I just asked him for a flight craft. That's all. Are you in business or not?"

Donavan nodded down at Davenport's chest. "*That's* what's wrong with him. He's back there gibbering and crying. He thought you came here for him."

Davenport looked down. Only then did he remember he was still wearing his star. "Oh. Sorry about that."

"How's life at Ultra Meridian? You're making quite a name for yourself as a lawman since you went straight."

"Making a name for yourself as a lawman is part of the job at Ultra Meridian. Not many legal transports come through."

Donavan cracked a grin. "By not many, I'm guessing you mean none."

"Something like that. Can you give me a flight craft or not?"

Donavan raised his eyebrows. "Give? No, I can't give you one."

"What kind of payment will you take? I can be a very useful guy to have around."

Donavan laughed. "Tell me something I don't know."

"You know me, man," Davenport went on. "Whatever you need, I'm at your disposal. Name your price."

"That depends on what kind of craft you want......but I think I might know a way you can get a craft without paying anything for it."

Now it was Davenport's turn to laugh. "Don't yank my chain. I've got a rap sheet, you know."

"I know."

"What do you have in mind? Don't keep me in suspense."

Donavan appraised him for a long moment. Then, instead of answering, he went to the taps, picked up a clean glass, and pulled a frosty pint of Ramrock—Davenport's favorite.

He set a coaster on the bar and deposited the glass on top of it. He gave Davenport a significant nod. "Sit down."

Davenport studied the beads of dew running down the glass and his mouth watered. How many years had it been since he even allowed himself to taste Ramrock?

This conversation was turning into something he didn't like at all—something he'd avoided for years. His past was coming back to haunt him.

He lowered himself onto a stool, but he didn't allow himself to touch the glass. If he tasted it, he might not be able to stop what was about to happen.

Donavan strolled down the bar and came back with a tray wrapped in tight, shrunk clear-film. The label on the outside read, *PureLife*. He tore off the wrapper and set the food in front of Davenport.

Davenport's practiced eye skimmed over the perfectly braised steak, the crisp, brilliant-green vegetables, the pasta dripping with succulent sauce, the flaky pie crust, and the juicy apple filling inside. It was a meal many people would kill for and quite a few already had.

Davenport dragged his eyes away from the food and locked his gaze on Donavan. "What's the deal? Tell me the truth."

Donavan rested both arms on the bar and returned Davenport's gaze without looking away. "There's a price on your head."

"I know that."

"No, I mean....Ekol Thaine put a price on your head."

"Ekol!" Davenport snorted. "That's impossible. I saved Ekol's life. He told me he would be in my debt for the rest of his miserable life. What is it now? Is he sending his hunters out to kill me so he doesn't have to repay me?"

"That's what I'm telling you, man. He put a price on your head to get you back. He posted a reward for anyone who convinces you to come back to him—to work for him again."

Davenport stared at the man in front of him. "You're bullshitting me."

Donavan waved at the communications link next to the taps. "I can show you the post on the wires if you don't believe me."

Davenport looked down at the bar. The PureLife meal and the frosty glass of Ram-Rock still waited for him there. Now he saw the whole game laid out in perfect detail. "Oh. I get it."

"If you go back to work for him, you can have any flight craft on the planet free of charge. You can take anything I've got on the lot, and as soon as you report to him, he'll give you the biggest, fastest, most heavily armed ship you can imagine. He'll give you any supplies and equipment you can dream of and a crew to boot."

"And all I have to do is go back to work for Ekol."

Donavan slammed his hand down flat on the bar. "Shit, man! What's the big deal? You got rich working for Ekol. There's nothing in the known universe stopping you from doing the same thing again."

"Yeah. I understand that."

"You don't have to slum it at Ultra Meridian anymore. When are you gonna stop punishing yourself? You paid your penance. Now you can come back to the land of the living."

Davenport felt his arm migrating forward. His fingers closed around the glass. He lifted it to his lips and the cool, luscious drink slid down his throat.

God damn, it tasted good! A flood of memories rushed into his mind. All the years he spent working for Ekol came back in a flash.

"What is it with you, anyway?" Donavan went on. "Did you really think you could walk away from a lifetime on the wires to become a lawman?"

Davenport set down his glass. "I am a lawman."

"Ekol won't be happy to hear you say that. He's as likely to slit your throat as look at any lawman."

"And you'll ride off into the sunset with the reward, right?"

Donavan blanched. "It ain't like that, man. Don't be like that. Besides, I won't get the reward unless you actually go to work for him. If I give you a craft on advance just to fly to his place and talk to him, well, that's a different story."

Davenport picked up his fork and stuck it in a piece of pasta. "And by 'working for', you mean 'on Ekol's payroll'."

"Sure. What else would I mean?"

Davenport picked up the knife and cut off a piece of steak. "All right. Send him a message and tell him I'm on my way."

Davenport finished his meal while Donavan scurried off to send a message to Ekol Thaine. Davenport took his time drinking his Ramrock. Who knew how many more years he'd have to wait before he drank another one?

As tempting as the prospect of working for Ekol might be, Davenport had a mission to complete. He actually enjoyed working at Ultra Meridian. His life actually started to mean something there, but he didn't expect people like Donavan to understand that.

Davenport's old associates saw his riches, his fame, his authority, his influence, his network, and his fleet of ships. They didn't understand why someone would sacrifice all that to haunt a lonely, remote, seedy outpost like Ultra Meridian issuing shipping stamps to smugglers, pilgrims, and ex-convicts on their way out of known space for the unknown of Sacron Enigma.

Davenport never would have believed he could prefer Ultra Meridian to his former high life, but he did.

This Ramrock filling him with a blissful feeling brought that home to him more than anything. He'd like nothing better than to slope off back to Ultra Meridian and disappear into his life as an unknown.

That would never happen now because the Ithium was still out there. He swore an oath to uphold the law, and unlike a lot of sheriffs on the Confederate roster, he took that oath to heart.

He didn't turn his back on all the benefits of his life outside the law under false pretenses. If he wanted to raise a one-fingered salute to the law, he didn't need to become a sheriff to do that.

Donavan would never understand that. None of them would, so Davenport could save his breath trying to explain it to them. He would save it for Ekol. Ekol might be able to understand it...or he might not.

Donavan came back. "The word is going out on the wires now. When you're ready, you can come with me to the hangar and pick out your craft."

Davenport drained the last of his Ramrock. "Did Ekol arrange payment?"

Donavan had the tact not to grin with ecstasy. "Yeah. He's covering it."

Davenport stood up and looked around the tavern. "While we're at it, put another two sidearms on his tab and a hundred-count of ammo cylinders."

Donavan couldn't trip over himself fast enough to hand them over. Davenport loaded the sidearms and reloaded the gun he took from the admiral. He stashed one sidearm behind his back and holstered the other two. Now he felt a little more human.

Donavan nodded down at Davenport's star. "You might want to take that off before you meet him."

"Why in the world would I want to do that?"

Donavan shrugged and looked away. "It's your funeral, man."

He walked around the bar and led the way outside. He escorted Davenport through the dusty streets and back into the ruin. They wound their way through many crumbling passages to a long, low, steel building hidden by creepers.

Donavan unlocked it and Davenport stepped into a hangar crowded with every high-tech ship imaginable. Skimmers, Vagrants, Daggers, Stalwarts, Bolts, Drifters, and Nitrols.

Donavan waved at them. "Take your pick, man. It's all covered."

Davenport meandered between them. He definitely didn't want a Stalwart or a Dagger. They were way too big for one man and Vagrants and Skimmers were too small.

He halted between a group of Drifters and three Nitrols. Their sleek, shiny lines and powerful engines thrilled his blood. He could already feel the throttles responding to his movements.

He pointed at the nearest Nitrol. "I'll take this one."

Chapter 19

"Quit shoving!"

"This isn't shoving. This is loading a weapon."

"Keep your elbows to yourself!"

"It's your fault we're in this mess. I never wanted to go to the bridge in the first place."

"Well, why didn't you say so BEFORE we went to the bridge?"

Fiddler peeked out from behind the crates that hid the fugitives in a less-than-ideal part of the cargo bay. "We can't stay here. The crew will finish cleaning up this bay and then they'll find us."

"We should make another attempt to commandeer the ship," Lyons suggested.

"Yeah, because our last attempt went over so well," Dice growled.

"Do you have a better idea? I'm listening."

"We should find a way to get off this ship."

"That is pure genius, muppet," Lyons sneered. "There isn't another spacecraft on board. We take the *Echo Omicron* or we ride all the damn way to Chiton's Hold."

Silence descended on the group. Fiddler didn't want to go to Chiton's Hold, and from the expressions on her companions' faces, none of them did, either.

"How the hell do we take the ship when it doesn't have any engines?" Beauty interjected. "If we break away from the *Agamemnon*, we'll be adrift just waiting for the Reserve Wing to come back and pick us up."

"And whatever you do," Dice boomed, "don't tell me we'll work it out after the fact. I am NOT listening to that shit anymore."

Lyons shut her mouth. She really had been about to say just that.

"I have an idea," Fiddler whispered.

"Well?" Lyons demanded. "What are you waiting for? Let's hear it."

"We ....." Fiddler broke off as rapid footsteps skidded around a nearby crate. She raised her weapon and almost fired before she recognized Emmet.

He slid the last few feet and crashed into their hiding place. "Where have you been?" he hissed. "I've been waiting ages for you to come back."

"Come back!" Dice roared. "We were here first. You were the one who just showed up."

"I think I might know where they're hiding the safe," he panted. "I followed one of their crewmen and he was messing with something behind the lockers in the crew lounge."

"Was it JimJams?" Beauty asked.

"No. I didn't see it, but I figured it had to be the safe because why would he hide it, right?"

Fiddler slumped down on the floor. "It wasn't the safe. The safe is on a different ship—the *Devil's Bane*. It's hundreds of lightyears from here."

Emmet frowned. "Are you sure?"

She nodded.

"Well, that's shit! How are we supposed to get it if it isn't even on this damn ship? Now the whole shit-ass Reserve Wing is after us."

"Keep your voice down," Fiddler hissed. "We were just trying to figure that out."

"Fiddler was just about to tell us her brilliant idea," Lyons minced.

"When you interrupted," Dice growled.

"What about getting to the....?" Emmet began.

"Quiet!" Lyons snapped. "We're listening to one idea at a time, and right now, Fiddler has the floor."

"Thank you. I was going to suggest that we ambush the clean-up crew. They keep migrating into unseen parts of the cargo hold. We sneak up on one or two and take 'em out. We whittle the clean-up crew down to a few we can overrun. Then, when they don't report and the bridge sends more personnel down here to see what the problem is, we jump out and ambush them, too. We keep that up until only the bridge staff is left. This ship doesn't have an unlimited number of people on board. It can't."

The others studied her. For a moment, no one reacted. Then Dice nodded. "Sounds like a good plan. I like it. Let's do it."

"Don't you at least want to hear Emmet's plan?" Lyons countered.

"I don't have a plan," Emmet interrupted. "I like Fiddler's plan. Let's do that."

"Doesn't anybody have any other ideas?" Lyons barked.

Dice rounded on her. "Do *you*?"

Lyons hesitated and then slouched. "No. Let's do it."

The group split up. They crept one silent inch at a time to different parts of the cargo hold. Fiddler hid herself just out of sight from the clean-up crew.

She heard footsteps approaching and her pulse quickened rotating her rifle forward. Two crewmen strolled around the crate in the middle of a cheerful conversation about their wives.

Fiddler struck without warning. She sprang out of her hiding place and nailed her rifle stock into one man's nose. He crumpled and she dropped the other with a cruel strike across the cheek.

She hauled the bodies farther back into the corners and repositioned herself. Thumps and bumps sounded all over the bay, but the crew didn't notice.

They went on with their work. Catlin's orders kept firing from near the hull breach. How long would he take to notice his crew dwindling by the second?

She didn't have long to wonder. The next time she sprang out to attack someone, she came face to face with Catlin himself. His eyes popped and she punched him as hard as she could in the nose.

He staggered and she leapt for him. She grabbed his neck in her left hand and tackled him to the floor. She straddled him punching for all she was worth.

She flashed back to the compartment where he subdued Dice. She wanted to kill this man, but he passed out before she got a chance.

When she returned to her position, she stole a peek around the debris to see five crewmen holding a conference near the hull breach. They were the only five left and, from the protective clothes and masks they wore, three of them were welders, not fighters.

Fiddler saw Dice creeping forward from the other side and she leapt out. She stormed toward the remaining crewmen and her raised rifle to fire. "Get your hands in the air. Get back against the wall!"

The crewmen threw their hands up and their eyes burst wide open. "Don't shoot! We're unarmed! Please don't kill us!"

Fiddler herded them toward the crates. "Get your hands up! Turn around and start walking!"

She marched them past Dice to the corner where the friends were just hiding. Lyons stared at Fiddler. "What are you doing? I thought we were going to neutralize these men."

"They are neutralized. This is the welding crew and they're unarmed. They won't give us any trouble."

"How are we going to guard them?" Lyons demanded. "We'd have to leave someone behind to make sure they won't retaliate against us."

Fiddler started to explain that the welding crew wouldn't retaliate. All they cared about was surviving this trip, but then Fiddler looked around her. She was looking for Emmet and spotted Beauty instead.

"Keep an eye on these men for me, will you, Beauty? You have my permission to shoot anyone who moves a muscle."

He squatted down at her side and waved a sidearm at the welding crew. He didn't appear capable of aiming it effectively. The muzzle swept across the welders' petrified faces and then pointed somewhere else.

The welders cowered in a huddle. They wedged themselves into a corner to get as far away from him as possible. He leered at them and they shuddered when he licked his lips.

Lyons groaned. "What next?"

"Let's set up our ambush by the bulkhead. We need to be ready when someone comes down here to check on the repair crew."

The friends returned to the bulkhead. Dice and Lyons took positions on either side of the door.

They flattened themselves against the wall ready to nab anyone who walked in. Emmet and Fiddler stationed themselves behind the nearest crate. They trained their weapons on the door just in case anyone gave the other two any trouble.

Fiddler held her breath. How long would she and her friends have to wait before the bridge staff noticed that no one was working in the cargo bay anymore?

A face appeared in the porthole and someone glanced into the bay. The door swung open. Lyons raised her weapon to strike, but she never got a chance.

A man walked in and stopped just inside the door. He glanced around and saw Dice and Lyons flanking him. His mouth opened, and at that moment, Dice raised his giant fist and brought it down in a smashing blow on top of the man's head.

The poor guy buckled on the spot. Dice grabbed his ankle and slid the body behind him. Fiddler watched open-mouthed as another ten guards entered the bay and met the same fate. Lyons, Emmet, and Fiddler never got a shot off. Dice took care of everything.

A long pause followed and no one came. Dice looked over at Fiddler and shrugged. Could they make a play for the bridge? Fiddler racked her brains to remember how many people Captain Boyne said were on this derelict. Was it forty or fifty?

Just when she got ready to signal Dice and Lyons to venture into the rest of the ship, another group of security guards arrived to be dispatched by Dice's Fists of Fury.

Another long pause followed. "I say we make a run for the bridge," Lyons whispered.

"I'll go first." Dice barged through the door into the corridor.

The others hustled after him, but they encountered no resistance—not any. They assembled outside the bridge and observed the bridge staff through the porthole. The Confederate personnel worked over their stations, totally oblivious that the ship had fallen into enemy hands.

Without warning, Dice stormed in bellowing in bone-shaking fury. His voice alone scared the bridge staff into retreating. They cowered before his wrath and paid no attention at all to anyone's weapons.

Fiddler raced to the gun range and held the second welding crew at gunpoint. "Everybody out! Get to the bridge—now!"

They did as they were told. The friends gathered the bridge staff and welders into one group and marched them down to the crew compartment where they left Boyne and his pals.

The friends then made a systematic search of the whole ship, one room after another. They put all the Confederate personnel in one room and locked them in.

"Now we can go get our safe." Dice growled.

"Not with all those Reserve Wing people on board, we can't," Lyons pointed out. "We need to put them off somewhere."

"Scion of Hubris is the closest," Fiddler interjected, "but we aren't going anywhere without engine power. We have to break away from the *Agamemnon*. We might as well stay put if we don't have the speed and maneuverability to get away from their guns."

"Do you have to be so damn reasonable all the time?" Lyons fired back. "Just when things start to look up for us, you rain on our parade with reality."

Fiddler had to smile at her. Despite Lyons's biting tone and withering sense of humor, she was starting to grow on Fiddler. Hell, maybe Lyons was starting to grow on Fiddler *because* of her biting tone and withering sense of humor.

"Go get Beauty and bring him to the bridge," Lyons told Dice. "We'll need his genius to get the engines running."

"There are no engines left to get running," Fiddler pointed out.

"Then we'll just have to take over the *Agamemnon*."

Fiddler burst out laughing. "I definitely won't shatter that fantasy with reality."

Lyons started to smile back at her, so maybe relations weren't as frosty between the two women as Fiddler thought.

They headed up the corridor for the bridge when a crash startled them into turning around. They peered through a doorway into the crew lounge.

Emmet, Fiddler, Dice, and Lyons stared at Beauty tearing open one cupboard after another. He seized boxes, containers, cartons, and packages, ripped them open, and tossed the refuse over his shoulder.

"My God!" Lyons groaned. "How many times do I have to tell you not to let Beauty get hungry?"

"Christ Almighty!" Dice snarled. "Do we have *any* JimJams in here?"

"Doesn't look like it," Emmet remarked.

Beauty built up an enormous mound of torn wrappers and dismembered boxes behind him, but he still didn't find anything that satisfied him. He emitted little grunts and squeaks of desperation as he emptied one cupboard after another.

This might have gone on for hours if he hadn't come to the last cupboard and disgorged its entire contents onto the floor. The four comrades watched him go through everything one container at a time.

He stopped waist-deep in trash and looked around him. He spotted the friends observing him from the doorway. His nostrils flared and his eyes took on an insane sheen.

"Hey, Beauty," Lyons called out. "Did you find any JimJams in there?"

"JimJams!" he gasped.

"Do we have any JimJams on board?" Lyons murmured out the side of her mouth.

"We're fresh out," Dice muttered back. "We didn't take any on board at our last stop. They didn't have any at Animus Delphi."

"We have to give him *something*."

Dice shrugged. "We might be out of luck."

"Here goes nothing." Lyons took a deep breath. "Hey, Beauty. We need you to come to the bridge and work on the engines."

His ears swiveled forward. "Engines?"

"Do you think you can do that? The sooner we break away from the *Agamemnon*, the sooner we can get you something to eat."

He brightened up even more. "Eat?"

"Come to the bridge, Beauty. We need you."

"Are you sure this is a good idea?" Fiddler whispered to Lyons. "He might flip out if his blood sugar falls too low."

"He'll flip out, but at least he'll flip out while he's working on the engines."

"What engines?" Emmet muttered.

Beauty loped toward them and no one said anything else on their way back to the bridge. Beauty hopped on top of the processor workstation as soon as he entered. "The Reserve Wing installed new engines."

Lyons spun around. "They did?"

"How convenient for us," Dice growled. "Are they operational?"

"Not yet." Beauty attacked the workstation. His long fingers waltzed over the controls adjusting, recalibrating, and checking everything. "They need to be activated."

"How do we do that?"

"I have to go down to the hull breach." He glanced around the bridge and his lips formed silent words that he didn't voice. Fiddler could just imagine him seeing food everywhere he looked.

"What do you have to do at the hull breach, Beauty?" Emmet asked.

"I have to go out onto the hull and activate the new engines."

Lyons and Fiddler exchanged glances. "You want to go out onto the hull while we're hurtling through space? How do you plan to do that without blowing into a million pieces?"

"Pressure suit."

"We don't have any pressure suits," Dice barked. "You know that."

"We don't, but the Reserve Wing does." Beauty looked up from his work and grimaced at his friends gaping at him. "How do you think they installed the engines in the first place?"

"How *did* they install them?" Lyons asked.

"By going out on the hull." Beauty hopped to the ground. "There's no wind out there. It's perfectly safe."

"Famous last words," Dice mumbled.

"If he flies off into space and disappears," Emmet interjected, "at least he won't be hungry anymore."

"And we'll be out of an engineer. I don't want you to go," Lyons told Beauty. "We can't afford anything happening to you."

Beauty was already scuttling toward the bulkhead. "If these engines take us somewhere with food, I'm going."

He slipped off the bridge and left the other four looking at each other. "He seems pretty determined to go," Dice remarked.

Lyons shrugged. "If anyone can do it, he can."

They walked out into the corridor to find Beauty already several paces ahead. He stopped and held up his hand. "You stay here. You'll get in my way."

"We won't let you go out there alone, Beauty," Lyons told him.

"You'll get me killed. Go back to the bridge and don't set foot in the cargo bay until I tell you to."

He dashed out of sight and left them standing there like fools. "He certainly acts like he knows what he's doing," Fiddler remarked.

She went back to the bridge and pulled up internal readings on the cargo bay. Emmet, Dice, and Lyons watched over her shoulder. Beauty entered the cargo bay and found some pressurized space suits in a compartment.

"How did he know they were there?" Lyons muttered. "He wasn't there when they installed the new engines."

"Look at that." Fiddler brought up the engine readings. "They're barely attached. They won't be able to stand the strain of activation. Their first thrust will tear them clean off."

"Then we're screwed," Dice boomed. "Call him back."

"Too late. He's already suited up."

Beauty looked comical dressed in a suit designed for a human. The sleeves and pant legs ended at his elbows and knees. They left at least seven inches of his extra-long limbs exposed, but his squat body left bulging masses of the suit sagging around his armpits and pelvis.

He hunched inside the suit and pulled the sleeves and pant legs down. He had to waddle along like an overstuffed toy. The gloves barely covered his hands and he winced when he sealed them to the rest of the suit.

Then came the protective helmet. He folded his ears inside it, but when he locked it to the collar, his small skull only filled a third of the helmet. His huge eyes barely showed above the neckpiece.

He attached the safety tether to his belt and took out the welders' toolbox. "I have a bad feeling about this," Emmet murmured.

Beauty shambled to the galvanic coil and it crackled against his suit when he stepped through it. His suit puffed into a perfect sphere that made it nearly impossible for Beauty to walk in.

In the end, he had to hop to the edge of the hull breach. He stood poised there for a moment and then jumped off into open space. The safety tether stretched to its farthest length.

"Where is he?" Lyons asked. "I don't see him."

"There." Fiddler pointed to a ball rotating through space at the very end of the tether. It floated behind the *Echo Omicron* which floated behind the *Agamemnon* in a ridiculous convoy.

The ball rolled over and over on itself. It took Fiddler a second to realize that Beauty was causing the revolving action deliberately. He turned himself over to wind the tether around his waist and pull himself nearer to the *Echo Omicron*.

"Somehow, I don't think the welding crew did it this way," Lyons remarked.

"Here he comes," Fiddler warned. "He's latching onto the hull."

Beauty used two magnetic grips to lock onto the hull and pull himself to the first engine housing. He went to work with the welders' tools and secured the housing to the hull.

A green indicator light flashed on the processor workstation when the ship's onboard systems registered that the housing was secure enough to withstand the strain of space-flight.

Fiddler didn't see what Beauty did next. He ran a current through the engines and tinkered with various components until another indicator blinked on the workstation. "It's activated!" Fiddler announced.

Beauty made his way to the second engine and activated that one, too. A moment later, the whole workstation exploded to life. "He did it! We're in business."

Lyons stepped onto the command podium and no one argued. "How much power do we need to break away from the *Agamemnon*?"

"I don't know, but I say we give it everything we've got the minute Beauty gets back inside. The *Agamemnon* will detect that our engines are now active. They'll know something is up."

"Do it! Full power to the engines. Dice, you man the gun range in case we need to....."

The instant she got the words out, the ship shuddered.

"The *Agamemnon* is cutting power. The gun range is powering up. They're turning around."

"Gun it!" Lyons roared. "Get us out of here!"

Emmet leapt to the navigation station. Fiddler checked once to make sure Beauty was safe. "He's inside! Go!"

Emmet slammed down the throttle. The *Echo Omicron* trembled again and, with a terrible ripping sound, it peeled off to starboard. The noise of the hull groaning sounded so much louder now than it did before, but everything held together.

The *Agamemnon* whirled around and charges exploded against the *Echo Omicron's* hull. Emmet didn't hesitate and the ship rocketed away into space.

Chapter 20

Dice, Fiddler, and Emmet aimed their XQs at the crew compartment while Lyons slotted Captain Boyne's security key into the door lock. It opened.

All the Reserve Wing personnel stood on their feet inside. Boyne glared at the friends with smoke billowing out of his ears. "You'll pay for this! You won't get away with this."

"Get off our ship," Lyons ordered. "You have enough to worry about just getting yourselves to safety. I wouldn't waste my breath with threats right now."

Boyne took one look at their weapons and stormed out of the compartment. His people followed him to the cargo bay, but when they saw the auxiliary town waiting for them, they hesitated to leave the ship.

"What the hell is this place? You can't leave us here. These people will tear us limb from limb."

"This is Scion of Hubris," Lyons told him, "and before you complain, just remember how you laughed when your admiral abandoned Davenport here. We're doing you a massive favor by putting you off on a friendly planet. Your intelligence station is about five miles that way."

"Five miles! We can't walk that far."

"We can fly you a thousand miles out into the ocean if you prefer."

He glared even more furiously, but he had no choice with Dice, Fiddler, and Emmet all holding him at gunpoint . He stormed down the dusty streets to the auxiliary town. His crew followed him casting terrified glances around them.

At the far end of town, they turned a corner and Fiddler lost sight of them. She lowered her XQ. "I'm going out there. I'm going to find Davenport."

"You're insane!" Lyons protested. "He could be anywhere."

"If he's alive, he'll be here. You heard what the admiral said. The intelligence station's security detail will be watching out for him. Either they captured him and he's already dead or he got away. If he got away, he's here or someone here will know where he is. I'm not leaving without him."

"Well, we are," Lyons yelled after her. "If you go out there, don't expect us to be here waiting when you get back."

Fiddler shot her a sneer over her shoulder. Fiddler might be a lot younger than Lyons, but she knew a hollow threat when she heard one.

She set her XQ in a corner of the cargo bay and strode out into the street. Emmet appeared at her side, and a minute later, Beauty, Dice, and Lyons caught up with them.

Lyons sniffed at the shabby surroundings. "This is the armpit of the universe. These people eat lawmen for breakfast."

"Davenport isn't an ordinary lawman." Fiddler didn't know how she knew this, but she knew it was true. "He's here.....somewhere."

She heard music coming from a rotten old watering hole on the corner. Fiddler stuck her head inside The place smelled of piss, unwashed bodies, and moldy beer. "This is the place."

"Davenport is probably bleeding out in their deep freeze by now," Lyons surmised.

Fiddler ignored her and approached the bar. A wizened Oziel worked behind the bar doing four jobs at once. "What'll you have?"

"Sheriff Mace Davenport from Ultra Meridian."

The Oziel didn't look up. "We don't supply sheriffs here. It's strictly food and drink."

Fiddler laughed in his face. "Who do you think you're fooling? You carry a lot more than that. Did you hear about a sheriff in town?"

The Oziel threw down his rag and mop and slouched out of the room. A second later, a tall man entered and cast a critical eye over each of the friends in turn. "So you're looking for Davenport."

"Do you know where he is?" Fiddler asked. "Did he come through here?"

The man raised his eyebrows at Dice and Lyons. "Who wants to know?"

"We're friends of his from Ultra Meridian."

The guy cast another doubtful look at Lyons, Dice, Beauty, Emmet, and then back at Fiddler. "I doubt that, somehow."

"Someone tried to kill him and he got stranded on this planet. We came to pick him up. If you know where he is, we'd be willing to pay to get him back."

"Have you completely cracked your nut?" Emmet muttered in her ear loud enough for the guy to hear. "We don't have a penny to our names, and even if we did, I wouldn't spend it to bail out a lawman who wants to put us all in jail."

"It doesn't matter," the man interrupted. "Davenport isn't here anymore. He was, but he's gone. He left about two hours ago."

"What?" Fiddler spun around. "How? Did the Reserve Wing take him?"

"He left in a ship supplied by Ekol Thaine. Davenport is back on Ekol's payroll as of today. It's all over the wires and Ekol advanced the money to fit him out with a ship, weapons—anything Davenport asked for. He's going home in style."

The friends stared up at him in shock. "He couldn't!" Fiddler whispered. "He wouldn't."

"He could, he would, and he did. He didn't take much convincing, either. If you ask me, he's been suffering in agony at Ultra Meridian these last seven years and he finally had enough. I don't blame him. Who would want to wallow in a pit like that when he could be living high on the hog at Ekol Thaine's right hand? A lot of people would pull some seriously hectic jobs to get Ekol to care about them the way he cares about Davenport."

Fiddler swallowed hard. Her whole idea of Davenport went spiraling down the drain. She never met a more dedicated lawman. He risked his life a dozen times to get that Ithium. He couldn't just turn his back on it to go work for Ekol Thaine of all people.

Lyons's voice cracked squeezing out the words in Fiddler's head. "I don't believe it. We've known Davenport for years. That guy took his job more seriously than any other lawman I've ever dealt with. He wouldn't turn to crime. He just wouldn't."

"Turns out you don't know half as much about him as you think you do, lady," the barman retorted. "Davenport worked for Ekol for ten years before he went up to Terminus Anathema. He didn't swear on with the Sheriff's Service until he got out. This whole purgatory thing at Ultra Meridian was always gonna be temporary until he came back to his real life. He's the most ruthless gunman this side of Sacron Enigma. He always was and he always will be."

He turned on his heel and left the room. A minute later, the Oziel returned to his work, but he didn't ask the group again if they wanted anything. Davenport—a hardened criminal? He couldn't be.

"I don't believe it," Lyons muttered again. "I don't care what he says. Davenport did NOT go to work for Ekol Thaine. He couldn't. He didn't. It's impossible."

"Maybe he was working for Ekol the whole time," Emmet suggested. "Maybe he only went to Ultra Meridian as a cover to make everybody think he went straight."

"That son of a bitch busted us a dozen times," Dice rumbled. "No sheriff ever searched us as thoroughly as he did. That asshole is as straight as they come. He's stone-cold dedicated to the law. He wouldn't turn—no way."

"Maybe he was a little too dedicated," Beauty interjected. "His dedication came back to bite him."

"So what's the plan?" Emmet asked. "We still have a payload to recapture."

"We're going after the safe," Fiddler announced, "but we won't be getting paid for it. We're sending that Ithium back to Helios Sanctus where it belongs."

The others gave her strange looks. When Fiddler confronted each one, she expected them to argue with her, but no one did. Each one looked away and Lyons finally nodded. "If we're going, we better go. We've got a long way to go to get to Altas Arcane."

Chapter 21

Davenport landed the Nitrol on the lawn and powered down the engines. He climbed down to the ground and looked around Ekol Thaine's palace on Nyx Anonyma.

Sprawling grounds stretched for a hundred acres in all directions. The island floated in a vast ocean covering the whole rest of the planet.

A fresh breeze blew out of the forest to the south. The sun glistened on the sandy beach where curling ivory waves lapped the shore. Everything about this place breathed wealth, luxury, ease, and comfort.

Davenport inhaled a deep breath. Nyx Anonyma smelled as delightful as ever. The stinging sand and burned smell of Ultra Meridian faded to a distant nightmare.

The smell brought back even more memories of his years as Ekol's right-hand man—his chief enforcer—his keeper of secrets. Davenport held Ekol in the palm of his hand then and he still held Ekol in the palm of his hand now.

Laughter and music drifted to his ears and Davenport turned to the palace. Towering spires of creamy marble graced the flawless blue sky. Colored flags flapped from the turrets. Armed guards patrolled the battlements and the grounds.

They hurried across the lawns to meet Davenport. "Mr. Thaine is expecting you, Sir."

Davenport didn't move....yet. He stood still and took in the whole scene. Nothing had changed in seven years—nothing but himself.

He changed into someone who preferred the sands of Ultra Meridian to all this wealth and beauty. He became someone who would rather live on the fringes at peace with himself and the law than be a king over a criminal empire.

Why was he here? Oh, yes. He was here for the Ithium—nothing more. Nothing—not all the riches in the universe—could entice him to go back to his old life. He only hoped Ekol would understand, because if he didn't, then Davenport was in serious trouble.

A deep, gruff voice drifted to his ears and he started walking. The security patrol surrounded him. The guards kept scanning the area for any threat—as if anyone would threaten Davenport here. No one would raise a finger against him.

He passed the crystal-clear swimming pool surrounded by beautiful people enjoying the sun, the water, and the refreshments. Their laughter played on the breeze with the music coming from the palace.

Ice sculptures decorated tables spread with delicacies. Flowering trees dotted the lawns. People played games in the sunshine, danced inside the beautiful halls, and lounged on spotless furniture.

None of them looked sideways at Davenport's dusty clothes or his star. No one ever questioned in Ekol's domain.

He approached the palace entrance and met Ekol coming out to meet him. The creature's hundreds of jointed arthropod legs scratched on the marble floor carrying his long body along in a flowing serpentine motion.

Ekol's head and thorax bobbed back and forth on a section of his body arched off the floor. This front section waved to and fro with the movement of his many legs. Six pairs of appendages extended from his thorax to grasp anything he wanted to hold or manipulate.

Small red eyes gleamed in his smooth, black head. Pinchers surrounded his mouth and waved in continuous motions of pushing tiny objects into his mouth even when he wasn't eating anything.

Ekol let out a low, sadistic chuckle when he spotted Davenport. "I always knew you'd come back to me, my friend. How nice it is to see you back home."

"I'm not home, Ekol. Ultra Meridian is my home and I'm still a lawman. I'm here because I'm on a mission and I need to call in the favor you owe me."

Ekol bared small, black teeth dotting his bottomless mouth, but he didn't hiss and spit curses the way he did when he got mad. "You're looking for the Ithium. I know it. Don't lie to me, Davenport."

Davenport didn't try to hide his surprise. "You know about it? Is it on Atlas Arcane now? Admiral Killian Joyce said he planned to take the Ithium there."

"I don't know where the Ithium is, but I brought you here to find it and get it for me."

"You want me to get the Ithium back—for *you*? I can't do that."

"You're the only one of my enforcers smart enough and resourceful enough to get it." Ekol waved at the people around the pool. "These fools are too stupid and fatuous to be of any use at all."

"You don't have to flatter me because I'm not here to sign on with you. I'm not going back on your payroll, Ekol, and even if I got the Ithium, I wouldn't give it to a crook like you."

"I don't want to use it," Ekol insisted. "I simply want to have it—to own it—just in case."

Davenport snorted. "That's a good one. If you brought me here to tell me stories, maybe you'll have better luck with your delightful friends out there. If I get the Ithium at all, I'll keep it until I can find a way to return it to Helios Sanctus where it was stolen from."

"My dear Davenport," Ekol husked, "you know me too well to play that innocent game with me. Do you think I don't know everything that happened on Ultra Meridian and again on Scion of Hubris?"

Davenport looked away. "If you know that much, you know I won't quit until I get the Ithium back. I have a job to do and I'll do it the same way I did all my jobs for you. I serve a different master now."

"Do you honestly believe you can just hand the Ithium back to Helios Sanctus and put it out of your mind? You can never go back, Davenport. The past is dead and gone. Whoever stole the Ithium from Helios Sanctus procured security codes from the Confederate Corps' highest ranks. If the Reserve Wing is that severely compromised, don't you think Helios Sanctus has been compromised as well?"

Davenport refused to look at him.

"If you returned the Ithium to Helios Sanctus, Admiral Joyce would only steal it again. He won't even have to steal it. He can just walk in and take it. No one would dare to question him. He can do the same no matter where you hide the Ithium—as you've seen these last few days. The Ithium will be much safer with me."

"I don't believe you. I know you too well, Ekol."

"The Ithium is rightfully mine. I sent my people to attack the *Echo Omicron* and steal the Ithium from them, but these incompetent fools lost the ship in space. The *Echo Omicron* dove into an ionizing radiation cloud and evaded capture."

Davenport raised his eyebrows. "That was an extremely foolhardy thing to do."

"It's exactly the kind of trick you used to pull in your heyday." Ekol put one of his jointed arms around Davenport's shoulders. Davenport resisted the urge to cringe away. "I'm so pleased you're here. These last seven years have been torture without you."

"You can paint this any way you want, but the Ithium isn't yours. Hiring a bunch of gunmen to attack a smuggler's ship so you could steal their cargo doesn't make the cargo yours."

"No, you do. You make the cargo mine by finding it and bringing it back for me. I'll give you anything you want, Davenport. Just name it. My whole empire is yours. I'll give you a ship and crew to take on the Reserve Wing....."

"Taking on the Reserve Wing will take more than one ship."

"Then take more than one. Take them all. I don't care."

"Now I know you're planning something with the Ithium. You wouldn't be so desperate to get it if you just wanted to have it."

"*You* want the Ithium, Davenport," Ekol pointed out. "How do you think you're going to get it away from Admiral Joyce without my help?"

Davenport wavered. Ekol was right. If he turned Ekol down, Davenport would have to give back the Nitrol. He wouldn't even have a way to get off this planet. He was stuck.

Ekol lowered his voice to a confidential whisper that went straight to Davenport's brain. "I would remind you, my dear friend, that you are on the run from the Reserve Wing now. You may consider yourself a dedicated lawman with the public trust resting on your shoulders, but to the Reserve Wing and the whole Confederacy, you are nothing but a petty thug on the wrong side of the law. You are as much a criminal as I am."

"Fine," Davenport returned. "I'll do it. I'm going to find the Ithium one way or the other, but I'm telling you right now. When this is all over, I'll be the one to decide what I do with it. If I think for a second that you plan to do anything nasty with it, I'll take it somewhere you'll never get it back."

Ekol burst into uproarious laughter. "Agreed. I'm so pleased to welcome you back! I dreamed of this day for so long."

"I suppose all your supply houses are in the same places. Is Babcock still your quartermaster?"

"Of course he is. I'm sure he'll be delighted to see you again."

"I'm sure he will be."

Ekol waved toward the pool again. "Won't you come and enjoy yourself for a while? I can have Krix bring you some new clothes and....." His eyes skimmed down to Davenport's star.

"No. I'm not changing my clothes."

"Davenport, Davenport, Davenport," Ekol chided. "What will the rest of my staff think?"

"I don't care what the rest of your staff thinks, and if you think for one instant that I'm taking off my star, you're sadly mistaken."

"You'll ruin my reputation. Word will spread on the wires that I'm employing a lawman."

"At least *my* reputation will still be intact. When this is over, I'll still be able to look myself in eye."

"How many times do I have to tell you, Davenport? This will never be over. You will never be able to go back to your boring little life at Ultra Meridian. Do you really think the Reserve Wing or the Sheriff's Service will ever forget everything you did to stick it up their noses?"

"We'll see." Davenport broke away. "I better get going."

"Stop, Davenport!" Ekol yelled after him. "I haven't finished yet."

"I have."

"Davenport! There is another component needed to trigger the Ithium."

Davenport stopped in his tracks gazing out at the party.

"A different operative was carrying a computer chip for the same client that hired the *Echo Omicron* to carry the Ithium cartridge."

"I know that."

"If properly connected to the release apparatus, the chip will amplify the Ithium's toxic capacity. It will release particulate Ithium ions into a plasma stream in space and broadcasts those ions across trillions of lightyears of space. The Ithium's lethal effects could be harnessed to attack hundreds of worlds—hundreds of solar systems—even hundreds of galaxies."

Goosebumps ran up Davenport's skin. Why was Ekol telling him this? Davenport already knew he had to get the Ithium back. So the chip turned the Ithium from a weapon of mass death and destruction into a weapon of universal death and destruction.

Why would an admiral in the Confederate Corps want to steal that? Why would he want to use it against the Confederacy?

Maybe he didn't plan to use it against the Confederacy. Maybe he planned to use it against a different people....but that made no sense. The Confederacy already had the Ithium. If Admiral Joyce planned to use it to defend the Confederacy against an external enemy....

That made no sense, either, especially if the chip made the Ithium that much more deadly. The ionized vapor could drift back to the Confederacy and.....

"Are you listening to me, Davenport?" Ekol asked.

"I'm listening."

"There is a third component, Davenport. That is what I am trying to tell you. Whoever stole the Ithium cartridge sent the three components they needed with three different agents. I don't know where they were sending them, but they need all three components to carry out their plan."

"What is the third component?"

"I don't know what it is. I only know you will have to retrieve all three if you hope to stop Admiral Joyce's plot—whatever that is."

"Do you know anything about what happened to the third component? Does Joyce already have it?"

"He doesn't have it and he doesn't know where it is. He would have it by now if he did know where it was."

Davenport turned around to examine his friend. "What makes you so sure of that?"

"Because the third component is at Ultra Meridian. The third ship carrying that component crashed on the planet and no one has been able to find it, though many have tried."

Davenport thought fast. What ship did he know of that crashed at Ultra Meridian? Ships crashed there all the time. More crashed out in the desert wastelands that Davenport never found out about. The third component could be anywhere.

"Davenport?" Ekol ventured. "Do you understand what you have to do?"

"Yeah. I understand."

He turned away, but before he could leave, Ekol fired one last parting shot. "Just remember, Davenport. If you succeed in capturing all three components, you'll be carrying the makings of the greatest disaster in galactic history. Every fanatical maniac on this side of Sacron Enigma will be after you to steal them from you."

Davenport strode out of the palace. He didn't need to hear anymore. He knew what he had to do. He just had to get on his way and go do it. Standing around talking about it didn't help.

He passed the pool a second time and the security guys moved in to surround him. Davenport waved them away. "You boys stay here. I can find my way by myself."

The security guys glanced at Ekol for confirmation, but when Ekol didn't move or say anything, they stayed behind and let Davenport walk away by himself.

He circled the refreshment tables heading for the west lawn, but before he got away, someone bumped someone else into the pool.

Water swelled out of the pool and splashed the tiles right in front of Davenport. It spattered his boots and he stopped where he was until the deluge subsided.

A few people held their breath to see how he would react, but when he only walked away, the party went back to its amusements.

Chapter 22

D avenport headed for a long building perched between the west lawn and the beach. It didn't look at all like it belonged to the rest of Ekol's kingdom. It bore no adornments or even any markings to show that it was probably the most important key piece in Ekol's massive criminal empire.

Davenport pulled the door open and walked into a hangar full of spacecraft, ground vehicles, and racks and racks of weapons, equipment, body armor, rations, and a thousand other things.

He migrated around a different Nitrol and spotted eight young men crowded around a Drifter not far away. They laughed, joked, and chatted while they worked on the ship.

Davenport observed them from a safe distance. A fat one with enormously thick glasses perched on the ship's roof tinkering with something inside an open access flap. "I heard Ekol say he's the best there ever was. Ekol said he's bloodthirsty and cruel. I don't want to work for someone like that."

"Go tell Ekol that, Alla," a skinny one called through the open cockpit window. "See what he says."

The others burst out laughing. "Fire the thrusters again, Coon," a burly character called from underneath the ship's belly. "See how much exhaust the ducts can handle."

"You got it," the skinny one replied. "Firing...."

"No!" a short, slight guy yelled from near the ship's tail. "I'm working back here, Bandit!"

"Oh," the chunky one replied. "Sorry. It can wait, then."

"When is he supposed to show up?" Alla asked.

"Whenever he pleases," Coon countered and the others laughed again. "I heard he went up to the...."

The whole group fell silent when Davenport stepped forward. They froze in startled terror and Davenport knew, in case he wasn't sure before this moment, that they had been talking about him. His reputation preceded him.

He stopped where they could all get a real good look at him and his star. He jutted his chin at the Drifter. "That's a real nice piece of machinery you boys got there."

Coon scrambled out through the cockpit window and sprang down in front of Davenport. "Yes, Sir, Sir. Ekol—he assigned us to you—Sir. We received word to fit out your ship for you and we were just...."

"How do you know I want this ship? I came over here to choose my own vessel. Why didn't you wait for me to tell you what to do?"

The whole group exploded in laughter. Alla turned his head and called out to no one in particular. "Did you hear what he said? How do we know he wants this ship!" The whole group exploded in gales of laughter all over again.

Coon struggled to hold back his mirth. "Sorry, Sir. You'll have to forgive the boys, Sir. They just...." He burst into giggles. "It's just that....."

"I'm waiting, boy," Davenport cut in. "Why were you so sure I would choose this Drifter and not a different ship?"

"The *Artemis Rex*, Sir....it's the best, Sir. I don't mean to step on your toes or anything, Sir, but....well, it's the best. Everybody knows that."

"Do they?" Davenport fired back. "What makes it the best?"

"Well, Sir...." Coon glanced over at his friends, who stared at Davenport as though he was out of his mind for even questioning their authority on the subject. "It just is."

Davenport scanned the hangar. He assessed the other ships around him, but he didn't see one that spoke to him. His attention migrated back to the Drifter. "Where's Babcock?"

"He went up to the house to receive instructions on fitting out your mission—Sir."

Davenport faced the young man in front of him. "First of all, I don't want you calling me, 'Sir'."

Coon snorted and immediately straightened his face. "What would you like me to call you, Sir—I mean....."

"Davenport. My name is Davenport."

Coon's eyes dipped to the star. "Sheriff Davenport?"

"Just Davenport. That goes for all of you. I don't want you calling me 'Sir' or anything else but Davenport. Understand?"

No one said anything. None of them moved.

Davenport stepped around Coon and measured the ship. It really was a very nice little craft. The engines had been juiced up to make it extra fast and it sported five Howitzers mounted under the wings. This would do nicely.

"Introduce me to your crew, Coon."

Coon rushed to Davenport's side. "Well, Sir—I mean.....We're the Chorion Team."

Davenport raised his eyebrows. "Excuse me?"

"That's what Ekol calls us, Sir, on account of.....Davenport....." Coon fumbled to a stop.

"He calls us the Chorion Team because he found us on Chorion Osiris," Alla piped up.

Davenport turned to face him instead. "Did he, now? And what were a bunch of kids like you doing on Chorion Osiris?"

"We was born there," Bandit replied.

Davenport's eyebrows really jumped at that. "Is that a fact?"

"Yes, Sir," Bandit replied. "I mean—Davenport."

Davenport discarded his first impression of these boys and started over from zero. If these children came from Chorion Osiris, they must be exceptionally strong, smart, resourceful—even ruthless.

They must have heard all the old horror stories about Davenport's past, but that was nothing compared to what the inhabitants of Chorion Osiris had to endure.

The planet's harsh climate, its deadly flora and fauna, its inhabitants' warlike and callous culture all added up to precious few young people ever making it to walking age, much less maturity.

Those that did survive grew to become the strongest, smartest, the most calculating, the most cunning, and the most determined of their kind. Many people all over the Confederacy speculated that Chorions weren't even human anymore.

Biologists hadn't yet confirmed this, but whispers and rumors told of the inhabitants interbreeding with monstrous native species. These interbreedings left them even stronger, faster, more perceptive, and more predatory than they were before.

Davenport took a deep breath. If this was his team, he could live with that.

The people of Chorion Osiris were known for their stubborn and independent nature.

Maybe these boys would actually be able to think for themselves and stand against Ekol when the time came to hand over the Ithium.

"All right, Chorion Team. Tell me your names. You're Coon. You're Alla and you're Bandit. Who are the rest of you?"

The kids came out from inside the ship, behind it, and underneath it. They arranged themselves before him and Coon introduced them. "This is Axel. This is Laub, Rodeo, Breeze, and Wolf."

Davenport committed their names to memory one after the other. Laub barely came up to Davenport's sternum, but Davenport could see the boy's body bulging with muscle. His head merged with a solid trunk of muscle that joined with his shoulders. He had virtually no neck at all.

Rodeo also wore glasses, but these were solid black and concealed his eyes. He didn't look at anyone when they spoke.

He must be blind, but he didn't grope around to find his way. He trailed one hand against the ship's hull, but when he ventured out into the open floor, he walked straight and true with no trouble.

Breeze was skinny and weedy like Bandit, but slightly shorter. Breeze tripped over, fell to the floor, and got tangled in his own legs on the way to join the rest.

When he finally presented himself for Davenport's inspection, he blushed and brushed his hair out of his eyes. "I meant to do that."

Wolf really looked like a wolf. Dense black hair covered every part of him except his eyelids and lips. Small, fierce black eyes glittered through his fur and sharp, pointed teeth peeked out of his mouth when he opened his lips.

Wolf made Davenport wonder again if the people of Chorion Osiris might carry alien DNA—not it mattered. He was stuck with these kids and they were stuck with him for better or for worse.

Davenport nodded to each of them in turn. "What still needs to be done to fit out the ship?"

"Nothing, Sir—I mean, Davenport," Bandit began. "The ship is all set to go—except for supplies, ammo, carry weapons, body armor, medical equipment....."

"Hold it right there." Davenport held up a hand to stop him. "It sounds like the ship doesn't have anything that can't be nailed down. You make it sound like we aren't ready to fly at all."

"Well....no, Sir—Davenport," Axel chimed in. "You need to clear all that with Babcock. We don't have the authority to fit out the ship—not with that stuff, at least."

"When will Babcock get back from the house?"

The Chorion Team exchanged glances. Coon shrugged and was about to say something when the hangar door crashed open.

A short, fat man with white hair and a white beard waddled in. "So sorry! So sorry I'm late! Phew! I tried to get here before you, but Ekol kept me talking. So sorry! Please forgive my rudeness. It's unforgivable, I know."

He pulled up in front of Davenport, panted to catch his breath, and mopped the sweat from his brow. Finally, he smiled up at Davenport. "So sorry, Davenport. I'm just....well, we're all just tickled pink to have you back."

"Don't enjoy yourself too much. I was just leaving."

Babcock burst out laughing and clapped him on the shoulder. "The same old Davenport! You're as funny as ever."

Axel stared at the two men. "You two know each other?"

"Of course we know each other." Babcock beamed at Davenport like he was welcoming home his own prodigal son. "It's wonderful to get you back. You don't know how much we all missed you."

"Thanks."

"So you picked out your ship, did you?" Babcock waved at the *Artemis Rex*. "An excellent choice. She's a first-rate Drifter—the best! Very responsive, powerfully gunned, state-of-the-art scanners, EM shields, stealth mode—the works!"

"I didn't pick it out," Davenport told him. "These kids picked it out for me."

"They're the best, too," Babcock informed him. "You can't get any better in all Ekol's service. It's true they don't look like much, but Ekol wouldn't send them out with you if they couldn't hold their own. They won't disappoint you."

The Chorion Team swelled at this praise and a few elbowed each other. "They were fitting it out when I showed up, but they said you had to authorize the expendables."

"Of course, of course! Well, consider them authorized. Ekol says you're to have the run of the warehouse. You take what you want. You could even take more than one ship if you wanted to."

Davenport took another turn around the Drifter. "We could take a Vagrant on board."

Babcock's smile slipped. "If you want to.....That won't leave much room for cargo."

"We'll be traveling light." Davenport sliced his finger at the Chorion Team. "You boys get back to whatever you were doing when I showed up."

The Chorion Team attacked the ship in a fury. They returned to their jobs, but they didn't go back to what they were doing. No matter where he went, Davenport discovered one of the kids glued to his side or under his feet.

Bandit took the first shift and shadowed Davenport to the cockpit. Bandit sat down in the pilot's cradle, gripped the stick in two white-knuckle fists, and crashed the cradle back and forth with powerful jerks. "This ship is a highly-tuned fighting machine, Sir—I mean, Davenport. It reacts on a dime and the firing triggers are super-sensitive."

"It won't be highly tuned when you finish with it. Why don't you take it easy on the poor thing so it still works when we get into battle against the Reserve Wing?"

Bandit looked up at him with huge eyes. "The Reserve Wing? Ekol didn't say anything about that."

"Did he tell you anything about our mission?"

"No, Sir—I mean, Davenport. He didn't say anything about it. He only ordered us to go with you and obey you the same way we would obey him."

"How do you boys know so much about this ship? You talk like you've flown it before."

Bandit turned bright red and started fiddling nervously with the controls. "Not this one, but I've flown other Drifters."

"Uh-huh." Davenport didn't believe a word of it. "You stay here and finish tuning it like you were before. I have to talk to Babcock."

Chapter 23

Davenport left the *Artemis Rex's* cockpit. Wolf appeared at his side the moment Davenport stepped out of the cockpit. The boy glared up at Davenport with piercing, feral eyes, but he didn't say anything.

He matched Davenport's movements step for step. When Davenport poked his head into the crew quarters and the mess, Wolf stopped at his side. The boy kept his eyes locked on Davenport's face and didn't look away once.

Davenport continued aft to the loading hatch between the engines. A shaft of light shone through an opening in the ceiling.

Davenport looked up through it to see Alla wrenching away on something. "What are you working on, Alla?"

"Just the EM shields, Sir—I mean, Davenport."

Davenport frowned. "The EM shields aren't up there, boy."

"They are on this ship, Sir—I mean, Davenport. The last crew that took this ship out moved them so direct enemy strikes wouldn't keep knocking them out every time the crew got into a firefight."

Davenport frowned. Now he knew for certain that this crew, the Chorion Team, must have been the last of Ekol's people to take this ship out into the field. They couldn't know so much about it otherwise.

He entered the loading hatch to find Axel, Breeze, and Rodeo maneuvering a Vagrant into the ship. Rodeo worked a remote crane arm while Axel and Breeze steered the little runabout into its position.

"Bring it to the left, Breeze!" Rodeo called out. "Your other left."

Breeze tried to correct, tripped over his own feet, and crashed backward onto his seat. The Vagrant twirled on the end of its chain until he scrambled to his feet. He colored when he saw Davenport watching. "I meant to do that."

"Are you finished screwing around?" Rodeo barked. "We're in the middle of a job here."

Breeze hustled back to the Vagrant. He made two more blunders during the operation, and both times, he claimed he meant to do it.

Davenport began to see a pattern to his clumsiness. Even when Breeze looked like he might seriously hurt himself, he always bounced back without too much trouble.

Rodeo fascinated Davenport more than all the others. He maneuvered the crane without messing up once.

The more Davenport watched him, the more convinced he became that Rodeo really was blind. He wasn't faking. He didn't look at the Vagrant or his comrades, but he pressed the buttons to move the crane with pinpoint precision.

He cocked his head from one side to the other and used his ears to check the Vagrant's position and direction. He set the Vagrant down exactly on its anchor points. Axel and Breeze attached the anchors and the job was done.

Axel called to Breeze and they both went off somewhere else. Davenport took the opportunity to sidle over to Rodeo. Wolf parked himself right at Davenport's side with the same ferocious expression on his shaggy little face.

"You're blind, aren't you, boy?" Davenport began.

"Yes, Sir," Rodeo replied. "Is that a problem, Sir?" Rodeo inclined his head in a different direction so his left ear pointed at Davenport.

"It isn't a problem for me if it isn't a problem for you. How do you manage to shoot if you can't see your target?"

"I can hear better than the rest of the boys can see. I can do pretty much anything except fly the ship and man the guns in an air battle. Put me on the ground and you won't be sorry, Sir."

Davenport studied him. "How old were you boys when Ekol took you away from Chorion Osiris?"

Rodeo cocked his head the other way. "Does it really matter, Sir?"

"I'm just curious. Did you grow up here or on your home planet?"

Instead of answering, Rodeo angled his head in a different direction. "You came from Ultra Meridian, didn't you, Sir?"

Davenport stiffened. "What if I did?"

"But you worked for Ekol before that, didn't you? Everybody says so."

"I guess I did."

"Would you call yourself a true believer in Ekol's entourage, Sir? Would you say you're one of his loyal foot soldiers....Sir?"

Something in the way he hesitated before he called Davenport 'Sir' made Davenport prickle. "Is this going somewhere, pal? Who I work for and when I worked for them isn't really relevant to our mission."

"And how long the boys and I lived on Chorion Osiris isn't really relevant to our mission, either, Sir. We're here now and we've earned Ekol's trust well enough for him to assign us to you. If that doesn't tell you everything you need to know about us, nothing will—and by that, I mean all of us. I'm as much a member of this crew as any of the others."

"I'm sure you are." Davenport meant it. He'd never met someone so young who impressed him so much. "One more question, Rodeo. Does your team have a chosen leader?"

"Sure." Rodeo cracked a huge grin. "I'm the leader."

"Are you sure? Coon isn't your leader?"

Rodeo burst out laughing. "Coon? Naw. He doesn't have the stones to lead anybody. He's a nice kid, but he's a little soft if you know what I mean."

Davenport didn't know what he meant, but he knew enough about Chorion Osiris to guess what Rodeo meant. "So where do you usually ride when the ship's in flight?"

"Sir? I ride in the tertiary cradle, of course. Bandit flies the ship. You ride in the secondary cradle for command, and I ride behind you for tactical. That's my position. The boys wouldn't have it any other way." Rodeo bit back another grin. "I used to ride in the command cradle, but now you're here so I guess you'll do that and I'll be your tactical."

Davenport's cheeks flamed. He didn't want to hurt the boy's feelings by demoting him out of the cockpit. "You won't mind if I choose a tactical who can actually see."

Rodeo only chuckled. "The boys didn't want to tell you that we had this ship before you, but I adjusted the controls so I could read them with my fingers. I can see better than you can.....Sir."

"I believe you." Davenport clapped him on the shoulder and left him to his work. If this kid modified the ship to put himself in command, Davenport wouldn't argue.

He found Babcock waiting for him out on the hangar floor. Babcock consulted a remote computer console while he itemized the contents of the ammo racks against the wall. "Take what you want and I'll update the inventory as you load up."

Davenport supervised the boys taking goods off the racks, loading them onto transport carts, and taking them into the ship. Laub piled his cart with ammo cylinders and then he picked up the entire cart in his beefy arms. He carried it into the ship and came back carrying an empty cart.

Coon and Breeze collected dozens of weapons and Breeze sighted down a rifle barrel. Davenport plucked the weapon from his hands. "Point that somewhere else, kid. Why don't you work on the rations?"

"You don't have to worry about Breeze, Sir—I mean, Davenport," Coon told him. "He's a crackerjack with any weapon."

"All the same, I'd rather wait until we're actually facing the enemy before I give him a weapon. Go see to the rations, Breeze."

Coon and Breeze glanced at each other and both burst into fits of laughter like Davenport just made a huge joke.

"Is something funny?" Davenport asked.

"Don't mind them," Babcock told him. "It's just that...well, they're right. Breeze might be a little clumsy, but he's steady in a fight. He's a brick."

The two boys turned back to their work. Breeze took one step toward the rations supplies, tripped, and plunged headfirst straight into stacks of ammo crates. They toppled onto his head and buried him under thousands of cylinders.

He flailed his arms and legs crawling out of the mess. "I meant to do that."

Davenport slung the rifle across his own torso to make absolutely certain Breeze couldn't get hold of it. "Like I said, I'll wait until we're actually facing the enemy before I issue him any weapon."

Laub, Bandit, and Alla came back from their last trip and started helping Breeze load up the rations. Davenport wandered over and watched what they took for their food supplies.

They helped themselves to all the usual ChunkyTenders, JuicyPies, and Universal Staples. Davenport didn't see anything unusual in that.

Just then, Davenport spotted a carton of JimJams on an upper shelf. He took it down and examined the label. They were blueberry flavored. That was perfect. He tucked the carton under his arm.

"Did you see that?" Coon whispered to Alla. "He took the blueberry JimJams for himself and left the grape ones for us."

"He's asking for a bullet pulling that right in front of us," Axel muttered.

"Sir!" Bandit called out. "I'll trade you ten ChunkyTenders for one blueberry JimJam."

"Don't listen to him, Sir!" Laub blurted out. "I'd give you fifty ChunkyTenders for one JimJam."

"These aren't for me. They're for a friend of mine."

The whole group exploded with laughter. "You don't have to shine our shoes with that shit, Sir," Alla told him. "If I was in command, I would take all the blueberry JimJams for myself, too. I'd leave the grape ones to my underlings."

He kicked Breeze in the ankle and that clumsy boy went down all over again. He upset a bottle of Zing pulp over his own head and his comrades choked with laughter. Bandit crumpled and pounded the floor with his fists while tears flowed down his cheeks.

Breeze tried to stand up, slipped in the puddle of Zing pulp oozing over the floor, and fell again.

The pulp splashed all over him and he swam and paddled like a beached fish while his friends busted themselves laughing.

Davenport bit back a smile watching them. If these boys handled themselves half as well as everyone said they would, he could indulge them in their juvenile fun. He didn't really like Zing pulp, anyway.

Breeze finally got to his feet and run his tongue over his lips and cheeks. He blinked at Davenport out of a face smeared with goo. "I meant to do that."

"I'll make you a deal, boys," Davenport announced. "If I've eaten even one of these blueberry JimJams by the time we get back to Nyx Anonyma, I'll buy each of you a Drifter just like the *Artemis Rex*. I give you my word as a sheriff."

The group fell instantly silent and the boys looked up at him with huge eyes. "You mean it?" Rodeo asked.

"You don't want to make a bargain like that, man," Babcock murmured in his ear. "Anything could happen. You might have to use the JimJams as emergency rations."

"If we have to use these JimJams as emergency rations," Davenport told the group, "you boys can eat these and I'll go hungry. Is it a bargain?"

The boys exchanged glances. "Is he serious?" Coon whispered.

"He gave his word as a sheriff," Alla pointed out. "He wouldn't wear that damn star in front of Ekol and everything if he didn't take it seriously."

"I'm dead serious," Davenport told them. "These JimJams aren't for me. They're for someone who needs them a damn sight more than I do—someone I made a promise to that I would find him some JimJams. I owe him. Maybe you'll meet him and then you'll see I'm telling the truth. I wouldn't take these for myself. I wouldn't deprive you of them if they were for me."

Rodeo straightened up, but he still didn't face directly toward Davenport. "All right. It's a bargain. We won't eat those JimJams, either, unless it's a life-threatening emergency. We'll save them for this friend of yours."

"Don't tell him that!" Laub hissed. "He's making it up."

"I'll do you one better," Davenport offered. "If the package is unopened when we return to Nyx Anonyma, you boys can divide them between yourselves. I won't eat a single one."

"Done!" Rodeo blurted out. "You got yourself a deal."

"Good. Load up and let's get out of here. Breeze....." Davenport trailed off examining the boy. He still dripped Zing pulp from every inch of his clothes.

"Sir?"

"Go straight to the infirmary and hose yourself off. If you meant to spill it all over yourself, you can clean it all up....and while you're at it, clean up every drip you leave on the gangway."

The others laughed their asses off at Breeze's hang-dog expression. They took the last of their goods to the loading hatch and their voices faded inside the ship.

"You're a genius!" Babcock whispered. "They'll do anything for blueberry JimJams."

"They aren't the only ones."

"I'll make sure to order in eight more Drifters while you're gone."

Now it was Davenport's turn to laugh. "Don't bother. You won't need 'em."

"No? Do you really think you can resist for the whole mission?"

"I don't have to resist because I don't like JimJams. Just don't tell anybody. I never liked them, but if you really want to know the truth, I don't think we'll be coming back from this mission at all. No one will ever eat those JimJams if the Reserve Wing has anything to say about it."

Chapter 24

Davenport dropped into the command cradle and the controls in front of him flickered on. The safety harness slithered over his torso and cinched him in tight against the seat. "Command locked into secondary cradle," Bandit reported. "Tertiary tactical locked in."

Davenport glanced over his shoulder to see Rodeo strapped in behind him. The boy's hands flew in a blur over the tactical controls as surely as if he saw them. "Tactical locked in and powering up for pre-flight."

"Pre-flight initiated," Bandit replied. "Standing by to launch on command."

Davenport scanned the ship. Six life signs showed up in the rear compartment. Alla, Breeze, Wolf, Laub, Axel, and Coon sat strapped into their accessory cradles on the gangway behind the cockpit. From here, they could man the Howitzers if the *Artemis Rex* ever got into a scrape—or rather, *when* it got into a scrape.

"Communications coming in from Ekol," Bandit reported. "It's for you, Sir."

Davenport accepted the signal from the palace and Ekol's face appeared on his console. "Good luck, Sheriff. Come back soon with your payload."

"Thank you. Keep the pool warm for me."

Ekol laughed. "You know you have your own pool, Davenport. We've been keeping it warm for you for seven years."

Bandit gasped. "Seven years!"

"Release launch bay doors," Davenport ordered.

"Launch bay doors released," Rodeo replied and a shaft of brilliant sunshine split the hangar's dim shadows.

The hangar roof levered open and tilted upward toward the sky. The ship shivered as the engines cycled up to full power. "Pre-flight complete," Rodeo told Davenport. "Clear to launch on command."

"Launch!" Davenport ordered.

Bandit pulled back on his stick and the *Artemis Rex* lifted off the floor. Babcock waved from the corner and the Drifter ascended through the roof.

It emerged into the blazing sunshine, but Davenport couldn't see the party from here. The partygoers saw ships coming and going from Ekol's domain all the time. One more made no difference to them.

The *Artemis Rex* hovered over the hangar for a moment and then, without warning, Bandit hit the throttle with unbelievable power.

The ship shot forward so fast that Davenport's head slammed against the cradle. His cheeks peeled back and his stomach turned from the incredible speed.

Bandit fought the helm with expert attention. Rodeo yelled orders and course corrections to him as the ship rocketed into the atmosphere, around the sun, and far away.

They traveled a hundred lightyears before Bandit asked, "Where are we going, Sir?"

"Set course for Atlas Arcane."

Bandit turned around in his cradle and his mouth fell open staring at Davenport.

"Atlas Arcane!" Rodeo barked. "You're out of your mind. That place is crawling with security."

"I know. They've even got a standing security flotilla stationed around the planet."

"And you want to go there?" Bandit smacked his lips. "It's suicide."

"We can't fly directly into the flotilla so we'll use stealth. Take us to Atlas Arcane and set down on Pandora's Needle."

Bandit stiffened in his seat, but he stopped himself from turning around to stare a second time. These boys were learning.

Rodeo got bolder by the second. "Pandora's Needle—that's the Confederate recreation satellite."

"I know what it is, son. I know people on the Needle who can give me information about Admiral Killian Joyce. The wires are on fire with the news that I'm Ekol's hound again. People will give me a passport to all my old underworld connections."

Bandit said nothing more. He turned the ship toward Atlas Arcane. He didn't have to check his navigation systems to plot the course. He steered there without even thinking about it. Davenport could well imagine why. These boys had a shitload more experience than they let on.

Rodeo ran his tactical regimes on the way. He fine-tuned the Howitzers and even brought online a couple of stealth Howitzers that didn't show on the ship's exterior so each accessory cradle had two guns instead of one.

The trip gave Davenport all the time he needed to watch Rodeo at work. The boy switched from one system to the next with unbelievable speed and accuracy. Even knowing Rodeo used his fingers to read the ship's instruments didn't explain his skill and expertise.

He increased power to the ship's EM shields and doubled the output on the stealth projectors that could conceal the ship from detection.

Davenport didn't understand half of what the kid did to the ship, but Rodeo obviously knew the Drifter better than Davenport ever would.

They flew for three hours and, after the first two, Davenport turned to his own work. He brought up the Reserve Wing roster for Pandora's Needle.

It didn't tell him anything he didn't already know. None of the ships docked at the Needle had visited Ultra Meridian recently.

Then he pulled up the criminal records of everyone charged by the Reserve Wing or the Sheriff's Service in the last seven years. This list proved far more enlightening and Davenport found many, many people he knew who still lived and operated on the Needle.

He performed a superficial scan of Atlas Arcane. Sure enough, he found the *Devil's Bane* docked at the Confederate Corps Command Unit in the city's very heart. That son of a bitch admiral was down there, and where he was, the Ithium would be. The question was how to get near him.

No doubt Admiral Joyce would hear the word sooner or later that Davenport went back on Ekol's books if the admiral hadn't heard already. He would know Davenport left Scion of Hubris alive and well.

He would expect Davenport to come after the Ithium. The Admiral would be a moron to think Davenport would turn his back on this case and the admiral was no moron.

"Pandora's Needle coming in fast," Bandit reported. "The local sheriff is signaling for our clearance to land."

"Send him this clearance code." Davenport punched a series of numbers into his console.

It transmitted instantly and the signal came bouncing back. "Clearance to land," Rodeo announced. "What did you do? Did you tell him you're a sheriff? Did you give him the secret sheriff handshake?"

"I gave him the secret Calyx Elkanon handshake. Calyx is a friend of mine and he has contacts on the Needle." Bandit turned around again, and this time, his lips moved in silent words.

Davenport only smiled at him until Rodeo called out, "Fly the ship, son. You're about to crash into the transmission antenna."

Bandit whipped around and grasped his stick with fresh energy. He concentrated all his attention on steering the ship toward Pandora's Needle.

The satellite hovered among the stars in orbit around Atlas Arcane. Those stars and millions of twinkling lights on the satellite tricked the untrained eye. The sight looked almost beautiful compared to what Davenport knew was really going on down there.

"Don't worry, boy," Davenport told Bandit. "Calyx isn't here."

"He's safely locked up in Terminus Anathema," Rodeo added.

"But his people are here," Bandit argued. "He must exercise a lot of influence if you....if he....if the damn Sheriff's Service accepted his signal to clear us."

"The Sheriff's Service didn't clear us," Davenport told him. "One of the gangs on the Needle controls the transmission antenna. They can let a transmission through or divert it depending on certain numerical keys. I entered my key to let them know I was coming. They'll send a dummy signal to the Sheriff's Service so we look like a normal civilian Drifter instead of one of Ekol's crews."

No one said anything else as the ship floated closer to the Needle. The millions of lights blotted out the stars and the satellite's superstructure loomed huge and awesome above the cockpit.

"Does.....?" Bandit shot Davenport a terrified glance. "Do Calyx's people have a preferred landing site?"

"You can land in the general allotment."

Once again, Bandit flew to the general allotment without having to look it up first. He knew exactly where it was.

He set down the *Artemis Rex* among hundreds of other spacecraft of all sizes. He popped the cockpit window and all three cradles unlocked to release their passengers.

Davenport stepped past Rodeo and met the rest of the Chorion Team on the gangway. "Are we really on Atlas Arcane?" Laub asked.

"Shut your mouth, fool," Axel countered. "We're on the Needle."

"Well, how was I supposed to know?"

"By listening to the cockpit the same as the rest of us," Coon countered. "Are we going out into the city, Sir?"

"Yeah. Arm up, all of you. You're with me."

The boys fell over each other in their haste to get to the loading hatch. They dug into the weapons they brought from Nyx Anonyma.

Davenport helped himself, but he didn't listen to the boys' chatter while he loaded his rifles and checked his sidearms. Instead, he ticked off the names he just read on the Sheriff's Service rap sheets.

Bandit and Rodeo joined them. Rodeo went through the same motions of loading an XQ-62, strapping on his sidearms, and hanging three rifles from his shoulders. His sensitive fingers explored his guns and didn't miss a trick.

Only Wolf stood apart. He watched the others with wary, hostile eyes and he didn't touch a single weapon. When they finished and stepped out onto the tarmac, Wolf went with them completely unarmed.

For some reason, this didn't bother Davenport at all. He couldn't explain why, but he trusted this kid. If Wolf didn't want or need a weapon, Davenport trusted him in that, too.

The satellite hummed with millions of voices, buzzed with millions of aircraft sailing here and there, and glistened with countless lights.

"Split up, all of you. Wolf, you and Rodeo come with me. Coon, you take Alla and Bandit. Axel, I'm putting you and Laub in charge of Breeze, and for the love of God, don't let him break anything."

"You hear that, Breeze?" Laub teased. "You break it, you buy it."

"I won't break anything, Sir," Breeze promised. "You can count on me."

"I hope so. Do me a favor, will you? Don't break any*one*, either, not even yourself. If you meant to destroy Babcock's ammo rack and go swimming in Zing pulp, you can stop yourself from getting yourself thrown in Terminus Anathema on your first.....or second mission."

The others laughed at him—all except Bandit. He looked up at the enormous antenna rising over the city. "Are you sure it's safe?"

"Don't worry, kid. They can't see you. Now listen carefully. Coon, I want you to go to the BabyFace Motel on Beachside Circus. Talk to Umea. She's the bony lady who works the concierge desk."

"The BabyFace Motel....." Alla interjected. "That's a brothel."

"Yeah?" Davenport asked. "Is that a problem?"

Alla and Bandit exchanged glances, but Coon only nodded. "We can do that. What should we talk to her about?"

"I want you to find out if she knows of any ships that crashed at Ultra Meridian lately—like in the last year."

Bandit frowned. "If they crashed at Ultra Meridian, shouldn't you already know about them?"

"You would think so. Axel, you, Laub, and Breeze will go to the swimming pool on Evasion Pier. I want you to talk to a bum who sits under the streetlamp by the stairs going down to the pool. Can you remember all that?"

Axel nodded. "What should I talk to him about?"

"I want you to give him a sequence of numbers—3827541. Can you remember that?"

"I can't, but Laub can." Axel jerked his thumb at his friend. "He can remember anything."

"Fine. Give him the numbers. He'll know what you're talking about and he should leave to meet me at the Windmill right away. You follow him back to the Windmill, but make sure you do it at a safe distance. Don't get too close to him or he might retaliate." The boys listened in rapt attention until he finished. "Do you all understand?" They nodded. "Good. Go on."

Chapter 25

Wolf stuck close at Davenport's side on their way into town. Davenport's nerves recalibrated themselves to this environment he understood so well. He rested his thumb on his sidearm the way he used to when he entered towns like this.

His eye skimmed the crowds all around him. Confederate personnel meandered in and out of establishments drinking, eating, buying, selling, engaging with street vendors of all kinds, and generally letting their hair down.

The townsfolk carried on their business with the Confederate people and with each other. They paid no attention to Davenport and his crew passing by. Nothing ever changed on Pandora's Needle, but Davenport changed.

He hadn't come back here since he went up to Terminus Anathema and changed his life. Now he saw it from a lawman's point of view. His practiced eye picked out details he wouldn't give a second thought as Ekol's man.

Illegal transactions went on all over the place. He noticed hidden objects concealed in people's clothing. He read their lips when they arranged price, location, sizes, weights, purities.....The possibilities were endless.

What would life be like as a sheriff in this town? He had his work cut out for him at Ultra Meridian with every smuggler trying to squeak their contraband cargo past him. His senses became attuned to every subtle attempt at subterfuge.

This town represented a law enforcement challenge on a grand scale. No one sheriff could patrol this town. The whole Sheriff's Service couldn't patrol it, so they didn't try.

Davenport kept the Ithium squarely in the forefront of his mind. He didn't have to solve humanity's problems. He only had to solve one of them.

He passed beyond the Confederate recreation areas and entered the seedy part of town, but the activity level didn't diminish here. Fewer people wore uniforms, but nothing else changed.

Rodeo didn't need any help navigating the crowded city. He kept inclining his head one way and then the other listening to everything. He even sniffed the air. He matched Davenport's movements exactly until the trio halted in front of the Windmill.

Davenport took up a position on the sidewalk across the street. He gazed through the windows at the familiar scene. Would he meet people in there who knew him? He already knew he would. The question was which people he would meet who knew him.

"What are we doing here?" Rodeo asked. "If the Ithium isn't here, why are we here?"

Davenport didn't ask how Rodeo knew about the Ithium. Rodeo must know everything about this mission. "We're here to get information."

"Information about Ultra Meridian," Rodeo finished. "If the Reserve Wing is here, we should be going to Ultra Meridian to look for our payload while they're occupied elsewhere."

"Our payload is here. The safe is here—or, more accurately, it's on Atlas Arcane."

Rodeo cocked his head. "What safe?"

"My safe. Come on."

Davenport led the boys into the Windmill. Two skyscraper casino towers of glittering glass raked the stars on either side of the establishment. Lights shone from thousands of windows. Laughter, music, and the jingle of falling coins came from all sides.

The Windmill slouched between these two luxury buildings. The one-story hovel squashed between their sheer walls with only two small, smoky windows that barely let light through.

Davenport had to duck to get through the entrance. A dense cloud of opiate smoke hung over the long, low room.

A few scruffy regulars played poker at three cracked tables near the bar. Threadbare couches, divans, and armchairs filled the rest of the room with inebriated people hanging out of them.

Davenport went to the bar. A few people who remained upright drew back from him. They eyed Wolf and Rodeo and examined Rodeo's weapons with curious expressions.

The boy kept scanning the room with his sensitive ears. Wolf snarled at the barman when he came too close.

"I'm sorry, Sheriff," the barman told Davenport, "but we don't allow Brikloids here. You'll have to ask your friend to leave."

Davenport didn't know what he meant until the barman shot a significant glance at Wolf. "Oh, you mean him? He isn't a Brikloid. He's a Chorion."

The barman wrinkled his nose at Wolf. "Either way, he isn't welcome here."

"Yes, he is. Get me a pint of ZoomZoom, a shot of BruteForce, and Vas Skrimhold."

The barman opened his mouth and shut it again. He hesitated a second time.

Ever so subtly, Davenport shifted his left hand to his sidearm, too. He didn't have to draw his gun or threaten this man. That movement told the barman everything he needed to know.

He got busy, pulled the pint, poured the shot, and hurried away. Wolf gave a low growl in Davenport's ear. "Don't pay any attention to him," Davenport murmured down to him. "If that's the worst we have to deal with in this town, we'll be lucky."

"Who's Vas Skrimhold?" Rodeo asked.

"Someone who won't be very happy to see me." Davenport slid the pint of ZoomZoom over in front of Rodeo. "Drink this. It's the most expensive drink in the house."

He placed the shot in front of Wolf, who seized the glass, tossed it back, grimaced, and then slammed it down like he drank in bars all the time. He probably did if he spent much time around Ekol.

Rodeo picked up the pint glass and took a sip. "ZoomZoom, you call this? It's delicious."

"Just be careful. It really makes you zoom."

The barman didn't come back. Instead, an enormously fat woman rolled out of the backroom.

She halted on the threshold and curled her lip at Davenport. "See what I mean?" he whispered to Rodeo.

She crossed the last few feet to where the friends waited. "You got a lot of nerve coming back in here, Davenport."

"It's wonderful to see you, too, Vas. Are you still looking for a bouncer?"

"I wouldn't hire you if you agreed to pay me for the privilege." She jerked her chin at his star. "What's that—your Halloween costume?"

Davenport laughed. He really was pleased to see her. "I'll take off mine if you take off yours."

"Get out, you back-stabbing son of a bitch!" she snarled. "Get out and take your gutter filth with you."

Wolf growled so loud it came out as a yowl. Davenport straightened his arm in front of the boy to hold him back. "You don't have to get nasty, Vas. I didn't stab you in the back."

"Your boss did and that's enough. Now, if you don't get out, I'll have to call in my Adik enforcer."

"Save your bullshit for the patsies who pay full price for your stuff after you cut it with shuliaite. There isn't an Adik alive in this town and you certainly don't have any enforcer. You can barely keep the lights on."

"What do you want?" she hissed. "State your business and get out."

"I don't have any business, Vas. I'm just here to entertain my young friends." He turned around so he presented his back to her, rested his elbow on the bar, and took a long pull from Rodeo's glass of ZoomZoom.

He could just feel her fuming behind him. That was good. The more she hated him, the less likely she would be to mention his visit to anyone who might decide to do something about it.

Rodeo took another sip from the same glass. "This stuff is great. I'm going to have to get me some of this."

"Just ask Ekol," Davenport told him. "He's got cellars full of it."

The tension behind Davenport spiked into the stratosphere when he mentioned Ekol. That would shut Vas up if anything did.

Davenport was just starting to feel the zooming sensation going to his head when an old man in rags shambled in.

He kept his head down and long, greying hair hung over his eyes. He didn't look up and Davenport spotted Axel, Laub, and Breeze on the sidewalk outside. They'd followed Davenport's instructions to the letter and brought the bum from the swimming pool.

Rodeo drew back automatically and made room for the man. The bum slotted up to the bar right next to Davenport and Davenport turned back around to stand at his side.

The man spoke in a raspy, dead tone. "Catalogue open."

"Ultra Meridian. Search one year prior to today. Shipwreck."

The old man hesitated. "Shipwreck unknown."

Davenport's heart skipped a beat. "Cross-reference criminal spacecraft, origin unknown. Cross-reference *Echo Omicron*, Ekol Thaine, and Helios Sanctus."

The old man stood silent for too long. "Shipwreck unknown."

"Maybe it isn't a wreck," Rodeo offered. "Maybe the ship survived."

"Ekol said it crashed," Davenport pointed out.

"Maybe he made a mistake. It's been known to happen."

Davenport's head spun. "If he made a mistake about the ship going down at Ultra Meridian, then we're up the shit creek. We could be searching until doomsday and never find the third component."

"Third component," the man blurted out. "Third component, *Blood Calliope*, dispatched from Helios Sanctus, rendezvoused *Echo Omicron*....."

Davenport whirled to stare at the side of the man's wrinkled face. "Where is it? Where is the *Blood Calliope*?"

"Location unknown. Destination: Sacron Enigma."

"That's impossible," Rodeo countered. "Ekol said they wanted to assemble the three components inside the Confederacy."

"Maybe they wanted to hold the three components in Sacron Enigma until they were ready to release it on their target." Davenport turned back to the old man. "Did the ship pass Ultra Meridian? Was it scheduled to pass through that section?"

"Passed Ultra Meridian. Last logged at DTF9Q."

Davenport's hand flew to his head. "Shit!"

"DTF9Q is between Ultra Meridian and Sacron Enigma," Rodeo pointed out.

"RWCC Stalwart *Devil's Bane*," Davenport went on. "Upcoming itinerary, cross-reference Vorax Summa, cross-reference Admiral Killian Joyce."

This one the old man found easy—of course. "Upcoming itinerary: scheduled departure one week. No scheduled return itinerary."

Davenport doubled over and collapsed with his elbows on the bar. One week. He had one week to get the Ithium and the chip away from Joyce before he sailed off to Vorax Summa.

If Joyce released the Ithium there, it would wipe out the whole Confederacy long before it made it to any other system. So much for using the Ithium for defense.

"We got a serious problem, man," Rodeo murmured.

Davenport didn't mind the kid dropping all pretense of rank and respect. He straightened up. "We have one week and we know Joyce is on Atlas Arcane. We have to catch him here before he leaves. That's all there is to it." He turned to the old man. "Thank you for coming over. I appreciate it. You can go now."

The old man turned and left. Axel and Laub stared after him, but they didn't follow him.

Davenport picked up the pint glass in front of Rodeo and drained it. "Let's get out of here. We got what we came for."

He turned around and stopped when a large crowd of uniformed Confederate personnel waltzed into the Windmill. They sneered at the many customers reclining in the couches and chairs. Then they headed for the bar.

A man and woman with their arms linked led the pack. Not one speck of dirt smudged their uniforms and both wore their hair so perfectly coiffured that a hurricane wouldn't dislodge it.

They pushed their way inside and the woman bumped into one of the gamblers.

She jostled his elbow just as he extended his hand to deposit his bet in the pot. His hand plowed into the pile of chips, coins, and tokens. The pot went flying.

"Watch what you're doing!" The guy reared back, kicked over his chair, and rocketed to his feet. His three companions got to their feet, too.

The Confederate people squared up to confront them. Vas hustled around the bar and tried to wedge herself between them. "Break it up, Samuels. It was an accident."

The Confederate lady turned her mocking eyes from the gambler to Vas. "Let's go next door, Ebert. If this is the kind of people who frequent this place, we can do better elsewhere."

"You don't belong here," Samuels snarled. "You're way out of your safe zone."

Ebert snorted at him. "We're attached to the Confederate Corps' ambassadors' service. We go where we like, and right now, we're going over there to get something to drink."

He glanced toward the bar and saw Davenport. Ebert's eyes slid down Davenport's vest to his star and then sideways toward Wolf.

The woman shuddered. "Ugh! Leeches!"

Wolf let out a shriek that stood Davenport's hair on end. Davenport barely caught the young man in time to stop Wolf from hurtling at the woman's throat in a murderous lunge.

Davenport saw the situation deteriorating rapidly. He didn't trust himself to hold Wolf back if these idiots insulted him again.

He wrestled Wolf toward the door and Rodeo inched after them. Rodeo swung one of his rifles forward and shifted between Davenport and the Confederate people.

Unfortunately, the Confederate crowd blocked the exit in such numbers that Davenport couldn't force his way through. They grimaced at Wolf which infuriated the boy even more. They flatly refused to move to let Davenport leave the building.

"Get.... the.... hell.... out!" Samuels snarled. "Turn around and walk away right now or the ambassadors' service will be dredging the plasma seam for your mutilated bodies."

The woman laughed extra loudly. "Do you hear that, Ebert? He threatened a Confederate officer! Arrest him."

Three more Confederate soldiers advanced. The gamblers saw them coming and pulled their sidearms.

Davenport ducked as the first shots rang out. He gave Wolf an almighty shove toward the door, but at the same moment, the Confederate crowd surged forward to help their friends.

They stampeded into Davenport and bowled him off his feet. He toppled, but the surge of bodies prevented him from hitting the floor. The impact knocked him so hard he lost his grip on Wolf.

The young man broke free and went berserk. He plunged into the crowd slashing, ripping, biting, and snapping bones in a blinding whirlwind of motion. Only the boy's blood-curdling screeches and the screams of his falling victims told Davenport where he was.

Chapter 26

Davenport huddled on the cold stone floor and did his best to make himself invisible among dozens of prisoners. Almost all of them got arrested along with him during the fight at the Windmill.

Wolf, Axel, and Laub flanked him. No one had seen Coon, Alla, Bandit, or Breeze since the crew split up at the *Artemis Rex*.

Wolf remained glued to Davenport's side except when the Sheriff's deputies took Wolf off to the sheriff's office for questioning.

Davenport could well imagine the joy the sheriff got out of the boy and Wolf came back more surly, more threatening, and more feral than before.

Random yells, sobs, and groans rose from the crowd packed into this dim, dank cell. The deputies didn't take it easy on the combatants, especially the ones not in Confederate uniform. They didn't know or care who started the fight. They threw everyone in together.

Wolf's ferocity during the fight didn't spare him the usual cuts and scratches, some worse than others, and Davenport didn't feel so well himself.

Axel and Laub kept themselves clear of the worst fighting, but they got arrested on general principle for the crime of being near the Windmill at the time.

A door slammed out of sight and the prisoners started yelling their heads off. They did this every time the deputies came near the cell.

The deputies marched their latest target down the bars, kicked away anyone too near the door, and flung Rodeo onto the floor at Davenport's feet.

Davenport grabbed the boy and towed him into their group. Rodeo's dark glasses were missing and his milk-white eyes stared around him at nothing.

"Are you okay, boy?" Davenport whispered. "How bad was it?"

Rodeo shook his head. "He didn't believe me—or he pretended not to. He didn't listen about the Confederate scum starting the fight. He said he'd heard it all before and he wasn't interested in that."

"What *was* he interested in?"

"He wanted to know where we came from and where we were going. I told him our cover story, but he didn't believe that, either."

"He's a lot smarter than your average sheriff." Axel glanced over at Davenport. "No offense, Sir, but you aren't exactly a sheriff anymore even if you do wear that star. It don't mean anything anymore."

Davenport checked the rest of his crew's reaction, but no one of them argued. Maybe they all thought the same thing. "You might be right, but I might have enough sheriff left in me to talk some sense into the guy."

They looked away, all except Rodeo. "He's onto you, man. He knows about that old bum who came to see you at the Windmill. He even knew the general gist of the questions you asked him."

"Did he say how he found out?"

"He didn't say, but I think he might have questioned the woman from the bar—what did you say her name was—Vas something? The woman you said wouldn't be happy to see you. She stood right there and listened to you question the guy."

"It doesn't matter. If he knows as much as that, maybe he'll realize I'm not here to make trouble."

Another crash made Davenport look up. The deputies were coming back. They stood beyond the bars and yelled over the noise. "Number 479!"

"That's you, Sir," Laub told Davenport. "You'll see for yourself when you meet him."

"All right. Sit tight and I'll be right back." Wolf tried to grab him. Davenport had to pry the boy's fingers off his arm. "Stay here and keep quiet. Don't give the deputies any reason to lash out. I'll be back soon and then we'll know better where we're at."

He stepped over bodies and made his way to the bars. The deputies held him at gunpoint while they opened the door.

They grabbed him and slammed him against the wall, twisted his arms behind his back, and dragged him off to the sheriff's office.

They flung him into a chair opposite the sheriff's desk. A plaque on the desk front read, *Lawrence Healey, Sheriff of Pandora's Needle.*

Davenport straightened up and found himself facing a middle-aged man with short brown hair and the worn face of a sheriff who works way too hard under an impossible caseload.

Grey flecked the two days growth of beard covering his face. His hands moved slowly over his console, but he sat up straight and his eyes flashed with an old fire that might have been there for decades.

His eyes slid once to Davenport's star and didn't acknowledge it again. "Do you mind telling me what you're doing bringing these Chorions into my town? Do you have any idea how dangerous they are? That hairy one killed fifteen people and the blind one shot ten—don't ask me how."

"They were defending themselves against attack," Davenport told him. "They got caught in that fight despite our best efforts to avoid it—but you already knew that, right? You must have heard the same thing from everyone who was there....and while we're at it, the last I checked, being Chorion doesn't make a person an outlaw. They're Confederate citizens and they have as much right to visit any Confederate town as every other citizen—as I'm sure you know, Sheriff."

"They aren't forbidden from coming to my town for being Chorion, Sheriff. They're forbidden from coming to my town for being Ekol Thaine's favored strike team—just as you are Ekol Thaine's favored enforcer....aren't you, *Sheriff*?"

Davenport did his best to ignore the sarcasm dripping from the sheriff's tone. "I'm not Ekol's enforcer. I'm here in the execution of my duties as Sheriff of Ultra Meridian. I'm hunting the people who stole a cartridge of Ithium from Helios Sanctus and are, at this very moment, planning to release it somewhere inside the Confederacy."

Healey didn't even blink. "And yet, here you are in Ekol's ship, commanding Ekol's crew, burning Ekol's fuel, shooting Ekol's weapons, and the wires are buzzing with the news that Sheriff Davenport from Ultra Meridian is back on Ekol's payroll where he belongs. Now what am I supposed to make of that?"

Davenport stiffened. This was going about as well as he expected. "Look, I realize it doesn't look good, but working with Ekol was the only way I could track the Ithium here. If you knew that a stolen cartridge of Ithium was somewhere at large on your Needle, wouldn't you do anything to get it?"

"I highly doubt I would partner with a known criminal who, by the way, also wants to acquire the Ithium for questionable purposes."

"Don't you care at all that someone is planning an Ithium attack against the Confederacy? Don't you care at all that a cartridge of Ithium is floating around out there somewhere unaccounted for—and might actually be on your Needle right now? Don't you care at all about your duty to at least investigate and hopefully stop them?"

"My duty is my business, not yours. You have enough to worry about breaching your own duty by turning to the enemy. We sheriffs have a hard enough time keeping on top of the crooks without one of our own helping them out."

"I'm not helping them out. I'm trying to stop them—unlike you. You sit behind your desk while these assholes use your satellite as a playground and you don't do anything."

Healey's expression hardened. "Don't you dare even suggest that I don't do anything! Don't you dare!"

Davenport pulled his head in real quick. "I'm sorry. I didn't mean it that way. It's just that I've been driving non-stop for almost four days now trying to stop these fools. I thought I might get some help from you and now you're accusing me of being one of them. I'm telling you I only partnered with Ekol because it was the only way to get the ships, guns, and personnel I needed to track down the Ithium. That's the only reason I'm here, believe me."

Healey pursed his lips, but at least he hadn't thrown Davenport out of his office yet. "All right, Sheriff. I'll give you five minutes to convince me."

Davenport's heart leapt. This was the opening he'd been waiting for. He started talking fast. "I inspected a known smuggler's ship at Ultra Meridian and seized the Ithium from their vessel. I put the Ithium in my safe and I was in the process of contacting my section chief about it when someone attacked my jail. They bombed the building from space and leveled it. My prisoners escaped, and while I was trying to recapture them, a bunch of Reserve Wing vessels landed on the planet and stole the safe."

Healey frowned. "How could the Reserve Wing steal it? They're tasked with defending the Confederacy, not putting it at risk."

"That's what I thought, but you have to admit that whoever stole the Ithium from Helios Sanctus must have had high-ranking security clearance. Even if I hadn't known that, I saw with my own eyes when one of the Reserve Wing officers took my safe on board their ship. I followed them, and when I got caught, Admiral Killian Joyce tried to kill me. He told me that he had my safe and then he attacked me. I had to run off to save my life."

Healey frowned. "I just can't believe that story, Sheriff. I'm sorry because I can see that you're sincere, but I just can't believe...." He trailed off and turned to stare out of the window.

"Listen, Sheriff," Davenport blurted out. "I really don't care if you think I'm Ekol's man. I don't even care what you do with me. Send me up to Terminus Anathema if you want to. I really don't care as long as someone stops the Ithium. If that's you, I really don't care. I swore an oath to uphold the law, and if that means going back to Terminus Anathema, I can live with that."

Healey jerked around and glared at him. "I'm sending you back to the cells now, Sheriff. I need to think about this and do some digging of my own. I can't promise you anything, but rest assured that I will look into this. I will verify everything you've told me—or not. What happens to you will depend on what I find out."

Davenport collapsed back in his chair. "Thank you!"

Chapter 27

Rodeo jerked upright and his blank eyes swiveled up toward the ceiling. "Did you hear that?"

"I heard a bunch of people talking and crying," Axel replied. "That's nothing new."

"Someone is plotting escape." Rodeo turned his head this way and that trying to catch the thread of conversation again. "Someone near us."

"What are their plans?" Laub asked.

"I can't tell. I don't think they have a plan yet. They're just grumbling."

"*We* should escape," Axel suggested. "We should get the hell out of here before that sheriff decides to do something not very nice with us."

"You mean like locking us in a windowless cell with a hundred other people?" Laub asked. "What could he do worse than that?"

"He could send us up to Terminus Anathema."

"He couldn't do that without sending all these people, too. He won't do that."

"And why won't he send them all up?"

"Because brawling in the streets is not an offense that can earn you a stretch in Terminus Anathema," Laub replied, "and we weren't even brawling in the streets."

"We were brawling in a tavern," Rodeo replied.

"*You* were brawling in a tavern," Laub countered. "I was standing on the sidewalk."

"You're as pure as the driven snow, aren't you?" Rodeo sneered.

"What do you say, Sir?" Axel asked. "We should escape, shouldn't we?"

Davenport glanced toward the bars. The deputies kept coming by and taking different prisoners off to Healey's office for questioning. They never took Davenport back. Did Healey blow smoke up Davenport's ass when he promised to investigate?

Davenport didn't want to escape. He wanted to be on hand to hear the good news that Healey had found out Davenport was telling the truth. Davenport wanted to earn Healey's trust by cooperating until Healey helped him.....do what?

Even if Healey did find evidence that Davenport was telling the truth, he wouldn't be able to free Davenport. He had to follow his protocols. If anything, he would have to notify Admiral Joyce about where Davenport was and the accusations Davenport made against him.

"Sir?" Laub prompted. "What about it? What about trying to escape?"

Davenport dragged his attention back to his team. "What's your plan?"

That shut them up for a while—all except Rodeo. "This cell is on the outside of the building. All we'd have to do is get through that wall over there and we'd be outside."

"Brilliant, genius," Axel sneered. "How exactly do we get through the wall without any weapons, explosives, or tools?"

Rodeo shrugged. "I'm just saying. We need a plan and the first step is to get through that wall."

"What about the deputies?" Laub suggested. "What about overrunning them the next time they open that door?"

"You'd be running straight into their guns," Rodeo argued. "Then, once you got out into the corridor, you'd have to run through a couple hundred more armed deputies to get out of the building. Like I said, going through the wall will be much easier."

"What do you say, Sir?" Axel asked. "Which do you vote for?"

"First of all," Davenport began, "I want to hear your plan for getting through the wall and defending yourself against the deputies. When I hear the two plans, I'll let you know which one I vote for."

Davenport went back to watching the deputies. Why did everything have to take so damn long? Why couldn't Healey call Davenport up and tell him what the hell was going on outside this stinking, fetid cell?

He put his head down on his elbows and shut his eyes. If only he could stop thinking about this damn case, he might be able to catch up on the sleep he lost since he left Ultra Meridian.

He couldn't stop thinking about it, though. It kept circling around and around in his head.

Another slam jolted him alert. He looked up to see the deputies coming back with some other prisoner. This went on day and night. The noise and the uncomfortable sitting position made sleep impossible anyway.

He put his head down again. He hardly heard the deputies call out, "Number 479!"

Laub nudged Davenport. "That's you! He's calling you up again."

Davenport looked up. "Huh?"

"You're called up! You have to go."

The boys propelled him to his feet. He stumbled over more than one person and almost pitched into the bars. He went through the same routine too numbed by sleep deprivation and constant stress to think clearly.

He slumped into the chair across from Healey's desk, but Healey wasn't sitting down. He paced up and down and almost attacked Davenport the minute the deputies left the room. "You've got a big problem, Davenport."

"Tell me something I don't know," Davenport mumbled.

"Listen to me, Davenport! Admiral Joyce knows where you are. He sent orders to transport you to Atlas Arcane. He sent orders to transport you there....*alone*."

That word echoed in Davenport's mind and woke him from his stupor. "What?"

"You have to listen to me, Davenport! This is important. I didn't tell anyone you were here. I don't know how he found out, but he did. Ordering any prisoner transported alone would be highly unusual on its own, but it means the admiral is worried. He's worried because you're getting too close to him."

Davenport shot out of his chair. "That proves it. He's got the Ithium on Atlas Arcane."

"He wants to get you isolated on Atlas Arcane where there's no chance you can get away from him a second time."

Davenport paced toward the door and stopped himself from walking out right in front of Healey. "I have to...." He marched back to Healey. "You have to get me out of here. You have to get my crew out. We have to find that Ithium before he leaves for Vorax Summa next week."

Healey straightened up and his features hardened again. He became a stoic sheriff again. Davenport was looking in the mirror. He knew exactly how this guy thought.

"I can't let you walk out and I can't free your crew. I'm sure you understand why, but I'll tell you this. You're scheduled to transport tomorrow morning. If you just so happened to escape before then, I wouldn't be too terribly disappointed."

Davenport's pulse quickened. Healey really was saying what Davenport thought he was saying.

Davenport's mind went into another tailspin. He had to escape. Thank goodness the boys were deep into planning to do exactly that.

Healey walked to the door and yelled something to his deputies. Their footsteps echoed in the hallway outside. They were coming back for Davenport right now.

Healey turned back into the room. Just before he returned to his desk, he murmured low enough for Davenport to hear, "It would be a terrible shame if those hardened criminals found out that there's a whole room full of explosives right next to their cell."

The next minute, the deputies trooped into the office and laid hold of Davenport. They yanked him around more roughly to get him away from their boss.

Davenport stewed in a fever of excitement all the way back to the cell. He kept himself under control until he got back to the boys. "Listen to me," he whispered. "I know a way we can escape."

They perked up immediately. "How?"

"This cell shares a wall with an explosives storage room. All we have to do is figure out which wall it is and get through it."

The news electrified Rodeo. He straightened up and started turning his head back and forth again. "The wall behind us leads outside, so that leaves the right and left walls."

He faced the right-hand wall. The group crouched right next to it. Rodeo started scanning the stone surface. His unseeing eyes traced the corners and indentations in the mortar. "This is it. This is the wall adjoining the explosives storage room."

"How can you tell?" Axel asked.

"The other wall joins up with a communications station. It's full of electronic equipment. I can hear it from here."

Laub started examining the wall in detail, too. "This mortar isn't very strong. We'd have to tunnel through it, get the explosives, and bring them back in here. We don't want to turn the whole building into a dust cloud—which is what would happen if we blew through the wall inside the explosives room."

Rodeo clapped him on the shoulder. "Now you're thinking, boy."

"Can you get through it?" Davenport asked Laub.

Laub extended his hand and scratched at the mortar holding the bricks together. A film of dust drifted to the floor. "I might, but it would go quicker if I had a tool of some kind."

The others started looking around for something, but Davenport got there first. He slipped the star off his vest and pushed it into Laub's hand. "Use this."

Laub stared at it and opened his mouth. The others gaped at Davenport as though he'd lost his natural mind. "You can't, Sir!" Axel whispered. "That....."

Davenport had to smile at them all. He was really starting to feel very affectionate toward them all, each in their own unique way.

"I guess Ekol was right about me. I'm on the run from the Reserve Wing the same as every other two-bit criminal. I'm not really a sheriff anymore. Use it to dig us out of here. It's the best tool we're gonna find in here."

The boys didn't move. All at once, Rodeo snatched the star out of Laub's hand and pressed it back into Davenport's hand. "You keep it. You're still a sheriff. You'll always be a sheriff and a sheriff needs a star. We'll find another way out of here."

Before Davenport had a chance to argue, Rodeo turned back the other way. Without looking, he slid his hand across the floor and slipped something from the pocket of another prisoner sitting right behind him.

He passed the object to Laub and Davenport got a good look at it. It was an old-fashioned pair of spectacles with wire rims surrounding two glass lenses.

Laub went to work at once. He unscrewed one of the ear bars and started scratching at the mortar.

"How long will this take?" Axel whispered.

"As long as it takes," Laub replied. "Oh, look. This mortar is ancient. It's crumbling with hardly any effort."

Laub put considerable pressure on the wire, but he kept it up. Rodeo discussed the situation with Davenport while Laub worked. "Once we bring the explosives back in here, we'll have to get all the rest of the prisoners involved. We'll have to explain that we want them to pull back from the wall while we blow it open."

"I don't think they'll offer much objection," Davenport remarked. "We'll have to time it so the deputies aren't here. The deputies will see the prisoners crowding nearer to the bars."

"We should wait until the deputies come for another prisoner. Once they leave, we can get everyone as far away from the explosion as possible."

Davenport nodded. "I can go along with that plan."

"I'm through!" Laub whispered.

The friends watched him scoop the last crumbs out of the hole he'd drilled. He scratched an opening big enough for one finger. Then he hooked the nearest brick and pulled it toward him.

"How big do you have to make it so we can go through?" Axel asked.

"We don't all have to go. We'll send Wolf. He can slip through smaller spaces than the rest of us."

Davenport glanced down at Wolf. "Do you know what explosives to get?"

"Don't worry about him," Rodeo told him. "Wolf knows explosives just fine."

Davenport didn't argue. Wolf might look like an animal, but he was smarter than he looked.

Laub started on the next brick. Then he cleared two more above the first two. He swept the debris away from the hole.

Rodeo pushed Wolf toward the opening. "Go!"

Chapter 28

Wolf crouched in front of the hole. He still looked way too big to get through, but when he put his head into the gap, he did something with his shoulders. He somehow collapsed his skeleton into a flexible cage that conformed to the bricks.

He slithered one arm through and then the other. One joint at a time, he adjusted his position until his hairy legs slipped out of sight. No light came from the storage room. What was he doing in there?

Davenport glanced around. None of the other prisoners paid any attention if they even noticed what the friends were doing. Laub and Axel moved their bodies in front of the hole to block anyone from seeing.

The prisoner whose glasses Rodeo stole didn't notice them missing, either. Rodeo took them and wound the screw back into the pin. He slipped the glasses into the man's pocket as though they'd never been anywhere else.

Laub jumped when Wolf bumped him in the back. Wolf handed him and Axel a few bundles and vanished into the dark.

Axel spread his bundles on the floor and went to work with fast, precise movements. "This is perfect—greprexsite charges..... Oh, Sweet Jesus, look at this! He found some Aswalt mines! God bless Wolf!"

Both boys jumped again when Wolf handed through another parcel with the greprexsite triggers. Laub and Axel worked at full speed to attach the triggers to the charges. They arranged the mines in rows.

A moment later, Wolf burrowed through the hole and rejoined them. He dusted the dirt off his fur and squatted down next to Davenport. Davenport patted him on the back. "Good job, boy. You done real good."

Wolf let out a low growl that sounded more like a purr than a threat. "I told you," Rodeo told him. "No one can get in and out like Wolf."

Davenport popped his head up and looked around. "Wrap that stuff up and let's get over by the back wall. Keep the goods hidden until we spread the word to the other prisoners."

Laub stripped off his shirt to reveal broad shoulders and a chest cut out of solid muscle. He wrapped the goods in his shirt and tucked it under his arm. Davenport pushed his way through the throng of prisoners with the four boys in tow.

The other prisoners cursed and threatened them, but Davenport didn't stop until he found the back wall—the one Rodeo said would open to the outside world.

Davenport pulled Rodeo to his side and pushed the other three against the mottled stone. "You three set up the blast while Rodeo and I spread the word."

He and Rodeo turned in opposite directions and Davenport whispered to the person sitting nearest him. "We're going to blow that wall and escape. When the deputies take the next prisoner, everyone press toward the bars and get away from the blast. Spread the word."

Rodeo repeated the message and Davenport turned to the next person. Whispers spread through the cell and a wave of excitement went with it.

People turned to look in their direction. The groans and complaints changed to murmured warnings and suggestions.

"We're ready!" Axel whispered.

Davenport glanced behind him. Ten charges rested at the base of the wall. A trigger stuck out of each, but he didn't see any mines. "Where are the Aswalts?"

Axel's eyes skipped sideways toward Rodeo, but the blind boy pretended not to hear. "Give the word, Sir," Laub hissed. "It's ready to blow. All we have to do is trip the trigger."

Davenport straightened up and peered over the other prisoners' heads. The deputies stood beyond the bars calling out their next victim.

He bent over and whispered in someone's ear. "As soon as they leave, rush the bars. Pass the word."

The word radiated outward from him with every prisoner taking up the message. People kept glancing toward Davenport and a few raised their eyebrows at his star, but he was way past caring about that now. He was getting the hell out of here with his boys.

The deputies opened the door to let their target out. The cell boomed louder than ever when they slammed the door. Their boots tramped down the corridor and out of sight. "Now!" Davenport yelled.

The whole mob of prisoners surged to its feet. They crushed the bars in a tidal wave of bodies.

Axel depressed the trigger and lunged after Davenport and the others. They made it halfway before the crowd blocked them from going any further.

Davenport grappled the boys to him and yanked them around. He rotated himself outside them so his body offered whatever small protection he could give them.

He barely tucked his chin and clamped his eyes shut when an almighty blast smashed him in the back. It hurled him against the crowd and he crushed Wolf beneath him.

Just as fast, Laub yanked Davenport away. "Move! Go!"

Davenport staggered after him. The charges had demolished half the cell and the prisoners streamed all around him. They jumped from the shattered edge of floor to the street outside. They raced away into the city, never to be seen again.

Wolf and Rodeo vaulted over the side. Wolf sprang down with catlike agility and landed in a crouch among scattered bricks and rubble on the ground.

Rodeo stumbled once and Laub tucked and rolled as the cell emptied of its occupants. Davenport judged the distance and jumped. He landed next to Laub and the boy caught his shoulder to steady him. "Let's get out of here."

The friends turned to run away when a howling streak of rocket fire plunged out of the sky. It smashed into the pavement behind Laub and the blast knocked all five off their feet.

Davenport huddled under his arms towing the boys to their feet. "Get up! We have to get out of here!"

Another five rockets plunged out of the atmosphere and exploded all around the jail. "The security fleet! They're bombarding the prisoners!" Davenport pushed Rodeo away. "Go! Run for it!"

The group set off for the nearest street where towering buildings would hide them from the bombardment. Laub and Axel went first with Rodeo followed by Davenport. He waited until he made sure Wolf caught up with him and then he burst into a sprint.

He got to the corner. The three boys raced ahead of him on their way back to the general allotment where they left the *Artemis Rex*.

Davenport put on speed when, out of nowhere, another rocket sliced through the air. It collided with the pavement right in front of him and exploded in his face.

He toppled back blinking stars out of his eyes when another blast hit him from behind. He staggered and felt himself falling.

Wolf charged to his side and grabbed him. Davenport felt the boy hauling him away when another rocket hit him in the side.

He hit the pavement hard and lay stunned and aching. He tried to push himself up when strong hands laid hold of him.

Davenport's body lifted off the ground and his legs straightened. He looked up and almost didn't believe his senses when Dice growled down at him. "The very next time this happens, I'm leaving you behind. You hear me?"

Another three concussions rocked the ground. Continuous explosions blasted the city to rubble all around them.

Davenport tried to turn back. "Wolf!"

"Don't even think about it!" Dice yanked him forward. "I didn't come here to watch you throw your miserable life away."

Davenport didn't hear him. He took a step toward the jail shrouded in dust and smoke. "Wolf!"

At that moment, a hundred deputies charged out of the jail raining ammo everywhere. Their XQs boomed and their rifles spat at Dice and Davenport.

Dice seized Davenport's shirt. "Move it, asshole!"

Davenport fought him off in his frenzy to get back to the jail. "Wolf! Wolf!"

Fiddler and Lyons rushed out of nowhere. They positioned themselves to defend Dice and Davenport from the deputies.

Another rocket smashed into the ground to Davenport's right. Gravel and concrete chips peppered his cheek and sides.

No matter where he searched, he didn't see Wolf anywhere. He couldn't leave the boy behind, but with more deputies piling into the fight, he finally gave it up and let Dice drag him away.

Dice shoved him around a corner and they bolted for an overturned vehicle not far off. Gunfire echoed off the walls behind them. Emmet poked his head over the vehicle as Dice and Davenport got nearer.

The two friends dove for cover and Davenport caught his breath. He still couldn't think of anything but going back to find Wolf.

He glanced over the vehicle and saw Lyons on the ground.

Fiddler backed toward Lyons unloading her rifle at a whole posse of deputies stalking closer. Fiddler faced down dozens of XQs and countless rifles aiming at her from all sides.

Lyons flipped onto her stomach and started dragging her useless legs toward the vehicle. She made it ten feet when an XQ charge hit Fiddler in the shoulder. She twirled on the spot and her gun flew out of her hand.

She turned a complete circle and toppled next to Lyons. Lyons rolled over onto her back again, pulled Fiddler's unconscious body toward her, and rotated her own XQ to aim at the deputies.

"Fiddler's hit!" Emmet yelled.

He sprang out from behind the vehicle before anyone could stop him. Davenport's instincts took over. He might not be able to save Wolf, but he could save Lyons and Fiddler.

Dice roared something inarticulate and the three men charged into the open. Emmet fired again and again, but he couldn't protect anyone from so many deputies, not even himself.

He ran a dozen yards when an XQ charge corkscrewed out of the enemy ranks. It spiraled toward the friends to blast them into eternity when Dice dove in front of Emmet, turned his body backward, and took the charge right between his shoulder blades.

He crumpled on the spot with a sickening grunt. Davenport left Fiddler and tried to run to him, but Dice only snarled at him. "Go! Get her out of here!"

Davenport sprang back to the injured pair to discover Emmet already bent over Fiddler. Davenport snatched Lyons's XQ and turned it on the deputies.

He fired once, twice, ten times. He backed up while Emmet dragged Fiddler away and Lyons crawled one painstaking inch at a time.

Dice alone remained hunched in agony where he'd fallen. Davenport laid down a carpet of charges, but he couldn't help Dice with his hands full of his weapon.

Emmet laid Fiddler behind the vehicle and came running back. He fired his rifle under Davenport's arms while Davenport backed them into their hiding place.

"In case you hadn't noticed," Lyons panted, "we have a serious problem here."

"No, we don't." Dice shook himself and jerked his chin at Emmet and Davenport. "You two cover me."

He didn't give Davenport a chance to figure out what he meant. Dice scooped up Lyons and slung her over his shoulder. Blood poured down her legs and stained his clothes, but he didn't notice. He collected Fiddler in his other arm and lunged into the open.

Emmet and Davenport jumped up and took up their positions behind Dice. They opened up with their weapons, but their retreat went off much quicker and more easily than Davenport expected.

The deputies hunkered behind corners to avoid the party's fire. Davenport fired three charges and the deputies hid while the friends made their last dash to freedom.

Dice led the way across intersections and through crowds to the general allotment. He ran past the *Artemis Rex* to the *Echo Omicron* waiting for them in a forgotten corner.

Davenport cast a wistful glance at the Drifter as he ran by. It was totally dark and deserted. The Chorion Team was nowhere to be seen.

Chapter 29

Sheriff Healey parked his skimmer on a street corner and climbed down. He checked his sidearm out of sheer habit even though he hadn't fired it since he put it on this morning.

Two of his deputies dismounted their skimmers nearby. They scanned the streets while they sidled over to him. "Are you sure you don't want us to come with you, Sir?"

"I'm sure." Healey pointed across the street. "Go over there and question that girl. Find out if her pimp imported another shipment of ZoomZoom."

Healey made sure the two deputies left to carry out his orders. Then he turned on his heel and strode down the steps to the swimming pool. He surveyed the area until he spotted a greasy, ragged bum crouched under a streetlamp.

Healey sauntered over to him and squatted down. "Search request, Healey, Sheriff."

The man didn't look up. His chin rested on his chest and he kept his eyes shut. His lanky hair hung over his face and he muttered like he might be talking in his sleep. "Search request granted."

"Search Ithium theft, Helios Sanctus."

"Search results returned."

"Cross-reference *Echo Omicron*, smugglers' vessel."

"Cross-reference *Blood Calliope*, dispatched from Helios," the man mumbled. "Cross-reference Ekol Thaine, rendezvoused *Echo Omicron*. Cross-reference Ultra Meridian."

Healey stared at him and his throat went dry. "Cross-reference Admiral Killian Joyce. Cross-reference Killian Joyce, RWCC Stalwart *Devil's Bane*, and Helios Sanctus."

"Admiral Killian Joyce, RWCC Stalwart *Devil's Bane*, arrived Helios Sanctus 17-04-63, departed Helios Sanctus 17-04-63. Admiral Killian Joyce, RWCC Stalwart *Devil's Bane*, arrived Ultra Meridian 18-04-63, departed Ultra Meridian 18-04-6. Admiral Killian Joyce, RWCC Stalwart *Devil's Bane* arrived Scion of Hubris 18-04-63, departed 18-04-63. Admiral Killian Joyce, RWCC Stalwart *Devil's Bane* arrived Altas Arcane 20-04-63."

Healey's mind whirled. So far, everything the old man told him confirmed Davenport's claims.

How convenient that Admiral Joyce erased his movements from the Reserve Wing records. He covered up the fact that he'd been on Helios Sanctus just before the Ithium went missing.

He left the planet just in time for someone else to perpetrate the theft so he'd have an alibi for the time of the robbery.

Then he went to Ultra Meridian just like Davenport said he did. How interesting that the Ultra Meridian jail should go up in smoke within the time window when the *Devil's Bane* was on the planet.

Transmissions from the planet confirmed that atmospheric rocket fire destroyed the jail building.

Then the *Devil's Bane* stopped off at Scion of Hubris, but Admiral Joyce didn't make contact with the intelligence station. No one at the intelligence station knew Admiral Joyce was in the area. How did that happen?

The wires listed Davenport's point of origin as Scion of Hubris. He re-entered Ekol Thaine's service from Scion of Hubris and left Scion of Hubris in a Nitrol paid for by Ekol.

Healey wasn't so stupid not to connect the dots. How did Davenport get from Ultra Meridian to Scion of Hubris in the same time window that Admiral Joyce went there?

Davenport didn't have any space-capable craft at Ultra Meridian. That left one possibility. He went there with the Reserve Wing—the same Reserve Wing he claimed tried to kill him.

He signed on with Ekol to get himself off Scion of Hubris and to get the resources to find the Ithium. He wouldn't come all the way to Pandora's Needle for any other reason.

Okay, so Ekol wanted Davenport to find the Ithium for him, but Healey's interview with Davenport convinced him that Davenport really did want to stop the Ithium attack, no matter who planned to perpetrate it.

Healey had been in this job long enough to recognize the truth when he heard it. No incarcerated criminal he ever met actually volunteered to spend the rest of their life in Terminus Anathema. Only a true-blue lawman would say something like that.

Healey straightened up and walked away, but he didn't go back to the stairs. He left his deputies to wonder where he was while Healey made his way to the Windmill.

He walked around the block and entered through an alley between the casinos. He slipped through the back door and entered a dingy office with a single bare light bulb hung over the desk.

Vas glared at him when he entered. "You aren't welcome here. Go back to the jail where you belong."

"I go where I like in this town, Vas—unless you want to go back to the jail with me. I can find transport for you to Terminus Anathema any time you say."

She hunched over her desk and pretended to ignore him. "What do you want?"

"I want to know the exact date and time you alerted Admiral Killian Joyce that Davenport was back in town and under arrest at the jail."

Her head shot up and he saw at a glance that he was right. She was the one who told the Admiral that Davenport was on the Needle.

Healey didn't need to hear or see anymore. He walked out and made his way to the general allotment.

He found the *Artemis Rex* and the eight boys gathered around the loading hatch. A chubby boy held a white carton in his hands. "I say we open it and divide it between us. What do we have to lose?"

"You've been sniffing the Apricot mint again, fool," a tall, skinny one returned. "Davenport would skin you alive if you so much as broke the seal."

"Davenport isn't here. Besides, we can buy him another carton to replace this one."

"None of you is touching Davenport's JimJams," the blind boy snapped. "If any of you breaks that seal, I'll break you. Now put it back, Alla. I don't want to find out any of you touched that carton until we get back to....."

The blind kid's head shot up and he frowned as Healey approached. Healey stopped in front of them and sized them up in a flash.

They didn't look like much, but he knew too many Chorions to be fooled by their appearance. "You boys are pretty far from home."

"What do you want?" the blind one snapped. "What did you do with Davenport?"

"I helped him escape which means I helped *you* escape. Who do you think told him where he could find those explosives?"

The other boys looked at each other, but the blind one never looked away. He cocked his head and listened hard to Healey's voice. "What do you want with us?"

"I have a proposition for you. Davenport is no longer on Pandora's Needle. He left. You boys are on your own."

The hairy boy bared his sharp teeth and snarled in Healey's face. "You're a liar!" the blind one snapped. "Davenport wouldn't leave without us."

"He had to. If he stayed, he would have been killed by my deputies. He didn't want to go. He wanted to come back and look for Wolf and the rest of you, but some other friends dragged him away before he could get his head blown off. He really cares about you boys. He has a good heart, does Davenport."

"Then it's your fault he had to leave," Alla fired back.

"It's my fault he got away before Admiral Joyce tried to kill him again and succeeded this time. As it is, I'm here to offer you boys a chance to get your mitts on the Ithium instead of Davenport. You can ride back to Nyx Anonyma clothed in glory and give Ekol what he wants. You'll be heroes and I'm sure Ekol will be very proud."

Alla looked down at the carton in his hands.

"What about Davenport?" the blind boy asked.

Healey shrugged. "He's on the run. Admiral Joyce knows he's after the Ithium and he'll send out the Reserve Wing to bring him in. Admiral Joyce doesn't know about you boys. That's why I'm here. I'm going to Atlas Arcane where the admiral is keeping both the Ithium and the computer chip that goes with it. If you come with me, I'll help you get it back."

"How?" a chunky boy asked.

"I'll explain my plan on the way, but you can't take this ship. It's tagged as belonging to Ekol, so you'll have to ride with me in my ship. It's back at the jail."

"We aren't going back to the jail," the blind boy snapped. "You can forget that. We'll go after Davenport ourselves."

Healey only smiled. "I didn't mean that you would go back to the jail. My deputies are looking all over town for you boys. If you tried to launch in this, the Reserve Wing would shoot you down in seconds. I'll go back to the jail, get my ship, bring it here, and pick you up. Are we agreed?"

The boys exchanged glances again Then the blind boy nodded. "Agreed. Just understand that, if you mess with us, we'll slit your throat and steal your ship for ourselves."

Healey nodded. "I wouldn't expect anything else."

An hour later, he sat in the cockpit of his own Nitrol, the *Prometheus Vox*. He launched from the general allotment with the eight boys on board. He sailed away from Pandora's Needle and entered the atmosphere of Atlas Arcane.

The Confederate headquarters covered the whole planet in a sprawling city of glass and marble. It sparkled in the sun rising over the horizon as Healey angled the *Prometheus Vox* toward the ground.

"This is a real bad idea," Laub muttered. "We shouldn't be doing this."

"Don't worry about it," Healey replied over his shoulder. "Most of the people on this planet don't even know you exist."

"Let's keep it that way," Laub replied. "This place is a den of vipers."

"They would probably say the same thing about Nyx Anonyma. You remember what I told you. The admiral will keep the cartridge and the chip close to him. You won't have to go more than fifty feet from his office."

"Which is where everyone on the planet who *does* know we exist will also be," Rodeo pointed out. "If any of them recognize us, you'll be in the shit."

Healey didn't reply. Everyone around the Reserve Wing Central Command Unit knew him. He was counting on it.

He landed his ship on the roof and turned to the boys. "Admiral Joyce's office is on the tenth floor. That's where I'll be and I suggest you concentrate your search near it. It's liable to be under heavy security, so be careful and don't get caught."

"How do we do that?" Coon demanded.

Healey waved behind him toward the hatch. "I don't know. Snoop around. You boys are good at that."

He left them to it and entered the Reserve Wing Central Command Unit. Towering glass ceilings let soft sunlight into a huge atrium. Live trees stretched their branches to the light. Confederate personnel worked on every level.

Healey checked in with reception. "I'm here to see Admiral Killian Joyce. He's expecting me."

"Go right in, Sheriff."

Healey made his way to Joyce's office, but he didn't look forward to the interview at all. He had to play it cool so the admiral didn't suspect that Healey found out the truth.

He entered an office as big as the entire Pandora's Needle jail. Huge windows behind the admiral's sprawling desk gave a magnificent view across Atlas Arcane and its ultra-advanced landscape.

"I'll be right with you, Sheriff," the admiral told him. "Please, take a seat."

Healey remained standing. He didn't want this admiral getting friendly with him.

Healey wasn't here to make friends and he already gathered enough information on the Needle.

He didn't need the admiral to confess or even to confirm that he had the Ithium in his possession. Healey only had to give the boys time to find it.

The admiral finished fiddling with something on his console and looked up. He actually had the nerve to smile at Healey. "What can I do for you, Sheriff?"

"I'm very sorry to tell you this, Sir," Healey began, "but Sheriff Davenport escaped from Pandora's Needle. He broke out of the jail before I had a chance to transport him to Atlas Arcane. His friends on the *Echo Omicron* snatched him and they got away. I'm sorry, Sir. I know I failed you.....but I think I might know where they went."

Admiral Joyce raised his eyebrows. "Really? Where do you think they went?"

"Well, Sir, Davenport appears to be out of his mind with this lunatic Ithium story of his. He probably thinks he can track down where it went. He probably went to Helios Sanctus. He probably thinks he can solve the mystery on his own if he can prove it really was stolen. Of course he's delusional, Sir. He must be a madman. He might even be trying to release the Ithium himself."

The admiral's eyes lit up just as Healey expected. This guy was a sucker for anyone telling him what he wanted to hear. "That's an interesting story, Sheriff. I have an idea. You can track down Davenport for me. You can bring him into custody and end this crime spree across the galaxy."

Healey froze. "I don't think that's possible, Sir. I have my duties on the Needle. I couldn't just up stakes and....."

The admiral bent over his desk. "It's all settled, then. I'm pulling you off the Needle and promoting you to full Confederate Marshall. Davenport is too dangerous to run free any longer. You bring him in and bring him back here."

Healey opened his mouth, but the admiral's fingers already entered the change into his console. Healey's heart sank, but at least he might be able to help Davenport in this position.

If he refused, the admiral would send out someone else—someone who didn't know Davenport was innocent. Maybe Healey and Davenport could work together to stop the admiral's plot.

The admiral straightened up and his bright eyes found Healey's. "Congratulations, Marshall. You can stop by the supply house on your way out of town and pick up anything you need. I'm looking forward to you bringing this disaster to a successful conclusion."

Healey turned on his heel. That interview didn't go as planned, but maybe it was for the best after all.

He stopped outside the office and looked around him. The Central Command Unit buzzed with its usual productive activity. Were the boys inside somewhere? He would probably never know.

He set off for the exit when a deafening alarm screeched above his head. The whole Command Unit erupted in mayhem.

The Confederate staff raced down the landings and corridors all heading for their mustering points. They re-emerged carrying weapons and wearing flack gear. They spread through the building and arranged themselves at every possible exit.

Healey hustled to the stairs in a desperate hope of getting back to the *Prometheus Vox*. He covered ten paces when a squad of armed Confederate guards charged him.

They turned into a room to his right. Through the open door, he spotted a wall safe standing open in the wall adjacent to the admiral's office.

Healey's eyes dropped out of their sockets. The boys! They found the Ithium cartridge and they may actually have succeeded in stealing it.

The next minute, soldiers' heads blocked Healey's view and he tore himself away. He shoved his way through more soldiers arriving every minute, but he didn't see the Chorion Team. Where were they?

If the soldiers hadn't captured the boys already, the boys would make their way back to the *Prometheus Vox*. Healey's ship was their only way off the planet.

He picked up speed, but when he turned toward the stairs, he almost collided with Bandit and Breeze charging him from the other direction.

The other boys followed hot on their heels. Breeze tripped over and bowled the rest of the way to Healey's feet.

He crashed into Healey's shins and the other boys skidded to a halt. Fifty soldiers rushed them from behind and they drew their weapons to fire on the boys.

Healey leapt over Breeze, yanked his star off his vest, and marched over to the soldiers. "Hold your fire! Confederate Marshall! I'm taking these boys into custody. Hold your fire!"

The soldiers didn't move. They didn't lower their weapons, either. Another squad charged into view from lower down the landing. They closed the boys in hundreds of guns.

For a terrible second, the two sides held the boys at gunpoint. If the soldiers opened fire, Healey couldn't save them. He would get caught in the middle and he would go down, too.

He swiveled his star around to show it to the newcomers. "Confederate Marshall! These boys are my prisoners! Hold your fire!"

"You traitorous son of a bitch!" Alla roared.

Before Healey could turn around, the boys charged the downstairs squad. Healey didn't see exactly what happened, but the next thing he knew, Breeze hit the carpet and rolled straight into the squad. He toppled dozens of soldiers in his path and guns started going off.

The boys plowed deeper into the squad. The noise of gunfire triggered the upstairs squad. Both groups aimed their guns at him and at each other.

Healey ducked and took off running in the only direction available to him. He charged the railing, planted his hand, and vaulted over the side.

Chapter 30

Healey hovered in space trying to think of a way to save his own life The atrium plunged four floors beneath him, but the next instant, his fingers caught the railing.

He flipped around and swung onto the third-floor landing below. Gunfire erupted above his head.

He took off running for the stairs when another squad thundered onto the landing in front of him. They aimed their guns in his face. "Freeze! Don't move!"

He held his star aloft. "Confederate Marshall! I'm hunting the same fugitives you are! Take me to Admiral Joyce. He can vouch for me."

They didn't listen. They cocked their rifles and someone in the rear yelled, "Fire! Take him down!"

"Stop!" another voice boomed out.

Admiral Joyce stormed between the soldiers and planted himself next to Healey. "Did you hear what he just said? This man is a Confederate Marshall. Didn't you see his star?"

The soldiers shrank from the rebuke and finally lowered their weapons so they wouldn't be threatening the admiral.

Admiral Joyce spun around and fumed at Healey through gritted teeth. "Those vermin broke into my safe! You'll go after them and hunt them down, Marshall. I want those little shits dragged back here in chains. I'll make sure to interrogate them before they go up to Terminus Anathema. Do I make myself perfectly clear, Marshall?"

So the boys got away. The admiral didn't say if they got the Ithium and Healey didn't ask.

"Yes, Sir," Healey panted. "I was just going to suggest.....They're known criminal elements on Ekol Thaine's payroll. They must be working with Davenport if they're going after the...."

"You have your orders, Marshall," the admiral interrupted. "Everything else is just standing around talking. You can go."

Healey took his chance and scooted back to the *Prometheus Vox*. He had one way to find out if the boys got the Ithium. They'd be hiding on the ship and chomping at the bit to get off Atlas Arcane before the soldiers found them.

He strode onto the ship....and stopped. No sound greeted him and he knew his own vessel well enough to know when someone else was on board.

He strode to the cockpit....and listened. Nothing. Should he stick around and wait for them?

If they weren't here, they'd be on the run somewhere on Atlas Arcane. They'd be on the run with a cartridge of toxic poison capable of annihilating the whole Confederate Corps Central Command Unit.

Then he had a brain wave. He powered up and scanned the area for Chorion life signs.

He frowned at the console. No Chorion life signs turned up anywhere in the Central Command Unit. Could the boys possibly have left that fast?

He launched and swooped over the city. He passed his scanners over every building. How the hell did they get away so fast?

They weren't in the Central Command Unit. They weren't in the city at all. In fact, they weren't on the planet at all.

Only one possibility remained. He pointed his nose to the heavens and streaked back to Pandora's Needle. He landed in the general allotment right next to the *Artemis Rex* and boy, did he pick up Chorion life signs there.

He strode into the loading hatch and found the boys debating breaking into the JimJam carton again. "Davenport isn't even on the satellite anymore," Alla argued. "We have no idea where he is or even if he's still alive. I say we eat them."

"We can't do that, man," Rodeo told him. "We have a code of honor as Ekol's....."

He broke off when he heard Healey's footsteps banging on the hatch ramp. The group turned to stare at Healey. Then they all relaxed and Bandit laughed nervously. "Howdy, Sheriff."

"That's Marshall to you boys. I've been promoted in the last hour." He surveyed them one after the other. "So you broke into Joyce's safe. I'm impressed."

"That was the plan, wasn't it?" Coon asked.

"Did you get the Ithium?"

The boys exchanged glances. No one answered.

"Do yourselves a favor and tell me the truth. I have the authority to ground your vessel on this satellite until you cooperate with me."

"Give us one good reason we should trust you....." Rodeo pulled his sidearm and aimed it straight at Healey's head. For a blind kid, he could aim well enough to get the job done. "Give me one reason I shouldn't shoot you right now. You tried to stop us. You tried to apprehend us and turn us over to the Confederacy. You're our enemy."

Healey snorted. "You think I was trying to arrest you? I was trying to cover for you. The guards were about to blow you away. I tried to intervene so I could get you away from them." He checked the others. "Do you really think I took you to Atlas Arcane to get you arrested? If I wanted to do that, I could have done that here."

Rodeo didn't back down. "We're leaving and you can't stop us. If you take one step toward us, they'll find your bullet-riddled body on the tarmac."

"Will you pull your head out of your ass, kid? Jesus, you might be tough and all that, but you aren't that smart. Admiral Joyce authorized me to go after Davenport—and you. I went along with it so I could help Davenport get the Ithium back and stop the admiral from releasing it. Now, if you tell me one way or the other if you got it or not, we can make a plan to get it off the Needle before the admiral catches on that I'm helping you."

Dead silence greeted this. The boys fidgeted and looked back and forth from one to the other for several minutes before Rodeo finally lowered his gun. "Fine. Yes, we got the cartridge and the chip but we aren't handing them over to anyone but Ekol and that's final."

"What about Davenport? Aren't you even interested to find out what happened to him?"

Bandit shrugged. "He won't dare go back to Ekol without the cartridge. If he's still alive, he'll join up with us and maybe we'll go back to Nyx Anonyma together....."

"Or not," Axel interjected and the whole group laughed.

"Either way," Alla pointed out, "we'll have enough JimJams to feed ourselves for the next ten years so I guess we don't really need these." He tossed the carton back on the shelf where he found it.

"So what's your plan?" Healey asked. "You're going back to Nyx Anonyma without Davenport? How will go down with Ekol?"

Their smiles vanished. Healey saw right through their bravado. They didn't dare go back to Ekol without Davenport any more than Davenport dared to go back to Ekol without the Ithium.

"I'll tell you what I'll do, boys," Healey went on. "I'll let you get off the Needle, but I have to pretend to hunt you down. I'll be right on your asses all the way, and if we ever get into the same space, I'll have to shoot at you."

Alla gave a nervous giggle. "If you have to shoot at us, I guess we'll have to shoot back at you. That's how accidents happen, you know."

"I know. That's why I'm telling you. I want you to tell Davenport when you catch up with him that I'm trying to help him. Can you do that?"

"Sure," Coon replied. "We got the message."

"Then get off my Needle and quit dirtying up my territory."

He turned on his heel and strode back to the *Prometheus Vox*. He slipped into his cradle in the cockpit and trained his scanners on the *Artemis Rex*. The boys powered up within seconds of his departure, so they must have gotten the message loud and clear.

They sent the same clearance code to the tower to request authorization to launch. The tower flagged that code when the *Artemis Rex* arrived on the Needle.

The Drifter would have been shot down when it tried to leave, but Healey intervened and sent the tower his own personal clearance to let the ship go.

It rocketed away into space. Healey didn't like letting the boys take the Ithium away, but hopefully, with his help, Ekol would at least keep it out of Admiral Joyce's hands. That was a start.

Healey settled down to wait. He would give them an hour's head start before he took off and followed them. He pulled up his own service record and stared at the words: *Promotion: Confederate Marshall.*

Most sheriffs didn't get promoted to Marshall for decades. Some never got promoted at all and died as sheriffs.

He wasn't sure he could be happy about this promotion. He could see the upside, but he'd almost rather stay on his own little satellite with his own little.....

An emergency transmission startled him out of his thoughts. "RWCC Stalwart *Bluebird* to Dagger *Clockwork*, transmitting location of target *Echo Omicron* moving two-hundred-eleven degrees port, sixty degrees ascendent, traveling seventeen lightyears per hour....."

Healey strained his ears to listen. So the Reserve Wing found the *Echo Omicron*.

Another voice came over the Central Command Unit's communications link. "Central Command mustering Reserve Wing Union company to intercept."

Healey's hands shot to his stick. He fired the engines and yanked back hard on the helm. He had to get airborne fast. If he flew at his top speed, he just might be able to get to the *Echo Omicron* in time to stop a bloodbath.

Chapter 31

L yons let out a blood-curdling bellow. "Aarrgh! Stop it, you sadistic bastard!"

"I'm trying to help you, you ungrateful bitch!" Dice snarled.

"Well, stop trying to help me." She struggled to sit up and shoved him away. "Go do something useful."

"Right, because saving your worthless waste of a life definitely would NOT be doing humanity any favors." Dice flung down the gauze pad he'd been using to sop up the blood on her leg. He stormed to the next table in the *Echo Omicron's* crew lounge and flung himself down on the bench next to Davenport. "That's the last time I try to be nice to you."

Lyons collapsed back on the table where Dice put her when he brought her on board. Blood dripped onto the floor and Beauty slipped in it when he slouched over to her.

He squatted next to her and started to lift the torn fabric of her pants away from the wound.

"Leave me alone!" Lyons snarled. "Go help Fiddler."

Beauty gave her a withering glare, hopped off the table, and slipped in the puddle of blood again. His gangly limbs flew in all directions and he slammed down on the floor before he got his feet under him.

Dice turned to Davenport. "Will you talk some sense into her for the love of Christ? If she bleeds to death on the table where we're supposed to eat, we'll never get the stains out."

Davenport didn't look up. He wrenched his spanner in the anionic reverter and snarled when the tool slipped. "I can't get it. You'll have to do it, Beauty. I don't know enough about these things to get the ship running."

"The ship is running fine," Dice countered. "What's wrong with it?"

Davenport made a face. "We're running at seventeen lightyears an hour. That's nowhere near fast enough to get us away if the Reserve Wing comes after us."

"If?" Beauty looked up and swiveled his ears toward Davenport. "I think you mean when."

"All the more reason we need to get moving." Davenport threw down his spanner. "I'm going to see if I can get that engine reattached. It was hanging by a thread the last I checked."

Dice stood up. "I'll come with you."

Davenport stopped in his tracks. "Do you know how to reattach it? I don't know for sure, but if I had to guess, I'd say you couldn't fit through the access crawlspace."

"He can't," Beauty called from his place crouching over Fiddler.

Davenport held up his hand. "You stay here. Go help Beauty."

"Don't help Beauty," Beauty countered.

"You see?" Dice told Davenport. "He has the situation under control here."

"Help Lyons," Davenport suggested.

"Don't help Lyons," Lyons countered.

"You see?" Dice asked. "She doesn't need help. She's just fine. She'll be right as the mail any second now."

"Well, you can't come with me," Davenport told him. "You're too big. Sorry, but you'll only get in the way."

"Well, what exactly am I supposed to do?"

At that moment, Fiddler shot off the table with an ear-piercing scream. She hurtled upright so fast that she bowled Beauty straight off the end of the table. He tumbled smack into the blood pool again. Fiddler stared around in petrified shock.

"That was sudden," Dice remarked.

Beauty flailed to get out of the muck on the floor, failed, and fell down again. Davenport went over and picked him up, but Beauty thrashed out of Davenport's grip, went down all over again, and finally wallowed over to a dry part of the floor.

He shot Davenport a hideous glare. "Liar!"

Davenport sighed. "I told you, Beauty. I got you a whole carton of JimJams, but...."

"Liar!" Beauty screeched. "You don't talk to me about JimJams! Never talk to me about JimJams again."

"You really did it this time," Dice observed. "You should know better than to tell him stories like that. You'll only make him mad."

"It isn't a story," Davenport replied. "It's the truth."

Dice only shook his head and Beauty turned his back on Davenport. He put his foot in the blood to go back to Fiddler's table again, but he drew back and shrank away from the spot that caused him so much trouble.

Davenport gave it up. "Fine. We won't talk about....*that*. How about you go help Dice get the ship moving a little faster? I'll take care of these two."

"I don't need taking care of," Lyons fired back.

Davenport turned around to say something, but at that moment, her eyes rolled back in her head and she flopped backward onto the table. Her arms fell off the table and hung from her shoulders. Her head lolled to the side.

Dice heaved a great sigh. "Thank Christ we won't have to listen to her attitude anymore."

Davenport went to work on Lyons's legs. Beauty had wrapped a loose bandage around them, but she interfered so much he hadn't been able to tighten them enough to stop the bleeding.

Davenport started to untie and retie them while he talked to Fiddler over his shoulder. "How you doing, girl? You've been out for hours. Do you have any pain anywhere?"

She glanced at him and then looked around in a daze. She opened her mouth a few times like she had no earthly clue where she was.

Finally, she looked down at her own body and pressed her hand to her sternum. "Here."

Davenport jerked his chin at her chest while he worked. "Let me see."

"Oh, I am SO sticking around to see this!" Dice crossed the lounge in one step, swung his leg over the bench, and sat back down at the table where he was before.

He propped his big ugly head in both hands and gaped at Fiddler with a huge shit-eating grin lighting up his dial.

Fiddler looked around again. "Am I....am I dead?"

"You aren't dead—just injured," Davenport told her. "Lift up your shirt."

Dice almost shot out of his seat when she pulled her belt loose, tugged her shirt out of her waistband, and hitched up her shirt. Dice wilted a second later when he saw her bra covering anything interesting he might have hoped to see.

"Huh!" he huffed. "So much for that. Come on, Beauty. The engines are more interesting than this."

He stalked out of the lounge followed by Beauty who left damp red footprints on his way out of sight.

Fiddler turned her eyes up to Davenport. "Am I gonna be all right?"

"You're gonna be fine." He scanned her chest. Blue-black bruises covered the left side of her ribs, her left collarbone, and even extended down to her stomach, but he didn't see any external injuries. "It doesn't hurt to breathe?"

"Not really."

"You're gonna be sore for a few days, but you should be fine." He left Lyons, went to the medical kit that Beauty left lying around, and came back with a syringe loaded with painkillers.

"I would give you a lot more of these, but I need you conscious and functional—just in case. If I gave you enough to totally knock out the pain, you'd be unconscious for three days. Roll up your sleeve. You can put your shirt down."

She obeyed him in a trance. She didn't notice when he injected the drugs into her elbow.

He put the syringe away. "I have to patch up Lyons now. You should maybe go to your quarters and lie down for a while. We might have to call you up at any time."

She looked around again and Davenport turned his attention to Lyons. He needed to stitch the wounds closed and probably give her a blood transfusion.

He brought the medical kit to her side and changed the bench that Beauty splashed blood on to a clean one.

He sat down when Emmet's voice echoed down the corridor outside. "We got company! You might want to come up here and take a look at this."

Davenport got to the bridge at the same time as Fiddler, Dice, and Beauty. "We got an unidentified Drifter coming out from the Needle," Emmet reported. "It's on an intercept course straight for us!"

Davenport took one look at the console under Emmet's hands. *Artemis Rex*. "It's friendly! Adjust course to rendezvous with them."

"Forget that!" Dice bellowed. "The Reserve Wing is on your ass. They must have followed you."

"Someone followed us, all right, and they're friendly. These are the boys I told you about. They're coming out to meet us. If we're lucky, we can transfer to the *Artemis Rex* and dump this broken-down crate for the fastest Drifter around. Alter course, Emmet."

Emmet scowled, but he did what Davenport told him to. He turned the *Echo Omicron*, but the crippled engines could barely limp. In the end, the *Artemis Rex* came to meet the ailing ship.

The communications link flickered to life and Rodeo's face appeared on the display. "*Echo Omicron*, this is *Artemis Rex*. Do you copy?"

"We copy, *Artemis Rex*." Davenport had to hold back the urge to laugh in relief. "Damn, it's good to see you, boy! Do you have all your crew on board?"

"Every last one of 'em—and two very small passengers—one cylindrical in shape and highly illegal—the other small, square, electronic, and also highly illegal. We met them in a safe on Atlas Arcane and they begged us for passage back to Nyx Anonyma."

"He's loopy," Dice grumbled.

"He's a genius!" Davenport breathed. "Congratulations, boy. I can't wait to return those passengers to their home planet. Do you also have a certain white package still on board and intact?"

Rodeo burst out laughing. "Don't let Alla hear you talking like that. We nearly lost it more than once when you went on your little vacation without us. We all had to work hard to stop him from helping himself."

"You're as crazy as he is," Emmet muttered over his shoulder.

"I hope so. Let's rendezvous somewhere. Are there any friendly planets nearby? This ship is falling apart around our ears. We need to jettison it and transfer to the *Artemis Rex*."

Rodeo frowned and did something on his instruments. "How many do you mean by 'we'?"

"Six including me."

"It'll be tight, but we'll manage it."

"It's only a short flight back to Nyx Anonyma," Davenport pointed out. "We can stand in the back if we have to."

"You just might. I'm transmitting coordinates for Argus Borealis. It's uninhabited. We can land there and make the transfer."

Just before Rodeo switched off, Bandit's face darted into view. "Hello, Sir!"

Rodeo shoved him out of the way. "Just fly the ship, boy!"

Davenport laughed and then the link cut out. "You are NOT jettisoning the *Echo Omicron*," Dice snarled. "Lyons will kill you."

"Then I guess it's a good thing she's out cold in the lounge." Davenport turned back to Rodeo. "We received your coordinates. We're on our way."

His hand moved to the link when Bandit screamed out, "Hold it! The Reserve Wing is leaving Pandora's Needle on an intercept course."

"An intercept course with who?" Emmet asked. "Are they after you or us?"

"Both! They're arming! This is gonna get messy."

Davenport rounded on his friends. "Man the gun range! Prepare to defend the ship!"

Dice, Beauty, Fiddler, and Davenport raced for the range and Davenport took his place with them. The targeting grid blinked on and showed the Reserve Wing closing in.

"I don't feel so good," Fiddler mumbled next to him.

Davenport glanced over at her. Her skin took on a greenish cast and her eyelids kept sinking like she might pass out at any moment.

"Just do your best. If you need to sit down, go ahead."

A scream of engine noise jerked him around to face his grid. The *Artemis Rex* whizzed past the *Echo Omicron* in a blinding streak. The Drifter gunned its engines and raced ahead to cut off the Reserve Wing, but that ruse could only buy the *Echo Omicron* a few seconds at most.

The *Artemis Rex* plunged into the Reserve Wing and the Howitzers opened up on all sides. The Reserve Wing obliged by rounding on the Drifter in swarms. They surrounded the *Artemis Rex*, but the Drifter flew way too fast for them to stop it.

The ship plummeted through the cloud and out the other side to draw the Reserve Wing away. Three Reserve Wing vessels followed, but the rest continued on their previous course to intercept the *Echo Omicron*.

"Here they come!" Dice bellowed.

Davenport swung his gun forward. "Open fire!"

He, Fiddler, Dice, and Beauty laid into the Reserve Wing with everything they had. For one moment, they battered the enemy to a standstill. A curtain of fire blocked the Reserve Wing's advance.

The *Artemis Rex* screamed around behind the Reserve Wing and came rocketing back to strike from behind. The Drifter careened into their midst and a bouquet of shots splintered from every corner. The Drifter's guns wheeled to match the speed and trajectory of everyone involved.

The three vessels pursuing the *Artemis Rex* saw the dragnet closing and dodged on either side. They screamed around the Drifter and pounded the crippled *Echo Omicron* with dozens of shots.

The gunners unloaded back at them, but the ancient smuggler's craft couldn't keep up with high-tech vessels like this. Two of the enemy concentrated on the bridge. Fiddler and Dice defended the ship, but Davenport smelled a rat.

Sure enough, the third ship zoomed around the *Echo Omicron* and struck the ship hard in the tail. The *Echo Omicron* wheeled out of control and the second engine ripped away with a bone-crunching screech that vibrated through the ship.

"We're finished!" Emmet yelled. "We've got nothing—absolutely nothing!"

Davenport swung his gun hard to starboard, but the attacker already pelted around the *Echo Omicron's* other side. Fiddler saw it sweeping in for another strike and she yanked her weapon hard to the left for a counterattack.

With only one gun protecting the ship in front, the other two attackers broke free of Dice's defense. They plunged in to help their comrades. At the same moment, the rest of the Reserve Wing overran the *Artemis Rex*.

The Drifter fell back to help the stricken *Echo Omicron*, but it was all too little too late. The Reserve Wing paid no attention to the *Artemis Rex* and surrounded the *Echo Omicron*. Another barrage sent one engine twirling off into space while the other detonated with a powerful thump against the hull.

The explosion knocked the ship sideways and it rolled onto its port wing. The Reserve Wing smashed the ship's exposed underside bowling it end over end and wing over wing.

Overpowering G-force tore Davenport's hands off his gun. He crashed into the ceiling and then tumbled into the wall.

Dice's enormous body landed on top of him and Davenport groaned in pain. A second later, another catastrophic blow hurled Dice away and flung everyone into a confused heap on top of their useless guns.

Screams and bellows of rage, pain, and confusion punctured Davenport's brain. He didn't stay in one position long enough to see whether the others were alive or dead. Incessant pounding deafened him and jostled his brain into a muddle.

Another devastating impact sent everyone careening out of the range. Fiddler slammed into the wall right next to the door leading to the bridge. "Emmet!" she screamed. "Help us!"

No one answered. Davenport caught one glimpse into the bridge. It was empty. An-other shot sizzled across the hull by his head and the ship creaked in agony.

Impossible force yanked him backward once again. He barely caught hold of the doorframe in time to stop himself from falling with the others.

He fought against pain and vertigo to haul himself onto the bridge. Every terminal lay dead and unresponsive to his touch.

He scrambled to the pilot's station and almost got hurled against the ceiling when the Reserve Wing pivoted around the *Echo Omicron's* nose.

Davenport stared at them in dumb shock. They targeted the bridge and there was no way in hell he could stop them. Five Daggers positioned themselves beyond the window where he couldn't miss them.

His hands fell off the terminal and he straightened up. He didn't bother to hold onto anything this time. The Daggers' guns swiveled to finish him off.

A scattered barrage of shots blasted toward the window. At that moment, the *Artemis Rex* vaulted into their path and took the shots across its starboard shields. The Drifter pirouetted and stalled there between the Reserve Wing and the *Echo Omicron*.

The next second, seven enormous Stalwarts rocketed into view. They joined their fire to the Daggers and blasted the *Artemis Rex* out of Davenport's view.

Another cataclysmic explosion went off somewhere behind Davenport's back. He couldn't see the rest of the Reserve Wing assaulting the *Echo Omicron* from behind.

The scene outside the window jerked to one side and every other ship vanished. The *Echo Omicron* went into a spin.

Davenport crouched on the floor holding onto the pilot's station. He hoped like hell the boys made it out of this with the Ithium intact. Nothing else mattered.

The stars whizzed aside beyond the window. The ship tumbled faster and faster until, to his horror, he spotted a blue and green planet coming closer each time the window rotated past it.

The *Echo Omicron* somersaulted one more time and then plummeted nose first for the densely foliated surface.

"Brace for impact!" he bellowed to anyone who might be able to hear him.

He told himself to duck and cover, but his addled brain refused to look away from the window. He must have a death wish. The ship screamed through the atmosphere until the thick forest blocked out all else. No way could the ship survive this impact.

He forced himself to turn away when, at the last second before the collision, the *Artemis Rex* rocketed in front of the *Echo Omicron*. The *Echo Omicron* glanced off the *Artemis Rex's* upper fuselage.

The *Artemis Rex* ricocheted off at an odd angle and smashed into the trees, but that one instant of shock took enough of the ship's momentum to soften its fall.

The *Echo Omicron* crashed into hundreds of trees. Thick trunks stabbed through the window and into the bulkhead behind. The ship plowed its nose into the soil and skidded for a mile before the forest stopped it.

Its fall ripped the hull apart and shot Davenport out of his hiding place. His spine cracked across the shattered window frame and he lost consciousness.

Chapter 32

"**Y**ou're bleeding." Fiddler shoved a square of gauze into Davenport's hand.

He swiped it across his eyebrow and threw it away soaked in blood and sweat. "Get the antibiotics, will you?"

She left him alone and he went back to stitching up Lyons's legs. He'd been at it for over an hour and he was almost finished with the first of ten long gashes. Fiddler came back and set the antibiotics ampule next to his elbow along with the syringe.

He didn't say anything. She wiped away the blood dripping into his eyes without asking. He knotted the next stitch when, also without asking, she sprayed some skin-tack on the cut.

He winced against the sting, but he didn't stop stitching. She left a second time and came back with a coil of plastic tubing, a wrapped needle cannula, and a few clamps. He didn't thank her. That would only cost valuable time.

Coon and Rodeo strolled into the *Echo Omicron's* crew lounge. Rodeo bent over to watch Davenport work like he could somehow see the stitches.

Whatever he might be able to sense must have met with his approval because he didn't comment on the sewing job. "The cabin's ready on the *Artemis Rex*."

"Good. Where's Beauty?"

"I don't know. No one has seen him since the wreck."

Davenport paused with his needle and forceps poised. "He's alive, isn't he? He survived the crash. Didn't he?"

"Dice says he saw Beauty slipping away into the forest."

Davenport went back to work. "As long as he survived the crash, he'll be fine."

"Do you need him for something?" Coon asked. "We could go out and find him."

"Do you need him to fix the *Artemis Rex*?" Davenport asked. "How bad is the damage?"

"We took some damage, but we can handle the repairs ourselves."

"Then leave Beauty alone."

Bandit walked in, marched straight up to Davenport, and took the forceps out of his hand. "I'll do that."

"No!" Davenport tried to fight him off, but Coon and Rodeo grabbed Davenport, too. They held him while Bandit took the clamp and suture out of his hands. "You're exhausted and you're injured. You're in no condition to fix up Lyons."

"Hey!" Davenport struggled against Coon and Rodeo's combined efforts to wrestle him out of the room. The minute they got him off the bench, Bandit sat down in Davenport's place and went to work with fast, sure movements.

Coon and Rodeo pushed Davenport toward the door. When he tried to get back inside, they barricaded his path.

"You have two choices," Rodeo informed him. "You can sit down and let Fiddler take a look at the gash on your forehead, or we can drag you off to the *Artemis Rex* where Laub and Alla will sedate you into next year while Fiddler takes a look at the gash on your forehead. It's up to you which one."

Davenport looked around him. Besides the two boys standing up to him, Bandit kept shooting determined glances over his shoulder. He barely looked at the stitches while he worked.

He would get up and help his friends restrain Davenport. Davenport never doubted that for an instant. He knew these boys too well to question their resolve when they set their minds to something.

Fiddler pulled him toward the door. "Come on, Davenport. Come over to the *Artemis Rex*. The *Echo Omicron* is finished. We'll abandon it as soon as Bandit finishes patching up Lyons. You'll be a lot more comfortable on the Drifter."

"What about....? Lyons needs a blood transfusion."

"What's your blood type?" Rodeo asked.

Davenport bowed his head. They had him. He couldn't think of one more decent excuse to stick around, but he didn't want to leave. He hated abandoning the *Echo Omicron* with an injured crewman on board, especially the captain.

Fiddler gave him one more tug and he gave it up. He let her lead him back to the *Artemis Rex*.

The huge gash the *Echo Omicron* carved in the forest sliced through compact vegetation all around them. The ship had slid nose first to the edge of a crystal mirror lake set between wooded mountains.

The *Artemis Rex* rested on its landing gear on the pebbled shore. Fiddler steered him toward the loading hatch, but Davenport paused on the beach to take in the sight. He'd been stranded at Ultra Meridian for so long he almost forgot about places like this.

He didn't forget they existed somewhere in the galaxy, but he forgot the feeling they gave him. He forgot about that expansive ache in his heart.

It made him feel like he was missing something. Pain and longing burned a hole in his heart that only a place like this could fill.

He spotted movement across the lake, but he didn't give it a second thought. He rummaged in his mind to remember something, something only this place could bring back to him.

"Davenport...." Fiddler began.

He glanced over at her, and for the first time, he noticed the concern in her eyes. Her brows came together in the middle and she scrutinized him with special intensity. "Don't worry, girl. I'm all right."

"Davenport.....You need to sit down—now."

He didn't understand that bite in her tone. He felt perfectly normal....except for a splitting headache, but that was normal considering how hard he hit when the ship crashed.

She took his elbow and led him inside the *Artemis Rex*. She took him to a random compartment. When he tried to remember which compartment it was, he came up blank.

She sat him on the bunk. Where exactly was he? Now that he stopped working and sat down, his mind seemed to be shutting down by the minute.

She rotated around him doing something. When she came back, she cupped his chin and held a device against his temple. "One of your pupils is distorted. You suffered a head injury. I have to anesthetize your skull and relieve the pressure."

"I told you I feel fine."

"Just sit still. This won't take long, but if we don't treat it now, you could die....and we wouldn't want that, would we?"

He looked up at her, and for a minute, he wasn't sure who she was. She looked like his older sister's best friend. Then she looked like a younger version of one of his aunts.

Then, when he blinked, she changed into a Friad assassin who used to work for Ekol, but she couldn't be her because that woman died in a raid fifteen years ago.

She dripped something ice-cold onto his scalp. The cold burned, but a moment later, the pain vanished.

Then she held a different device against his head. It hummed and buzzed. A rush of hot fluid oozed down his cheek and his mind cleared. He could think as well as ever.

She walked away and arranged her toolbox on a table by the door. Now he recognized where he was. He was in the *Artemis Rex's* tiny sick bay.

She came back with another tool. "I'll just fuse the skull closed. You'll probably feel sore for a while, but I'll keep an eye on you and open it up again if you need it. I'll give you some painkillers, but not very much. We need you conscious, just in case."

He looked up at her and laughed. "You have a very comforting bedside manner for a smuggler."

She beamed down at him and her eyes shone even more. "I learn from the best. Roll up your sleeve." She gave him an injection. "Can you stand without getting dizzy?"

He stood up. "I feel fine."

She shone a light in both his eyes to check his pupils. "The distortion is disappearing. You can go."

"Thank you, Doctor." He left the sick bay and would have walked back to the *Echo Omicron* when he remembered.

He turned off to the loading hatch and found the crates and containers of food the boys took from Ekol's storehouse.

He rummaged everywhere, but he didn't find what he was looking for. Then he remembered what Rodeo said about Alla wanting to eat the JimJams when Davenport vanished.

He went to one of the *Artemis Rex's* three crew cabins. As he expected, he found the carton on a shelf next to Alla's bunk. The seal was still intact. Amazing. These boys must have taken their agreement seriously, but then again, Davenport knew they would.

He took the carton back to the beach and took a bearing where he'd seen the movement across the lake. Rodeo said this planet was uninhabited, which meant only one thing could be moving out there.

He took off hiking. He followed the lakeshore to its opposite side and found Beauty squatting on a rock. The lake's glassy surface perfectly reflected every detail of the surrounding mountains.

Beauty snarled at Davenport. "You go away! Filthy liar!"

Davenport held out the carton. "These are for you, Beauty. You can eat them all right here where no one can see you. You don't have to share them with anyone and you don't have to tell anybody you ate them all, but I would really appreciate it if you told the boys I gave them to you. They don't believe I didn't bring them for myself."

Beauty glanced down at the carton and back at Davenport. He snarled and bared his teeth. "Did you steal my JimJams, filthy JimJam thief?"

"The seal is intact. See?" Davenport rotated the carton so Beauty could see the seal. "I didn't steal them. Ekol Thaine gave them to me so I could give them to you and I didn't take even one of them. Do you know, Beauty, I don't even like JimJams? These are all for you. I brought them for you."

Beauty's gaze darted to the carton. Davenport held it out to him. "Take it. I want you to have these."

Beauty's scrawny arm shot out and he stripped the carton from Davenport's grasp. Beauty clutched the carton to his chest, but he didn't once take his suspicious eyes off Davenport.

They regarded each other for a moment, but when Davenport still didn't move, Beauty shut his eyes, turned up his nose, and inhaled a long, deep sniff. "JimJams!"

"Aren't you going to eat them?"

Beauty lowered his eyes to the carton. He beamed at it with undisguised longing, but he didn't tear into it. He didn't even break the seal. "JimJams!" he breathed.

Davenport chuckled and walked all the way back to the *Echo Omicron*, but he didn't find anyone on board, not even Lyons. The lounge was as bloody and desecrated as he left it.

He made his way over to the *Artemis Rex* and found all eight boys, Fiddler, Emmet, and Dice sitting on crates just inside the loading hatch. Davenport pulled up a seat next to Alla. A pristine white carton lay open on the boy's knees.

Alla picked out a perfectly round, purple rubber disc and bit into it. He rolled his eyes in ecstasy. "Mmm. The blueberry ones really are the best."

"Have you had that on board all this time?" Davenport demanded. "Were you eyeing Beauty's JimJams when you had your own stash all along?"

"Oh, you don't ever want to underestimate Alla's appetite," Axel called. "He never goes anywhere without a guaranteed supply."

"You better not let Beauty hear you say that," Dice interjected. "He can sniff out hidden food like no one else. If he finds your stash, you won't have any stash left at all."

Rodeo pulled a sealed plastic bag out of a crate near his ankle. "Are you hungry, Sir? You don't want to miss out."

"Sure," Davenport replied. "What do you have?"

"Dominos." Rodeo tore the bag open and pulled out a fistful of black squares dotted with white. He stuck one in his mouth and handed the bag to Davenport.

Davenport took some, too, and munched them listening to the banter flying around the circle.

Dice unlatched a crate and jerked away when he bent over to examine the contents. "Ugh! ChunkyTenders! We ate nothing but ChunkyTenders for the last year and a half. I don't think I can look at another ChunkyTender as long as I live."

"Send 'em over here," Fiddler told him. "I'll trade you the ChunkyTenders for the BoilBuns."

"Deal." Dice gave the crate a shove and sent it sliding across the floor. It bumped into Fiddler's seat.

She wound back her arm and tossed him another bag full of spherical doughballs congealed into a solid mass of starch. Dice caught it and pried one of the BoilBuns off the blob.

"Hey, look at this!" Bandit called out. "I found a bottle of Ramrock. Did any of you boys load that on?"

"Ramrock?" Coon turned in Bandit's direction. "We aren't allowed swill like that on missions."

"Or at all," Axel replied. "Ekol doesn't allow any of his staff to drink."

Davenport pricked up his ears and turned to see Bandit holding a square bottle full of the amber liquid. The seal on that hadn't been broken, either.

"Did you know Babcock had this stuff in his warehouse?" Bandit asked Rodeo.

"Babcock doesn't keep swill in his warehouse. Ekol wouldn't allow him to have it on Nyx Anonyma, either."

"Then how did it end up in our gear?" Coon asked. "If none of us put it there, who did?"

Bandit glanced up at Davenport. "You didn't bring it, did you, Sir?"

"Don't ask him that, twerp!" Rodeo snapped. "If he brought a full, unsealed bottle of Ramrock on board, he sure as hell wouldn't leave it lying around in our ration crates for you to find. Of course he didn't bring it."

Rodeo stood up, strode across the floor, and snatched the bottle out of his friend's hand. He shoved it toward Davenport, deposited it in Davenport's empty grasp, and walked back to his seat.

"What are you doing, fool?" Axel demanded.

"Who you calling fool, fool?" Rodeo fired back. "Use the brain God gave you for once in your life. If you didn't put it there and I didn't put it there and we aren't even allowed swill like that on Nyx Anonyma or off of it, there's only one answer. Babcock must have put it there and there's only one person on board he could have left it for."

All eyes turned to Davenport, but he couldn't look away from the label. A whole bottle of Ramrock all to himself!

"Aren't you going to open it, Sir?" Alla asked hopefully. "Aren't you going to drink it?"

Davenport rotated the bottle in his hands. He felt exactly like Beauty with his unopened box of JimJams. Ramrock!

That word sent a flood of bliss through him. He didn't have to drink it. He only wanted to have it, to gaze at it, and know it was all his. It would be waiting for him when he finally got to the end of his tether and cracked that seal.

He looked up to find Wolf sitting at his heel. The boy held a box of JuicyPies in one hand. With the other, he scooped out one pie after another, tore the wrappers off with his teeth, and crammed them into his mouth. He barely finished chewing before he attacked the next one.

"Here's what I want to know," Dice began. "We have the Ithium and the chip, so what are we going to do with them?"

"We can't take them back to Helios Sanctus," Fiddler remarked. "Admiral Joyce or whoever would only steal them again."

"We aren't really handing them over to Ekol Thaine, are we?" Emmet asked. "Please tell me we haven't sunk as low as that."

"We aren't giving them to Ekol because we haven't completed our mission." Davenport stuck the bottle of Ramrock into his jacket pocket and pulled his attention back to the present. "There's a third component and we still have to retrieve it to stop this plot."

"Third component?" Fiddler asked. "What third component?"

"We don't know what it is. A ship called the *Blood Calliope* was carrying the third component when it crashed somewhere near Ultra Meridian. We're going back there to find it."

Dice frowned. "*Blood Calliope*? I know that ship."

"Our contact on Pandora's Needle said the *Blood Calliope* rendezvoused with the *Echo Omicron* after leaving Helios Sanctus."

Dice nodded. "I remember now. They handed off the Ithium. They were the ones who stole it from Helios Sanctus and they passed it to us for transport to Sacron Enigma."

Davenport stiffened. "You were taking the Ithium to Sacron Enigma?"

"Sure. Why else would we need to get a stamp from Ultra Meridian? Our job was to get it across the boundary so the Confederate Corps couldn't find it."

"Why does that matter?" Fiddler asked. "If the third component is near Ultra Meridian, it should be easy enough to find."

"I said it's *near* Ultra Meridian. I didn't say it was on the planet. Ekol said the *Blood Calliope* crashed on the planet, but our contact at the Needle says the ship had already left Ultra Meridian when it disappeared. DTF9Q logged the ship before it vanished."

"That doesn't help much, does it?" Bandit remarked. "The ship could be anywhere."

"I'm just telling you what I heard. I'd much rather believe it was on solid ground at Ultra Meridian than floating somewhere in the vastness of space."

"I never heard of any *Blood Calliope* going down on Ultra Meridian," Fiddler added.

Davenport glanced at her out of the corner of his eye. He didn't even bother to ask why she thought she'd know of every shipwreck on the planet. She and her friends must know a damn sight more about what went on at Ultra Meridian than he ever did.

"If we're going back to Ultra Meridian or anywhere else to search for this mysterious third component," Emmet asked, "shouldn't we find a safe place to stash the Ithium first? Surely there must be a safer place for an Ithium cartridge than on board a Drifter whizzing around the galaxy getting into epic battles against the Reserve Wing."

"Admiral Joyce needs all three components to launch his attack—whatever that is."

"So he'll be even more obsessed with wiping us out once we get the third component," Rodeo pointed out. "I agree with Emmet. We should hide the Ithium and the chip. That way, if we get caught—or more likely killed—he won't be able to find them."

"You're forgetting one thing," Dice countered. "He knows where we are. The Reserve Wing saw us crash on this planet, which means they'll be watching for us to try to leave. We can either hide the Ithium here, in which case they'll look here, or we can hide it somewhere else, in which case we have to fight our way off this planet just to get there—wherever there is."

Davenport pointed at him. "Give that man a cigar. I'm impressed, Dice. I didn't know you had it in you."

Dice snarled at him. "I'm more than just a pretty face, pal."

"So we're going back to Ultra Meridian." Emmet huffed. "I can't shittin' wait."

"First, we have to dig up as much intel on the *Blood Calliope* as we can. We need to come up with some identifying feature so we can scan Ultra Meridian from orbit to see if the ship is on the planet."

"No, we don't," Fiddler countered. "All we have to do is ask Friend. If it's on the planet, she can tell us."

Davenport shrugged and helped himself to another Domino. At the rate he was going, he might not get another decent meal for a while. "Fine. We'll ask Friend, but if it isn't on the planet and we have to search Sacron Enigma, we'll still need some traceable feature we can scan for."

"No. You don't," Fiddler repeated. "You just ask Friend. She'll be able to transmit any traceable feature so you can scan for the *Blood Calliope*."

"Now just hold the phone, lady," Dice growled. "How do you know Friend will be able to identify one ship out of billions? If it didn't go down on the planet....."

"The *Blood Calliope* is attached to the Reserve Wing, isn't it? It must have been—or it was." Fiddler glanced over at Davenport. "It would have to be if it got clearance to land at Helios Sanctus. It's an ex-Reserve Wing vessel."

"I'm willing to bite. So Friend has statistics on every Reserve Wing vessel?" Why did Davenport even bother to ask? Of course Friend had statistics on every Reserve Wing vessel and a lot more besides. She probably had statistics on every smuggler's vessel, every gang vessel, every criminal syndicate vessel, every Ekol Thaine vessel, and every other vessel in creation.

"That settles it, then." Rodeo put down his bag of Dominos. "The feast is over. It's time to get back to work"

Chapter 33

Rodeo, Wolf, and Davenport stood up. The others took longer finishing their snacks. Alla didn't move and neither did Dice or Emmet. They just kept right on eating.

Davenport stuffed the last Domino into his mouth and wadded up the wrapper when a strange crunching noise came from the open hatch. He and Rodeo looked outside.

Davenport stared at dozens of large, armored creatures digging their way out of the ground. Their domed carapaces concealed everything except hundreds of tiny legs carrying them along the ground.

As soon as they popped out of the soil, they took flight. Davenport didn't see how they did it. Maybe they jumped.

They sailed through the air and stuck with a clank to the *Echo Omicron's* hull.

As soon as they landed, they started crunching into the metal. They chewed their way in tangled curlicue patterns. They wove in and out of each other eating the hull to shreds.

"Please tell me you moved Lyons over to the *Artemis Rex*," Davenport murmured.

"She's in one of the crew compartments," Rodeo replied. "We cleared as much gear off the *Echo Omicron* as we could."

Davenport started to relax at those words. He could lose the *Echo Omicron*, but in a few seconds, so many of the creatures clustered on the *Echo Omicron's* crumpled fuselage that they kept bumping into each other.

One or two popped off and soared toward the *Artemis Rex*. The first three hit the dirt and then bounced up. They stuck to the Drifter and started chewing.

Davenport rocketed from the opening and yanked his sidearm. "Power up the engines! Get us off the surface—quick!"

Rodeo vanished inside. Davenport jumped down the hatch ramp and spun around. He fired at the creatures eating into the ship, but his shots only deflected off their shells. He was just planning to go inside and get a Howitzer when the engines screamed to life.

The ship started to lift off the ground. He hustled back to the ramp and ducked inside. The Drifter wheeled over the forest with the creatures still clinging to the hull. Their crunching bites resounded through the ship.

Davenport raced to the cockpit, but by the time he got there, the creatures had dislodged themselves and fallen back to the surface. They returned to the *Echo Omicron*. As the *Artemis Rex* lifted higher into the atmosphere, the *Echo Omicron* crumbled and vanished under hundreds of bodies.

"Damn!" Dice growled. "I was just beginning to like that place."

"Reserve Wing coming in fast!" Bandit yelled from the pilot's cradle.

Davenport dropped into his seat between Bandit and Rodeo. He could already see the Reserve Wing closing around Argus Borealis to cut off the *Artemis Rex's* escape.

"Stand by to fire!" Rodeo ordered. "We have to break through and get to Ultra Meridian."

"Wait!" Davenport called back. "Not so fast."

"You're kidding, right?" Rodeo sneered. "If we get shot down here, we're finished. Those bug things will devour our ship and the Reserve Wing will finish us off."

"Take a tour through the Reserve Wing, Bandit," Davenport ordered. "You boys stand by to fire, but don't break through. Annoy them enough to follow us."

"Follow us!" Rodeo snorted. "Where are they going to follow us to?"

"Get the Reserve Wing hounding our tail. Then return to Argus Borealis and land......"

"NO!" a dozen voices shrieked from behind the cockpit.

"Just listen, will you?" Davenport roared. "Land in the treetops by the lake. Make it look like we're hiding from them."

Rodeo frowned. "I don't follow you."

A scatter of gunfire ricocheted off the ship. Bandit dodged, but with so many Reserve Wing vessels closing in, he only flew into the path of more shots coming from all directions. "Just do it!" Davenport ordered. "Get down on Argus Borealis! Hurry!"

Bandit ripped the Drifter into a sideways roll. He plummeted away and took off at a blistering speed.

The Reserve Wing hurtled after the ship firing all the way. Bandit made a dive for Argus Borealis, but the Reserve Wing cut him off.

"He he he," he chortled. "That's right, suckers. Make me run."

The boys' fire erupted from the ship's tail and scattered through the pursuers. Davenport added his fire to their efforts, but the *Artemis Rex* couldn't hold the Reserve Wing at bay.

The *Artemis Rex* streaked into Argus Borealis's outer orbit and then Bandit made another sprint for outer space. The Reserve Wing fanned out to cut the ship off, but Bandit outpaced them.

"Stand by to come about!" he bellowed to his friends.

Davenport almost asked what he meant when Bandit broke orbit and zoomed away. He almost made it when five Reserve Wing ships put on a burst of speed. They came within range of the boy's guns.

Bandit whipped the *Artemis Rex* backward with a brutal wrench of the controls. He killed the engines and the ship's forward momentum carried it deeper into space. All the boys swung their accessory cradles and plastered their pursuers.

Four of the five attackers exploded in the *Artemis Rex's* wake. Bandit gunned the engines hard and the ship punched through the Reserve Wing line. He sent the ship into a death spiral over the planet.

"Now, Bandit!" Davenport roared. "Get us down on the surface."

"That's what I'm trying to do!" the boy screeched back. "This isn't as easy as I make it look."

Rodeo guffawed behind Davenport's back. "Put us down right next to the *Echo Omicron*."

"Where is it?" Davenport checked the edge of the lake. "I don't see it."

"Those things must have finished it off. Do you have the coordinates, Bandit?"

Bandit didn't answer. He rotated the ship over and over on its wing plummeting for the lake. The blue expanse rushed at the ship's nose way too fast.

Davenport checked his instruments. The Reserve Wing entered orbit and raced to intercept the ship exactly the way Davenport hoped.

At the last second, Bandit ripped the nose up and reversed his engines. He lowered the *Artemis Rex* into the canopy only a few yards from their former position. The ship sank into the treetops with a dozen Reserve Wing craft buzzing overhead.

"Now just sit tight," Davenport ordered.

The enemy came back and hovered directly overhead. They fired at the *Artemis Rex*, but they stopped before they inflicted any damage.

A long, pregnant silence descended over the ship. Davenport held his breath waiting to see what the Reserve Wing would do next. The fate of everyone on board depended on him being right.

Dice stuck his head into the cockpit. "Where are they? What are they doing?"

Bandit, Rodeo, and Davenport all spun around. "Shh!" they hissed. "Keep quiet!"

"Why?" he boomed. "They already know where we are. Asking what they're doing won't exactly give away our position."

"Do you mind?" Davenport fired back. "We're trying to concentrate here."

"You're concentrating on where they are and what they're doing, aren't you?"

Davenport pursed his lips, but before he could come up with a sufficiently scathing reply, a Stalwart floated down to land in front of the *Artemis Rex*.

The giant ship touched its landing gear right on the spot where the *Artemis Rex* and the ill-fated *Echo Omicron* had been just a few minutes before.

Dice sucked his breath between his teeth. "Holy shit!"

"Do you want me to put the boys on standby to fire?" Bandit breathed over his shoulder.

"No," Davenport replied. "We aren't firing. We're running."

Another Stalwart, several Nitrols, and at least a dozen Daggers descended on the *Artemis Rex's* location. They arranged themselves at strategic intervals around the lakeshore. Their gleaming metal sides shone in the sun.

Soldiers, officers, and teams of guards streamed from the ships. They surrounded the trees where the *Artemis Rex* swayed in the branches.

The Reserve Wing personnel pointed up at the Drifter. A few put their weapons to their shoulders only for their friends to yank them down. Davenport could just hear the wheels turning in their heads.

"It looks like an illegal cartridge of a highly toxic substance is the best defense around," Dice observed.

"They've been shooting at us for days and they destroyed the Echo Omicron thinking it had the Ithium on board," Davenport countered. "They don't care about that."

"They still might find a way to bring us down," Rodeo added

"How—grappling hooks?"

Bandit whipped around fast. "Shh!"

Dice pulled his head in. "What's wrong with you? Do you really think my saying that could give them the idea?"

Davenport didn't respond and focused on his instruments instead. The soldiers set up a perimeter detail around the trees as if the *Artemis Rex* crew might suddenly take it into their heads to go down to the ground.

Then the officers pointed outward and the soldiers turned their backs to the trees as though some unseen strangers would appear out of the atmosphere and steal the *Artemis Rex* from them.

"How long do we have to wait for those things to come back?" Bandit fretted.

"We were here for over an hour before they came for the *Echo Omicron*," Rodeo observed.

"An hour!" Bandit rubbed his hands together. "I don't think I can wait that long."

"You might not have to. Look!" Davenport pointed at Bandit's controls.

The scanners picked up movement under the ground. Some burrowing creature made convoluted trails just a few inches beneath the topsoil. They migrated around the soldiers' feet, but none of the Reserve Wing personnel noticed them.

Dice chuckled low. "It looks like someone is coming to dinner."

"Put the boys on standby," Davenport murmured.

Bandit glanced over his shoulder. "Are you sure?"

Davenport nodded. "We'll meet resistance in the atmosphere. The Reserve Wing won't send all its ships down here to capture us. They don't make mistakes like that."

"Sir!" Rodeo's voice came too loud in the silence. At the same moment, he brought something up on Davenport's controls.

Davenport looked down at a scan of the area of space around Argus Borealis. He almost asked what Rodeo wanted to show him when he saw a small blip coming from another system.

An unarmed freighter crossed Argus Borealis's orbit on its way somewhere else. The Reserve Wing completely ignored it.

"Are you thinking what I'm thinking?" Rodeo asked

Davenport's heart skipped a beat. "Can you make contact?"

"Already done it."

"Don't transmit until I give the word."

"What are you two scheming about?" Dice rumbled.

"Just inviting someone else to the birthday feast." Rodeo's fingers danced over his controls, but the *Artemis Rex* remained motionless and quiet.

Bandit signaled the accessory cradles to stand by for hostilities. The boys signaled back that they were ready and standing by.

Davenport strained his eyes to see the movement underground. Were those creatures getting ready to make their presence known? How long before they.....?

All of a sudden, they erupted out of the ground. They attacked so much faster this time and in vast numbers.

They didn't dig into view and then spring onto their meal. This time, they rocketed out of the ground without warning. In a split second, they latched onto the Reserve Wing vessels by the thousands.

A black cloud of them catapulted for the Stalwart. They stuck with such a resounding thwack that Davenport heard it inside the *Artemis Rex's* protective cockpit. In a blink, that sickening sound of countless mouths chewing filled the air.

"Ugh!" Dice snarled. "They're disgusting!"

"Are you sure they can't get to us here?" Bandit quavered.

Davenport stared in unblinking amazement as more and more of the things materializing out of the soil. They blanketed the Reserve Wing ships until he couldn't see their hulls at all. "If they could see us, they would be on top of us already."

The soldiers on guard didn't notice anything amiss. Their orders didn't include watching out for native creatures who ate ships for lunch. No one told them what to do or what to watch for.

No one noticed anything until the Stalwart's landing gear gave out on the port side. The ship banged down on its belly and tipped at a dangerous angle. A few crewmen charged outside. Davenport could see their mouths moving in desperate explanations.

The officers and soldiers whirled away, the *Artemis Rex* forgotten. They raced back to their ships and tried to fire on the creatures the way Davenport did, but to no avail.

One of the Daggers even tried to use its onboard Howitzer to shoot the things off. It fired at its own engine housing and the engine exploded in a massive ball of flame that engulfed the Nitrol parked next to it.

The Reserve Wing personnel went into a confused flurry of chaotic activity. They raced toward their ships. Then they dodged and ran somewhere else. The officers yelled so many orders that no one knew whether to go blind or wind their watches.

"Now, Sir?" Rodeo asked.

"Not yet."

Three officers tried to get near the Stalwart, but when they approached the aft gangway, the creatures ate their way into the fuel stores. The ship detonated with an unholy kaboom that resounded across the lake.

"Now!" Davenport bellowed.

Chapter 34

B andit must have been clutching the controls with sweat-damp palms because the *Artemis Rex* catapulted into Argus Borealis's atmosphere so fast the acceleration knocked Dice off his feet. He tumbled out of the cockpit, but Davenport didn't have time to worry about him.

The *Artemis Rex* zoomed skyward, and at the same instant, Rodeo transmitted his signal to the freighter.

The blue sky turned black. Stars pricked the ionosphere and Davenport prepared to fire when the rebounded signal came back. An alarm went off on the controls. *Proximity Alert. Imminent Attack.*

"The freighter is wheeling!" Rodeo yelled. "It's working!"

The *Artemis Rex* vaulted into the heavens just in time to see a massive fleet of Reserve Wing ships arrayed around Argus Borealis. They blockaded the planet exactly the way Davenport expected, but the instant the *Artemis Rex* appeared, the Reserve Wing split off.

The *Artemis Rex* plummeted on a collision course for the whole battalion when the Reserve Wing ripped sideways and took off in a blur.

They streaked toward the freighter. The little craft bobbed along at a snail's pace and never saw the Reserve Wing coming.

"Stand by to fire!" Davenport roared.

"Wait for it!" Rodeo corrected.

Sure enough, the Reserve Wing charged the freighter with every gun blazing. Dozens of fighter craft surrounded the tiny ship and bombarded it with countless charges. They didn't even check to see if it was capable of fighting back.

"Alter course for Ultra Meridian!" Davenport ordered.

"That will take us directly into the Reserve Wing's path!" Bandit screamed.

"Do it!" Davenport countered. "Run straight through 'em if you have to—the quicker the better."

Bandit hunched his shoulders, gritted his teeth, and slammed the throttle to the wall. The ship streaked up behind the Reserve Wing at a punishing speed and overtook the freighter just as the hull disintegrated under the Reserve Wing's assault.

The *Artemis Rex* plunged nose first into the explosion and a flash of orange-yellow enveloped the ship.

"Swing backward!" Rodeo yelled to the accessory cradles. "Prepare to defend our tail!"

The *Artemis Rex* broke through into clear, open space and the Reserve Wing realized the ruse. They gunned their engines and fell into pursuit.

Bandit huddled low in his cradle. Sweat beaded the back of his neck and his knuckles went white on his stick. He fought the ship on as straight a course as possible while gunshots peppered the shields.

The Reserve Wing pummeled the *Artemis Rex* from side to side, but Bandit paid no attention to the attack. More shots spouted from the Drifter's Howitzers. Davenport heard the boys yelling to each other down in the accessory cradles.

"We can't keep this up for long!" Rodeo called over the noise. "They're coming up on us. They'll...."

As he said those words, a Dagger whizzed up on the starboard wing. It scattered fire across the *Artemis Rex's* flank and pirouetted in front of the ship trying to block its path.

Davenport inhaled to warn Bandit, but the boy reacted before Davenport could get the words out. Bandit ripped back the stick and sailed straight over the Dagger before diving past in a dizzying rush.

The boys in the accessory cradles spun their weapons around and plastered the Dagger with a punishing barrage. They followed the Dagger as the *Artemis Rex* zoomed away and the Dagger exploded in its wake.

"Here comes another one!" Rodeo called. "Correction: here comes *all* of 'em!"

Davenport barely had time to see dozens of Reserve Wing ships creeping up on the *Artemis Rex* from behind. The next instant, they swarmed around the Drifter. So many charges hammered the ship that Davenport couldn't see beyond the flashes covering the cockpit window.

"We got a problem!" Rodeo yelled.

"Don't tell me that!" Bandit screeched. "Just tell me how the hell we can get out of it."

Davenport glanced down at his instruments. He couldn't even see Ultra Meridian on the chart. Even as he looked, five Stalwarts and a bunch of Daggers cut into the *Artemis Rex's* path. They wheeled to aim their guns at the Drifter.

Bandit tried to dodge again, but too many Daggers blocked the ship. He wheeled from port to starboard and back again, but an enemy moved in front no matter where he turned.

"Any ideas?" Rodeo asked.

No one answered him. Bandit never let up on the engines. He swooped aside and rocketed across the Daggers' bows. He turned back toward Argus Borealis only to come face to face with the rest of the Reserve Wing moving in for the kill.

Bandit circled one more time, but the Reserve Wing tightened the dragnet. Guns exploded everywhere. The hull boomed and crashed in a steady din.

Davenport checked the scanners for any way out. A particularly vicious assault punched the ship's nose from starboard. The *Artemis Rex* staggered and Bandit roared in fury. "Bastards! Get the hell off!"

Davenport expanded his chart. Ultra Meridian hovered several lightyears off....way out of reach. Then he saw it.

"Bandit!" he barked. "The Stalwarts!"

"What?" Rodeo called back. "What about them?"

"Gun it, Bandit! Set a collision course for......" Davenport surveyed the Reserve Wing and picked a ship at random. "The *Empress*! Go—now!"

Bandit hesitated only a second and then punched the engines with all his might. The *Artemis Rex* sprang forward in a death dive.

"What the hell are you doing?" Rodeo bellowed. "You want us to destroy ourselves on a Stalwart? We won't even scratch the *Empress's* paint job."

Davenport ignored him. Bandit never wavered. He narrowed his eyes at the *Empress* looming huge and deadly over the *Artemis Rex*. The Drifter never seemed so small.

The Stalwart swung its guns forward. Blasts pummeled the hull one more time, but the Daggers didn't pursue. They held their position and waited for the *Artemis Rex* to destroy itself on the Stalwart's enormous bulk.

The *Empress* covered the cockpit window. Davenport stared up at the ship and the rest of the world vanished from his awareness.

"Five seconds to impact!" Rodeo called. "Two seconds!"

"Now, Bandit!" Davenport thundered.

Bandit yanked the stick and the *Artemis Rex* whistled within inches of the *Empress's* sides. None of the other Stalwarts could turn in time. The *Artemis Rex* hurtled clear and Bandit put on speed to escape.

Whoops and cheers drifted to the cockpit from the accessory cradles. Davenport caught a few, "Go, Bandit!" and "Show 'em, boy!", but the advantage only lasted an instant.

The *Artemis Rex* made it forty lightyears before the Daggers caught up. They started their old game of cutting the *Artemis Rex* off and closing it in a deadly ring of guns.

"We're screwed!" Rodeo roared. "I hope you have a backup plan."

Davenport shook his head. "Sorry. I'm fresh out."

More Reserve Wing ships charged the ship from all over. So many closed the *Artemis Rex* in a lethal trap that Davenport lost track of them all.

His eyes skimmed the chart, but he couldn't see any way out until Rodeo let out a shriek that stood Davenport's hair on end. "The *Assassin Polaris*! It's the *Assassin Polaris*!"

Davenport barely had a chance to look around when another fleet of fast-moving vessels rocketed into view. They lambasted the Reserve Wing with so many shots that the Reserve Wing didn't have time to break off pursuing the *Artemis Rex*.

"Ekol to the rescue!" Bandit cheered.

"Fly the ship, boy!" Davenport bellowed. "Get us to Ultra Meridian and don't spare the horses! Don't look back!"

The *Artemis Rex* raced away, but the battle followed hot on the ship's heels. The Reserve Wing rounded on Ekol's fleet, but the *Assassin Polaris* blasted through the Reserve Wing so fast that the Reserve Wing followed almost on top of the *Artemis Rex*.

Scattered shots missed the enemy and exploded on all sides. The *Artemis Rex* shuddered under the bombardment against Bandit's efforts to keep the ship on course.

The *Artemis Rex* shot forward, but at that moment, the *Assassin Polaris* plowed past the *Empress*. The Stalwarts hammered the huge pirate ship with dozens of guns. They didn't damage Ekol's flagship, but they did knock it into the *Artemis Rex*.

The impact hurled the *Artemis Rex* hard to starboard. "We're hit!" Bandit yelled.

"How bad is the damage?" Davenport called. "I don't see anything on the read-outs."

"There's no damage.....but still," Bandit replied.

Davenport turned his attention back to the battle raging all around him. The *Assassin Polaris* tried to block the Reserve Wing from getting to the *Artemis Rex*. Ekol's other spacecraft whizzed between the Reserve Wing ships exchanging continuous shots.

"Get us out of this shit, Bandit!" Rodeo bellowed.

"I'm trying!" Bandit yelled back. "The *Assassin Polaris*—it's too big!"

As he spoke, the Stalwarts overtook the *Assassin Polaris*. Ekol spun the ship backward to face them down. The giant pirate ship slipped in behind the *Artemis Rex*.

The Drifter whizzed away while the Reserve Wing surrounded the *Assassin Polaris*—at least, the Stalwarts did. The Daggers avoided everything and dropped in behind the *Artemis Rex*.

Davenport's heart took another nosedive into his stomach when he saw the Daggers closing in for the last time.

Another ship whistled across the *Artemis Rex's* trajectory. The strange vessel thundered into view so fast the Daggers didn't see it. The newcomer punched its guns into three Daggers and two of them exploded.

The strange ship whipped around for another pass and all the Daggers cut off their pursuit to attack. "What the hell is that?" Davenport barked.

"It's the *Prometheus Vox*," Rodeo reported. "It's Sheriff Healey's ship!"

Chapter 35

The *Artemis Rex* made the last sprint to Ultra Meridian, but Davenport didn't see any Reserve Wing craft following them. He didn't see the *Assassin Polaris*, either. He hated to think about what might have happened to Ekol, but another blip on his instruments distracted him.

"The *Prometheus Vox* is making a circuit around the planet," Rodeo reported.

"Get Fiddler up here," Davenport ordered.

She stuck her head into the cockpit. "What's on your mind?"

"I need you to get in touch with Friend. Find out if the *Blood Calliope* is on the planet."

She practically had to sit on Rodeo's lap to tap something into his controls. Rodeo cocked his head and listened to her finger taps, but Davenport couldn't figure out what she was doing. She sent an encoded signal that bounced off the Mount Refractory communications array on the planet's other side.

"What are you doing?" Rodeo asked.

"I'm sending a message to Friend like Davenport asked me to. What does it look like I'm doing?"

Rodeo snorted, but before he could argue, another screed of numbers streamed across the *Artemis Rex's* instruments.

"It's coordinates," Rodeo reported. "The *Blood Calliope*—it's here!"

The numbers looked like gibberish, but Fiddler read them with no trouble. "The ship crashed here. Friend says the registration at DTF9Q is a decoy. It was sent ten days before the *Blood Calliope* crashed here to cover the thieves' tracks."

"Set course for those coordinates," Davenport ordered, "and scan for any contraband or toxic elements. We don't know what we'll find down there."

Bandit started to turn the ship in that direction. "Hold it!" Fiddler cut in. "You have to land near the old jail site."

"What for?" Bandit asked. "That's miles away from the ship."

"If we land right next to the *Blood Calliope*, the Reserve Wing will spot us and they'll come after the third component, too. We have to land at the jail and cross the country on foot. The *Blood Calliope* is hidden in a chasm beyond the Khuntan Reserve. It will be difficult to access. "

Bandit groaned. "Oh, please no!"

"Oh, please yes." Fiddler got to her feet. "Set us down. I'll go tell the others."

"You heard the lady," Davenport told him. "Set us down at the old jail site."

"What *old* jail site?" Rodeo asked. "It's perfectly intact."

Davenport checked the readouts and stared in amazement when he saw that Rodeo was right.

The desert around his old outpost showed all the signs of dozens of ships landing. Building equipment tracks crisscrossed the dusty soil. Someone had mined quite a bit of stone from the nearby hills. The jail looked exactly the same as before.

"The Reserve Wing must have rebuilt it," Rodeo remarked.

"Which means they've been all over this planet looking for the *Blood Calliope*." Davenport climbed out of his cradle. "As soon as we're on the ground, get to the loading hatch and get suited up for a walk in the park. Rodeo, you're with me."

Bandit bowed his head and let out a little whimper. "A walk in the park! What did I do to deserve this?"

Davenport found everyone standing around inside the loading hatch. Dice, Fiddler, Emmet, and the boys loaded themselves with weapons and supplies. Only Lyons was missing.....and Beauty. "Where's Beauty?"

"Don't ask," Dice boomed.

"I just did. Where is he?"

Laub and Axel exchanged glances. "Do you want to tell him?" Axel asked.

"No," Laub replied. "You do it,"

"He's in that crate over there." Emmet jerked his thumb at a steel box strapped to the bulkhead. It was nearly as tall as Davenport.

"What is he doing in there?" Davenport asked. "He should be getting ready to go with us."

Dice rolled his eyes to heaven. "What is he doing? I'll give you three guesses and the first two don't count."

"Those JimJams should have lasted him a week at least," Coon remarked.

"He moved on from JimJams a long time ago," Laub explained.

"He's saving the JimJams for Carlisle," Alla added.

"Who's Carlisle?" Davenport asked.

"It's an expression," Rodeo told him. "It means he's saving them for later—indefinite-ly."

"Oh. I get it. So….he's eating."

"Give yourself a gold medal and advance to kindergarten," Dice sneered. "I didn't think you had it in you."

Davenport laughed, but Wolf rounded on Dice and gave him such a vicious snarl that Dice bristled.

Davenport pulled Wolf back before the joke turned to bloodshed. "Take it easy. Dice, go get Beauty out of the crate. We need him on this job."

Dice snapped shut the ammunition cylinder on his XQ-85. "*You* go get him out of the crate. Since when am I your puppy dog?"

"You can be my puppy dog anytime, Dice," Fiddler teased. "I promise I'll make sure you get all the ChunkyTenders you can eat."

"Promises, promises!" Emmet interjected. "Don't listen to her, Dice. She's always tempting me with all the ChunkyTenders I can eat and….."

"And you fall for it every time, don't you?" Dice fired back. "You'll forgive me if I don't take life advice from *you*."

Davenport holstered the sidearm he just finished checking and strode around the crate. The outer lock had been jimmied and the cover stood ajar. A flash of light winked inside and then blipped out.

Davenport slid the cover back with his toe. Light flooded the crate's interior and he peered inside to find Beauty crouched in a corner.

The creature raised his huge eyes to meet Davenport's. To Davenport's surprise, he didn't see a single JimJam in sight….or a ChunkyTender or a JuicyPie or a BoilBun. In fact, the crate contained no food at all.

Beauty clutched what looked like a jumble of wires and trash in his long spindly fingers. He blinked up at Davenport with a decidedly guilty expression and his large ears drooped.

"What are you doing, Beauty?"

Beauty held up the jumble of whatever it was for Davenport to see. Davenport squinted at it, but he couldn't make it out until Beauty rotated it over in one hand.

He showed Davenport the back of it and a light went on in Davenport's head. The device was the doppler refractor scavenged onto the back of a primitive scanning chip from the *Artemis Rex's* main array.

Davenport opened his mouth to say something, but Beauty raised a finger to his lips. He held out the device for Davenport to take.

Davenport almost said something else, but Beauty shook his head and shoved the contraption into Davenport's hand. Beauty waved him away and pulled the cover shut to block himself in.

Davenport looked down at the thing Beauty had given him. If this device was what he thought it was, it should lead him directly to the third component.

The doppler refractor would detect any radiation interface resisters. The third component would need those to interact with the Ithium. The whole concept was so basic and yet so brilliant.

"Yo!" Dice thundered from behind him. "We're landing! Are you coming or not?"

Davenport pocketed the device without a word and stepped back into view. He strode over to his companions just as Bandit set the ship down.

"What is it this time?" Alla asked. "Is he pigging out on Salacious M's Spicy Delights?"

Coon turned to stare at him. "Did we bring any?"

"Of course not, fool," Alla countered. "If we had, we would be eating them ourselves."

"*You* would be eating them, you mean," Rodeo cut in.

"Don't tell me we have to wait for Beauty to suit up before can go," Dice grumbled. "This could take all day."

"Leave him alone," Davenport replied. "Beauty isn't coming with us."

"Why not?" Fiddler asked. "You said we needed him."

"I changed my mind. Beauty is staying here."

"Alone?" Alla groaned. "We'll have no food left by the time we get back."

"Do you ever think about anything but food?" Emmet asked.

"All the time," Alla replied. "Beauty is the one who never thinks about anything else."

"I said leave him alone," Davenport cut in. "Let's go."

Bandit raced down from the cockpit and grabbed himself two XQs. The hatch opened and Davenport pulled his goggles down over his eyes. He tugged his shirt collar over his nose and mouth.

As soon as he stepped outside with the others, the smell hit him between the eyes. He was back at Ultra Meridian.

Fiddler yelled over the howling wind. "The Khuntan Reserve is this way."

"How far is it?" Emmet called back.

"Only a few miles. As soon as we get into the chasms, the wind won't bother us so much. Let's move out."

Davenport fell in line behind her. The boys ranged in front and in back. They scanned the area, but no other ships descended to land. The crew had the place to themselves.

Davenport cast a nostalgic glance toward the jail. Did the Reserve Wing restore it completely? What would it be like inside?

He wouldn't find out anytime soon. Fiddler, Emmet, and Rodeo passed the building and Davenport put it out of his mind. He had some mileage to cover before he got back here—if he ever made it back at all.

The wind scoured as fiercely as ever. He tasted the dust through his shirt and a steady tapping sound filled his ears as millions of sand grains peppered his goggles. It was the taste and sound of home.

The others bowed their heads and pressed on until Fiddler led them into the northern hills. In all his time at Ultra Meridian, Davenport had never explored this part of the planet.

He didn't have to. The gangs and crime syndicates who populated the hills all lived to the south. He didn't get much leisure time to go off into parts unknown.

Fiddler and her Armageddon Core must have explored them, though. She found a tiny trail barely wide enough for a single person. It wound into the hills with no end in sight.

Davenport looked back before he turned the first corner. The *Artemis Rex* looked tiny and vulnerable parked next to the jail. Would it still be there when he got back? Should he be happy or sad if it wasn't?

Rodeo bumped into him from behind. The blind boy dragged his fingertips along the sandstone wall at his left to guide his way. Sound and smell didn't help him orient himself in this environment.

The next moment, the group turned the corner and the wind died. The sound cut off and silence descended.

Fiddler propped her goggles on her forehead and listened, but nothing disturbed the desert quiet. The friends nodded to each other and kept on going.

They hiked for at least an hour without stopping or talking. Fiddle wound from one labyrinthine chasm to another. She turned so many corners and took so many hidden passages that Davenport long since lost track of where they were going.

She finally held up her hand in a tight gully almost too small for Dice to fit into. She flattened her spine against the wall and peeked behind it to the next channel ahead. "We're about to enter the Khuntan Reserve. How do we find the component?"

Davenport pulled out the device that Beauty gave him. He flicked it on and a faint red light flashed on its surface. "What the holy hell.....?" Rodeo snarled.

"That's.....that's the doppler refractor....." Bandit choked. "Did that come from the *Artemis Rex*?"

"Yes." Davenport swiveled around Fiddler to take the lead. "Follow me."

He ventured deeper into the Reserve. Stone arches covered the path. The doppler refractor led them through dim caverns and under low-hanging ledges.

Davenport paused at every intersection and checked the blip on the doppler refractor. It quickened drawing him closer to the *Blood Calliope*. He slowed his pace as the blip got faster. His heartbeat increased to match it. He was so close.

He stopped a lot more often to listen. When would the Reserve Wing attack to stop him? They wouldn't just let the Ithium go.

He scanned the skies, but no one came. Could this be another trick? Was Admiral Joyce waiting for the crew to lead him to the third component? If so, why was he trying so hard to kill the crew?

Fiddler got Davenport's attention by tapping his elbow. "That arch up there marks the end of the Reserve. The ship shouldn't be far beyond that point."

Davenport held up the doppler refractor. The light on its top flashed so fast it practically stayed on continuously. This was it. The third component must be here.

The crew inched into a wider channel lined with sheer, sandy walls. The sun blistered down through the thin crack overhead. Dice and Emmet passed their XQ barrels across the visible sky, but no one could see the crew on the ground.

Davenport tiptoed to the arch. Another crooked passage led deeper into the mountains. He couldn't see any ship.

His eyes darted to the doppler refractor. It no longer blinked. The device seemed to read the third component right under the crew's feet.

He eased to the end of the passage. It ended at another narrow threshold leading onto another vast, desolate expanse like the one at Ultra Meridian, but without the jail. The hills dotting the horizon occupied different positions. Other than that, he might as well not have gone anywhere.

A giant destroyed ship perched upended in the middle of the plane. Its nose lay buried in a giant gash sliced in the baked soil. The ship's wings extended undamaged at ground level.

The ship showed signs of gunshots on its tail and rear flanks. It must have been shot down here, but the four Howitzers on the near side appeared unharmed.

He held up the doppler refractor. The light shone at a steady brightness without fading. "It's here," he whispered. "It's on board that ship."

Bandit leaned forward. He extended his head into the open and squinted up at the sky. "It looks all clear. Let's......"

A shrieking missile plummeted right in front of his nose and pounded into the ground. A crater of soil sprayed in the crew's faces.

"Holy shit!" Bandit shot backward so fast he collided with Fiddler and Alla.

"What were you just saying?" Emmet yelled over the noise.

"Withdraw!" Davenport shoved them back into the chasm.

In answer to his words, a whole flock of Daggers and Vagrants whistled overhead. They hammered the maze of gorges with more rockets. They cut off the crew's retreat.

Davenport grabbed Fiddler and dove into the open, right into the path of the Daggers' bombardment. "Everybody forward! To the ship!"

Fiddler tried to pull back. "No way! You're crazy.....!"

Another devastating kaboom cut Davenport off from answering her. She ripped her arm out of his grasp and tried to pull back, only to get overrun by Dice, Bandit, and Wolf charging from behind.

More shots pounded up the canyon coming closer by the second. Davenport couldn't wait anymore. He zigzagged between more eruptions of sand and dust in his headlong sprint to get to the *Blood Calliope.*

The boys ran in a cluster and caught Fiddler and Emmet in their undertow. In seconds, the whole party swarmed onto the plane amid ground-shaking explosions going off all around them.

Dice, Laub, and Alla swiveled outward to aim their XQs to the skies, but Davenport crouched under his upraised arms and concentrated everything on running. The ship offered their only protection with more Reserve Wing ships materializing out of nowhere.

Vagrants shrieked back and forth over the crashed ship. Daggers raced up the canyons driving everyone into the Vagrants' guns.

A Dagger rotated over Davenport's head and came screaming back. Two converging lines of gunfire chewed through the powdery soil eating their way closer to his legs. He danced right and then left, but they tracked him everywhere he went.

Dice bellowed at the top of his lungs. Davenport sprang back to avoid another brutal volley. Rodeo collided with him from behind and Davenport caught hold of the boy.

Wolf and Breeze crowded close to them firing off rifle shots by the dozen, but the Vagrants only soared out of range. The friends couldn't hit them from the ground.

Davenport squinted through curtains of dust and flying rock. The *Blood Calliope* hovered so close, but the Reserve Wing blocked him from getting to it. They must be able to read as well as he could that the third component was right inside the wreck.

He only had to cross two dozen yards to get to a large breach in the hull. Pounding rockets shook the planet beneath his feet. The group couldn't stay here, frozen in fear and indecision.

He prepared to make another dash for it when three Daggers swiveled in front of his eyes. They descended close to the ground and zoomed up the side canyons on a dead course for the crew trapped in the open.

Their gunports locked on him and Davenport's heart stopped. He tightened his grip on his XQ ready to fire back when a cannon blast ripped the canyon wall in half. A giant burst of shattered rock and boulders sprayed out of the cliff face and massive blocks smashed into two Daggers.

The Daggers skidded sideways with a catastrophic screech. One of the Reserve Wing ships exploded. The other hit the cliff wall, rotated sideways, and detonated.

The third dodged the blast only to get caught by another missile fired from the cliffside. Davenport spun around and stared at a deep, dark tunnel cut straight out of the rock. The massive Howitzer rested inside it with a small, slight, brown-clad girl sitting on the seat.

She ripped the enormous gun from right to left blowing Daggers out of the sky. The Vagrants gathered from all over and turned their fire on her only to get caught in her sights.

Davenport shoved Rodeo toward the *Blood Calliope*. "Go! They're covering for us. Go! Go!"

The boys raced for the ship with Dice, Davenport, and Emmet bringing up the rear. More Daggers whizzed over the slit of sky above the canyon, but Armageddon Core guns belched from all sides and left the Reserve Wing vessels spinning to earth in balls of fire.

Davenport didn't stick around to see the rest. He lunged for the hull breach and then dove into the shadows.

Chapter 36

Davenport looked around at his comrades. Laub and Coon propped their hands on their knees catching their breath.

Dice wrenched his XQ open and started reloading rapidly. "Don't take a tea break now, boys. Those girls won't be able to hold off the Reserve Wing forever."

Fiddler turned to Davenport. "Where's the third component?"

He fished the doppler refractor out of his pocket and held it up. "It isn't reading anymore."

Bandit snatched it out of his hand. "Give me that. That little shit stole it from the *Artemis Rex*, but he obviously didn't know what he was doing. I'll recalibrate it."

"You can do that?" Emmet asked.

Bandit snorted. "I could do a hell of a lot more if it was attached to the ship where it belongs, but I guess that isn't going to happen."

"Of course it isn't, genius," Dice barked. "We couldn't fly the ship here without all of us getting our asses handed to us."

"Just calibrate it," Davenport told Bandit. "We have to find that component."

Bandit pursed his lips, bowed over the device, and started fiddling with it. Axel surveyed the ship's interior and kicked a stray crate lying overturned on the floor....except that it wasn't the floor.

The ship had crashed nose first into the ground so the crew stood on one of the walls turned horizontally. Random crap, loose equipment, and a few skeletons lay scattered all over the place.

"What do you think made them crash?" Fiddler asked.

"Probably another Reserve Wing attack." Rodeo approached a control panel near the bulkhead door at his feet. He tapped at the panel, but nothing happened. "If we can link into the power supply....."

A deep groaning boom vibrated the wreck. Everyone looked up at the ceiling and listened....all except Bandit.

He held up the device. "Got it! It's working now."

The light blinked much more slowly now, but when Bandit moved it around the compartment, the blinking sped up when he aimed it at the bulkhead Rodeo was messing with.

Davenport's boot heels crunched through sand and broken glass. He squatted down next to Rodeo. "Can you get it open?"

Another groan trembled the ship and then, without warning, gunfire stuttered the hull right near the breach where the crew entered.

Davenport and Fiddler sprang to the gap and aimed their XQs outside. The boys raced over to join them and Bandit started to put the doppler refractor down on the floor.

"Find that component!" Davenport ordered. "We'll hold 'em off as long as we can."

Four Vagrants cartwheeled past the breach. Dice joined Davenport and Fiddler. They spat gunfire at the Reserve Wing ships, but the Vagrants were already out of sight.

The low, dull thump of Howitzer fire sounded out of sight. The Reserve Wing must have found a way to evade the Armageddon Core's shots.

Rodeo left the panel and groped along the wall to another bulkhead. "Over here! Come this way—all of you!"

"What are you doing?" Fiddler demanded. "They'll blast the ship apart."

"The gun range! It's this way."

Rodeo wedged his fingertips between the two sliding door panels and pried them apart. They slid open to reveal a service ladder running sideways. It ran between the bulkheads leading to the ship's upper decks.

Rodeo crawled into the space and started climbing. Dice and Davenport exchanged glances, but the rest of the boys were already following Rodeo.

Fiddler stayed where she was and kept firing at the assembled Daggers, but she still couldn't hit any of them.

Davenport crouched into the crawlspace and followed the boys. Dice tried to enter and banged his giant shoulders on the partition. "Cocksucking filthy stinking piece of....."

"Stay here," Davenport told him. "You and Fiddler keep an eye on things. Warn us if the Reserve Wing tries to board the ship."

"I won't have to." Dice's snarling voice got farther away as he moved back to the breach. "You'll get plenty of warning. Believe me."

Rodeo, Alla, and Coon vanished at the top of the shaft. They climbed out somewhere and the rest of the Chorion Team followed.

Davenport clambered out into the range to find Rodeo, Laub, and Coon all manning the *Blood Calliope's* Howitzers. Rodeo swung his weapon hard to the left and sprayed rockets into the sky beyond the window, but the grid didn't show up.

The boys had to lie down on the rear bulkhead and wedge their legs against the vertical wall to work the guns. "On your right, Laub!" Rodeo called. "Here they come, Coon! Fire!"

Davenport sprang into the nearest seat. Bandit and Axel fumbled over the control panel to one side. "I'm trying to reroute power to the grid!" Bandit called over the deafening noise. "The ship still has full power, but the diverter was damaged in the crash."

"Forget the grid!" Davenport told him. "Find the component."

Bandit hesitated and then snatched the doppler refractor from the floor where he dropped it. He checked the light indicator, moved the device around, and followed the signal to another bulkhead on the far side.

He tried to pull it open, but nothing would budge it. "We need the power up to open this door. It's protected by....."

"I got it!" Axel called back. "The grid is up!"

The grid winked into view in front of Davenport's eyes. It slowed everything down. He could target the Daggers now.

The grid acquired targets and exactly matched the Howitzers' tracking nodes to the incoming ships. Davenport fired again and again. Daggers ruptured in clouds of fire outside the ship.

"Woo-hoo!" Laub whooped. "That's right, bitches! You better run!"

"Another grouping coming in hot!" Rodeo informed him. "How much ammo do we have left?"

Axel's fingers danced over the panel checking all the ship's systems. "Fully loaded. It's all yours."

"All mine," Rodeo murmured. "I like the sound of that."

Another posse of Vagrants whistled across the grid. Howitzer shots zoomed out of nowhere and hit two of them. The Vagrants pivoted to the *Blood Calliope's* other side where the Armageddon Core couldn't hit them.

They concentrated their fire on the hull breach. A few bright streaks soared away from the ship, but Dice and Fiddler couldn't hit such fast-moving ships from their hiding place.

"Come on, you chickshits!" Coon hissed. "Stick your necks out so I can cut them....."

In answer to his taunt, seven Vagrants rocketed upward. They lifted out of Dice and Fiddler's range and hammered the *Blood Calliope's* tail. The broken fuselage tottered on its smashed nose.

"Be careful what you wish for!" Rodeo yelled. "Hit 'em with everything we've got, boys!"

Davenport slammed his gun as far back as he could, but his shots still fell short. The Vagrants alternately bombarded the ship's tail threatening to knock the wreck over and raining fire and brimstone on the hull breach where Dice and Fiddler hid.

"Bandit!" Davenport roared over his shoulder. "How much longer before we can get out of here?"

No one answered him. Davenport stole a glance over his shoulder. Neither Bandit nor Axel was on the gun range anymore. Did they abandon the rest of the crew?

He shook those thoughts out of his head as more Vagrants materialized out of nowhere. They turned their fire into the cliffs and devastated the Armageddon Core's gun placements.

The Armageddon Core's Howitzers no longer fired at all. The girls must have retreated and Davenport didn't blame them. They got the crew onto the *Blood Calliope*. Davenport couldn't ask for more than that.

He checked one more time for Bandit and Axel. If they didn't find the component, he would pull out. The crew's lives were much more important.

With the Armageddon Core either neutralized or preoccupied, the Daggers moved in and assaulted the *Blood Calliope* from all sides. The grid showed the hull collapsing on multiple decks and the grid itself flickered.

"The power is failing!" Rodeo reported. "Time to pack it in."

Davenport nodded, but at that moment, another ship pelted into the battle from far to the left. It hurtled out of the canyon and opened fire.

Missiles erupted all over the battlefield. Davenport and Laub instinctively wheeled their guns around and Davenport locked the grid on the incoming ship.

"Don't shoot!" Rodeo bellowed. "It's the *Prometheus Vox*!"

Davenport hesitated a fraction of a second, but he never got a chance to identify the ship before it plunged into the battle. Missiles spurted from its gunports and ten Vagrants woofed into flame.

"Bale out!" Davenport ordered. "Evacuate!"

Rodeo left his gun and stood up. Davenport returned to the crawlspace where they entered the gun range. He paused there to make sure the other boys made it out.

He glanced back to see the *Prometheus Vox* hurtle past the grid one more time. It made pass after pass leaving a carpet of destruction in its wake.

Rodeo, Laub, and Coon hustled over to the ladder and Davenport pushed them into the hole. "Get back to the hull breach. We'll get into the canyons while Healey ties them up."

The boys crawled back onto the ladder, but before Davenport could join them, a call floated to his ear. "Davenport! Over here."

Bandit's voice came from the other end of the gun range. Davenport stuck his head inside to see Axel peering back at him. "We found something."

"Is it the component?" Davenport ducked through the opening and joined the two boys standing in what might have been a repair conduit.

There was barely enough room for the two boys. They squashed together to let Davenport in.

Bandit aimed the doppler refractor at something on the floor. "It must have gotten damaged in the crash."

"What is it?" Davenport asked.

Axel prodded something that looked like an open cake tin with his boot. "It looks like a food storage flask."

Davenport grimaced at the walls surrounding them. "Are you seriously telling me someone stashed food in here? This is a repair conduit. Who would store food in *here*?"

Axel shrugged. "Beauty?"

"Alla," Bandit added. "Anyone who didn't want anyone to find it."

"There are crumbs in it," Axel pointed out.

Davenport bent down to pick up the tin, but Bandit held him back. "Don't touch it! The particles are radioactive. That's what signaled the refractor to show us this tin."

Davenport frowned at the tin and then at the doppler refractor. "Are you saying someone stashed the third component with their GoGo Yogurt Bombs?"

Bandit cracked a grin. "Stranger things have happened."

Davenport scowled at the surroundings—what there was of them. "Is there anywhere else on the ship the component might be hidden?"

Bandit shook his head. "This tin shows the strongest signal. If the component isn't here, it isn't anywhere else on this ship."

"I checked the ship's onboard sensors, too," Axel added. "The only radioactive signal on board comes from this conduit. It isn't here."

"You don't think....?" Bandit suggested.

"It's obvious," Davenport interrupted. "Someone beat us to it. Someone scavenged the ship before us and took the component."

"Who would do that?" Axel asked.

"The Reserve Wing could have done it," Bandit replied. "They searched the whole area. We all saw that. They must have found this ship."

"They wouldn't be so hot to stop us from getting it if they already had it." Davenport bumped Axel's arm. "Let's get the hell out of here. This place is a death trap."

The three of them returned to the hull breach, but this time, Dice, Fiddler, and Emmet stood around with their XQs propped on their shoulders. None of them manned the breach anymore.

"Did you get it?" Fiddler asked.

"It isn't here," Bandit replied. "Someone rifled the place already."

"Probably the Armageddon Core," Dice rumbled.

Fiddler sneered at him. "I would have told you if they did. We could have just walked into their headquarters and asked them for it instead of running in front of a bunch of fighter craft."

"It doesn't matter who got it. It isn't here." Davenport squinted out at the dusty terrain. "The *Prometheus Vox* is coming in to land."

"Any sign of the Reserve Wing?" Laub asked.

"Healey probably convinced them to let him take us in to the admiral on his own." Rodeo headed for the breach. "We better go turn ourselves in."

The friends climbed down to the ground. Davenport kept checking the skies, but the Reserve Wing didn't come back.

Healey stepped out of his cockpit and crossed the dusty ground to meet them. He broke into a grin when he got close enough to meet Davenport's gaze. "I didn't think it was possible for a crew to become even more wanted than you are now, but you proved me wrong."

"For someone who's supposed to be hunting us down, you aren't doing a very good job," Davenport shot back. "For a little while there, it actually looked like you were shooting at the Reserve Wing. You need a few targeting lessons because you missed us completely."

Healey frowned and rubbed his chin. "Yeah, I might have to have an awkward conversation with Admiral Joyce about that." He immediately brightened up. "But, hey, I never did have much difficulty talking my way out of trouble."

"Maybe you could give me lessons on that."

Healey laughed "I'm afraid I'm gonna have to pass on that. I think I have to go search the Zalus Sector for a fugitive crew who is wanted by the Confederate Corps. Last I heard, they were flying a stolen smugglers' craft called the *Echo Omicron*, but it hasn't been seen in days. The search could take a lot longer than I expect."

Davenport beamed back at him. He hated to think of flying away from this man. Davenport really needed people like Healey right now—people who weren't wanted and who might be able to help him. "Good luck with that. I hope you find them."

"Me, too."

"I sure wish you could come with us," Davenport added. "We could use a man of your skills and talents."

Healey laughed out loud. "Of course you would! You'd love to have me gunning away from you instead of toward you, but thanks for the offer. I'd like nothing better than to go hunting for buried treasure in a dusty old ruin like Ultra Meridian, but my place is at the Needle. I can do you more good there, now that Admiral Joyce thinks I'm hunting for you."

"How will you explain to him about driving the Reserve Wing away from us?"

Healey shrugged. "I won't explain it. I'll say I was trying to hit the Blood Calliope and the Reserve Wing pilots must have mistaken my intentions. I'll insist that they fired on me first and maybe the ships that got hit went down from friendly fire. The brass will believe anything as long as military incompetence is involved. They expect it."

"If he ever catches on to what you're really up to, you always have a place with us."

Healey grinned even more broadly. His eyes shone with warmth and understanding, something they definitely didn't shine with back at the Pandora's Needle jail. "Thanks. I just might take you up on that."

Davenport hesitated to leave. "There's another component—a third component Joyce needs to make the Ithium even more destructive. He won't act until he has all three."

"So I hear," Healey replied.

"We heard it was here—on Ultra Meridian. Maybe you could keep an eye on things in case it turns up in the wrong hands."

Healey's cheeks colored and he turned away. "Sorry, man, but Ultra Meridian already has a sheriff and I have another job to do. See you around sometime."

He returned to his ship, and in a minute, the *Prometheus Vox* rocketed away and vanished into the atmosphere. Davenport watched it go with a heavy heart.

Davenport wasn't the Sheriff of Ultra Meridian. He was still a lawman and he still bore the responsibility of saving humanity from Admiral Joyce's plans, but Davenport wasn't the Sheriff of Ultra Meridian anymore. He didn't know what he was.

Wolf brought him back to his senses. The young man brushed Davenport's elbow when Wolf approached his side. Wolf always had a way of steering Davenport where he most needed to go.

"Let's get out of here."

"Where are we going this time?" Breeze asked.

"Somewhere you won't be able to do any damage," Laub replied.

"Somewhere we can get Lyons some medical attention," Fiddler reminded them.

"We're going to Sacron Enigma," Davenport decided.

A gasp went through the group. Even Dice jolted and stared at Davenport in horror .

"Sacron Enigma!" Bandit whispered. "We can't go there! It's beyond the boundaries of known space."

"No, it isn't," Davenport replied. "It's just outside the Confederacy's control. There are plenty of people there who might help us."

"There are also plenty of people there who would slit our throats to steal an Ithium cartridge without any traceable line of ownership," Dice growled.

"Since when did you grow a pair?" Davenport asked. "You and Lyons were on your way to take the Ithium to Sacron Enigma when you got busted at Ultra Meridian."

"Busted by you," Dice hissed.

"We might as well go there as anywhere else," Rodeo added. "Ekol knows people there."

"He *knew* them, you mean," Coon corrected.

The Chorion Team turned away from each other. Davenport suffered a pang of regret when he thought about Ekol falling to the Reserve Wing fighters, but he couldn't help Ekol now.

He motioned for the others to follow him and they started the trek back to Ultra Meridian. Davenport gave the doppler refractor back to Bandit and the boy tinkered with it all the way back to the ship.

They climbed on board and Davenport hesitated at the cargo hatch for one last long, heartfelt look at the Ultra Meridian jail. He didn't know when he left it last time that he wouldn't be coming back.

Now he knew. The *Artemis Rex's* engines fired up and billowing dust clouds swept across his view. It was time to leave. The others had already gone inside the ship. They were only waiting for him, waiting for him to say goodbye.

The engines wound up to full power. The boys were sending him a clear message. He tore himself away and the hatch closed.

He wandered up to the cockpit, but he didn't sit down in his cradle. Bandit and Rodeo already occupied their places. This was their ship. He was just a passenger.

He almost walked away again. His thoughts turned back to Lyons. Maybe he should drop her off at the nearest Confederate hospital station before.....

A blast glanced off the *Artemis Rex's* tail. The ship skidded sideways before Bandit could correct.

"Fourteen Nitrols coming in fast!" Rodeo announced. "It doesn't look like they're too happy about someone raiding their WhifflePops."

"We didn't!" Bandit shrieked as another blast ricocheted off the cockpit cover. "Hey—assholes! We didn't take your......"

Rodeo twisted his sightless eyes toward Davenport. "Get the boys strapped in. We're in for a fight."

"No!" Davenport countered. "Don't fight them."

"Don't what?" Bandit hollered over his shoulder.

"Don't fight them," Davenport repeated. "Forget it. Get us to Sacron Enigma. Gun it!"

<u>End of Book 1.</u>

If you enjoyed this book, please consider leaving a review. You can also support me on Patreon at <u>www.patreon.com/InvisiblePublishing</u>.

Keep Reading

Ultra Meridian Series: Book 2: Artemis Rex

Powerful forces are amassing from every corner of the galaxy and they all want the doomsday weapon Sheriff Mace Davenport is carrying. The ultimate battle for the fate of humanity spills over into the unknown reaches of Sacron Enigma, the vast stretch of space beyond which only the foolhardy dare to tread.

Davenport and his friends have already lost everything that matters. They have only each other and the mission they've all sworn to carry—to keep the weapon away from Admiral Killian Joyce, the madman who will stop at nothing to get it back.

Admiral Joyce is about to learn that he isn't the only psychopathic murderer in the Confederacy and beyond it. They're as determined as Joyce to steal the weapon and they won't let him stand in their way. The final confrontation will leave the world in ruins unless Davenport's crew can find a way to stop it without getting their heads blown off in the process.

You can find it at your favorite book retailer.

Sign Up Once--Get all Theo Mann's free books including brand new releases

S ign Up Once--Get all Theo Mann's free books including brand new releases

Humanity on the brink of annihilation.

A mysterious package, a corrupt officer, and a conspiracy that goes all the way to the top? What could possibly go wrong?

When a routine mission goes horribly wrong, Warrant Officer Ewing Archer and a handful of faithful friends get trapped in a battle to save the last survivors of Earth.

The human race has abandoned the ecological disaster of Earth. Now all that remains is a network of interconnected ships, stations, and satellites surrounding the planet.

But when war breaks out, Archer becomes a firebrand that could destroy it all....or save it.

Sign up at www.theomann.com to read it for free

About Theo Mann

I write 70 books per year—and yes, before you ask, all these books are my original creative work. Nothing written under my name is AI-generated or ghostwritten because I write better than AI and any ghostwriter out there.

People don't read fiction for entertainment or to escape from reality. People read fiction to see their humanity reflected in another person's character and story.

This is my promise to you. When you read my books, you'll see your own humanity reflected in the characters and stories. I take this commitment to my readers very seriously. My books are an intimate form of communication between us. I would never disrespect my readers by turning that over to a machine or another writer. This is my bond between me and you as my reader.

I write 20,000 words per day as my daily work output. If anyone with a public platform would like to challenge me to prove this in a controlled environment, feel free to contact me on this website's contact page.

I worked as a professional ghostwriter for fifteen years. Now I'm on a mission to set a Guinness World Record by writing 700 books over the next ten years and 1400 books over the next twenty years, all originally written by me. See my website for the full book list.

I'm also the author of *Proof for the Existence of God* and the *Crimes Against Fiction* blog. You can find all my nonfiction work at www.crimes-against-fiction.com.

If you have a story idea, or if you would like me to explore a series in more depth, or if you'd like me to explore a character by writing a spinoff series about that character or world, leave me a message on my website's contact page. I answer all reader emails, so ask me anything, tell me what you liked and didn't like, and let me know where you'd like your favorite series to go. I would love to hear your ideas and find out what you'd like to read next.

Find out more at www.theomann.com.

Also by Theo Mann (so far)